Snakes and Daggers

The Haunted Past Series Book 2

Bow before the queen,

Or face the viper's wrath.

by Sharon Jackson

Snakes and Daggers 1

Acknowledgements 5

Chapter One 9

Chapter Two 22

Chapter Three 38

Chapter Four 50

Chapter Five 64

Chapter Six 76

Chapter Seven 92

Chapter Eight 109

Chapter Nine 122

Chapter Ten 137

Chapter Eleven 149

Chapter Twelve 162

Chapter Thirteen 173

Chapter Fourteen 187

Chapter Fifteen 200

Chapter Sixteen 215

Chapter Seventeen 227

Chapter Eighteen 238

Chapter Nineteen 253

Chapter Twenty 264

Chapter Twenty-One 280

Chapter Twenty-Two 294

Epilogue 303

Copyright©copyrighthouse2023 the moral rights of the author have been asserted. Written by: Sharon Jackson

All rights reserved. By payment of the required fees, you have been granted the non-exclusive, non-transferable right to access and read the text of this book. No part of this text may be reproduced, transmitted, downloaded, decompiled, reverse engineered, stored in or introduced into any information storage and retrieval system in any form, by any means, whether electronic and mechanical, now known or herein invented without the express written permission of Sharon Jackson.

Acknowledgements

I would like to thank my family "the Jackson clan" for always being there for me. We are a wolf pack in human form. I would remiss in not thanking my work colleagues for their encouragement and help with my Schrodinger's cat problem and would like to send a shout out to my wingman Jean for reading along, sometimes while I'm still typing, your support as always is appreciated.

Of course Open Eye Editing for their work editing this manuscript and I can't forget the magnificent Creative Paramita for yet another stunning cover. Many thanks to the Delinquent Minxes, I'm happy to have you on board.

And finally a special thank you to Moreno's café for allowing me use of their business name as the café my characters use and of course for the delightful cafe itself.

Thank you all.

Disclaimer

This is a work of fiction. Names, characters, places, and incidents are either a product of the author's imagination or used fictitiously. Any resemblance to actual persons dead or alive, events or locales is entirely coincidental.

Content warning

This is a crime thriller story about a detective dealing with the past that includes violence and abuse. As such, the content contains triggering elements, including graphic or explicit violence/deaths on a page, Sexual violence, abuse, graphic medical descriptions or bodily fluids, especially blood or internal body parts described on the page, harm and abuse to children, removal of body parts, drug abuse, stalking, flashbacks to violence, domestic violence, kidnapping, torture and other criminal activities.

If any part of this list disturbs you in any way, then it is probably best to read no further. Otherwise, enjoy the book!

*Dedicated to my delightful readers.
Thanks for sticking with me.*

Chapter One

August 12th, 2014

Keri McNamara knew what she had done by sending that package. She knew it was going to be the catalyst. It might not entirely clear her brother, but it would leave room for reasonable doubt. And where there was doubt, the case couldn't be closed. So now she was going to have to face the consequences of her choice to help her brother, whatever that might entail. That being said, she didn't plan to go down without a fight. It was time to make a plan.

"If I'm going to fight with the viper, I'm going to need some anti-venom," she muttered absently.

She'd been trained for this exact situation; to manipulate and anticipate, to plot and prepare. She only hoped that the student could surpass the master. The stakes were the highest they had ever been. Before she had dabbled, and believed herself more capable than she'd proved to be in their first battle. But the war wasn't over, yet, and her very life would depend on her winning. She couldn't really be any more motivated considering the odds, but she had beaten the odds before.

This time she had called in help from unlikely sources. She had never imagined she would ever ally herself with the "enemy".

"It just goes to show that you never can tell what paths you might take, or what levels you would be prepared to stoop to, when the right circumstances align," she mumbled to herself.

She supposed if she were being entirely honest, it was Keir for whom the troops were rallying. It would appear that her brother had more support than he seemed to believe. She had made but one call and it had caused a domino effect; a call to arms, one might even say.

They were going to need all the troops they could muster by the time this ugliness had seen its end. While they worked on the side of the law, she would be working from the opposing angle. When you corner a snake after all, you have to be prepared for the strike. That was what she would be bringing to the table, only those with the right skills would be able to tackle a viper in its nest. Sometimes it took somebody with the same ruthlessness to do what needed to be done. They—the innocent—wouldn't have the inclination, but Keri would see to that, if she got the chance.

Let the game begin.

****

Dev still wasn't entirely sure what to make of everything that had happened in the last week. He'd begun this case trying to catch a rapist, then a murderer, and now he was–somehow– in custody because of a past he didn't fully recall. Since his shocking arrest, he'd been suffering from flashbacks, or more specifically, a single flashback on repeat.

It was dark when he woke, and cold, hard bands restrained his arms to his sides. Groggily, Dev looked behind him, and gaped at the headless corpse which was hugging him.

Since that memory had surfaced, he'd been plagued with subsequent, fragmented flashes of the events, leading from waking up in a corpse's arms all the way to sustaining his injury during a hit and run incident. The last twenty-four hours had been both confusing and illuminating. He'd learned that he and Kier Whelan were one and the same, thanks to Mary McNamara, the wife of the latest nursery rhyme victim and, now that he considered it, also his Aunt.

However he couldn't say he was sorry to have been unaware of her existence until recently. If that were an example of the family he had, then perhaps it had been better to have grown up a foster child. The woman was a cold-hearted shrew and having now had time to evaluate their first meeting, she had been a little too quick to twist the knife.

"Suspicious," Dev uttered.

He wondered how much truth there had been to her intimation she had been unaware of her husband's part in his family's demise. Apparently there was a videotape he had yet to see, showing a pretty graphic demonstration of violence and torture towards his birth family and himself. Shouldn't he recall such vicious things? Yet he still had no memory of those events.

When he'd finally re-emerged from his first flashback, he'd been surprised to find Stephen, his foster brother, sitting across from him in the small room. They'd grown up together, placed in the same foster family; he was the closest thing Dev had to family. They hadn't seen each other for years, however here he was and had been since Dev's arrest. Being a successful defence attorney, Stephen had promptly questioned when he had begun to suffer from flashbacks. He had informed him that, to his knowledge, this had been the first one or at least the first he had recalled and could remember upon coming out of the strange fog he'd fallen into.

Stephen also asked about his knowledge of the crimes he was supposed to have witnessed as a child, yet it was still blank. The only memories he possessed of his youth before the age of eight was the new one that had been repeating through his mind and those fragmented pieces.

"That's all I remember," he mumbled with self-derision, before going on to tell Stephen about the resurgence of his childhood nightmares, which had increased in regularity since Dev had begun working on the case involving Vincent Walker. He also admitted to the strange sleepwalking incidents he believed he'd been experiencing. Stating that because of these incidents, he couldn't categorically attest to no wrongdoing since he had no memory of what transpired during these missing periods of time.

"More memories I can't recall," he murmured in frustration. "Why the hell not?"

He then recounted finding his front door open and finding himself fully clothed when he hadn't recalled dressing, which had been why he'd contacted Stephen regarding his childhood sleeping habits. He'd also given an overview of waking up unaware of his surroundings, with no clue how he had come to be there and the discovery of his birth mother's grave. Dev finally finished by adding that he'd also noticed odd things such as waking to find himself with sore, dirty feet as though he'd wandered around outside with no shoes on, but he had never again found himself somewhere other than in his home.

Stephen had listened to all this intently, a frown forming on his face as he assessed Dev's current predicament. He had informed him that the DCI, Richard Head, had suggested a psychologist, and they would like to have him evaluated to ascertain if he was responsible for the crimes he had been arrested for, and whether he truly had no memory of the events.

At Stephen's insistence, it had been decided that it was to be someone Stephen had worked with in the past. She'd dealt with numerous clients Stephen had represented and had experience dealing with people who suffered due to past trauma. He'd also stated that, while it was true the unveiling of his real identity and the circumstances surrounding it had made him a person of interest, it did not in fact prove he had been responsible for the crimes committed. Therefore, since there was no physical evidence to link him to the crime scenes or victims, he expected Dev to be released pending further investigation.

"At least one of us has his shit together," Dev mused.

He had of course been found at the scene of Chastity's remains and the tape had proved he had buried her under duress. It had also shown that he was not involved in her death. The only real crime they could prove categorically was that he hadn't reported the crime, but with his memory being in question and his age at the time, it was unlikely they could justify keeping him in custody. Overall, Dev was stuck here temporarily until they'd had him evaluated and ran out of time to hold him before they were either forced to charge him or release him. He would have nothing but time to review what had happened in detail, how he'd ended up here and the betrayal that still stung.

"Bad memory *and* bad judgement," Dev muttered bitterly.

Wren had not even allowed him the time to accept the shocking news of his past before she'd had him in cuffs. He'd thought that they had been making tentative steps towards something more, something a bit more romantic and less work focused. But she had shattered that illusion. Shattered it at a time when he'd been reeling from news that had been both disarming and devastating. She had decided at that moment that he was nothing more than a tidy answer to the case causing her problems. She had assumed he was guilty without even hesitating and, worse than that, she had made him doubt himself too.

Dev didn't know who he had been before he'd forgotten his identity, however he knew who he'd been since, and he'd been Devlin Doyle for far longer. Given the life he had lived as Dev, there should've at least been some doubt he had committed the crimes. To his knowledge he had lived his life as an honest, upstanding member of society. That alone should have given them cause to question his guilt. He'd just started to feel as though he was finally part of something, that he belonged somewhere, only to have it cruelly ripped from him.

"Some people are just meant to be alone," he murmured sadly.

Before, he had always felt as though he'd been living in a force field; he had been present, but nobody could really reach him. That hadn't been the case since he had come here, and he had believed that he was becoming a part of their family; they had told him he had and, for the first time, he'd started to believe he could be. But that was gone now. He was as alone as he'd ever been. He'd managed to exist that way before so he should have no problem doing so again.

That left him with one problem, admittedly a huge one, if he hadn't committed the crime, then who had? Someone knew about his past enough to frame him for this, manipulated him into this corner by luring him to his own detriment. Stephen's support had reminded him of who he was, where Wren's doubt had made him question it.

Dev was going to get out of here and when he did, he was going to figure out who had set him up and settle this, for the last time. He was no longer eight years old; he wasn't afraid to go head-to-head with evil and take them out of play. Heck, he'd been putting monsters like them where they belonged for over 10 years. He would do what he always remembered doing up to this point and that was seeing that criminals answered for their crimes. "I'm coming for you, asshole," Dev promised under his breath.

With his resolve set, he began to plan where he intended to start. They might have caught him off guard this time, and his shock at the latest information had thrown him off balance, but Dev knew the law. They didn't have enough to charge him for this, he was getting out and, when he did, he was bringing hell with him.

****

Wren was recalling the moment the parcel had arrived in the incident room. Everyone had frozen with the arrival of death in a package. After the initial shock, Wren had gone into autopilot and the DCI had been informed. Being of African American descent and being in his position within the force, he was familiar with all manners of racism and violence that not everyone could comprehend with less experience under their belt. However, even he had blanched at the contents sitting on her desk, and after a slight pause he'd seen that the correct procedures for such an occurrence were followed and the evidence at hand collected appropriately. Now a day later, Wren had a gnawing feeling of guilt eating away at her gut.

"It fits. The pieces fit," she reminded herself, or at least they had, until they hadn't.

She remembered her coldness and anger upon learning of Dev's past, the mistrust and suspicion of his motives, she'd felt betrayed and used, which had made her feel out of control, and she hadn't liked the feeling one bit.

But then she'd watched the video tape of his childhood torment. It had forced her to rethink the feelings she'd had and some of that anger had diminished.

She'd understood his motives, even if she couldn't dismiss his actions as acceptable. Now though, she had undeniable thoughts running around her head; thoughts that questioned her own actions. Had she jumped to conclusions because of her emotions? If she had then she might have made a horrendous mistake. If Dev were innocent, she had taken a traumatised person who had—despite his past—become a well-balanced, admirable adult and stomped all over him, at a time when he'd been vulnerable and in shock.

Then, when he'd reached for her needing help and support, her need to protect herself from the truth had caused her to level him with a blow of her own. She'd rejected his plea to trust him, in favour of her own selfish need to cling onto control of her own feelings.

"I was just doing my job," she murmured, trying to justify it to herself.

If it turned out that Dev was innocent in all of this, she wasn't sure he'd ever be able to forgive her. Mary may have been the one delivering the news, but she had been the one to hang him out to dry. That sour thought made her stomach churn and her chest tighten. Would there be a way to make it up to him? She didn't know because if the shoe had been on the other foot, then she would have held onto that grudge indefinitely. She could only hope that Dev was more forgiving than she herself was. All she could do now was play the cards she had been dealt and hope she had a winning hand.

"When luck was handed out, I was passed over," Wren mused gloomily.

It was of course also possible that he wasn't innocent; it wasn't a foregone conclusion either way. He may have an accomplice who'd posted the parcel to cast doubt on his guilt. If that was the case, then who? If it were concluded in the evaluation that he didn't remember his past, as his medical history implied, then how could he have had help? It would only be plausible for him to have plotted this with aid if he had known of his previous identity. Otherwise, what would his motive be?

Deciding to try another angle, she took Dev out of consideration. If Dev were not involved in this sorry mess, who would be her prime suspect? She could only produce two viable candidates in answer to this question, Kelly Whelan, and Mary McNamara.

She could use the same motives Dev possessed when considering Kelly, however what was Mary's motive? She would have known about her sister's fate long ago, despite her implying otherwise. She was far too shrewd not to have seen her husband for what he was, in Wren's opinion at least. So why now? What had changed in the here and now that would prompt this sudden need to see her husband and his followers meet their end in such dramatic fashion?

They had yet to receive the preliminary report from Jack and Jilly's murders, which would give them something that might better explain Mary's motives if she was in fact the perpetrator.

"She certainly has the temperament to be a cold-hearted bitch," Wren surmised with disdain, but finding the proof to substantiate the theory might be more difficult though.

This was where Wren could focus her attention until Dev's evaluation had been completed. She pulled her phone from her pocket and placed a call to the pathologist, Dr Jodie Malone. A few minutes later when the call had ended, she had a plan. Tomorrow she would meet with the pathologist in person and go over the preliminary report in as much detail as she could give her. However, that was a task for the morning, for now she needed to go home and try to sleep. She was going to need her wits about her if she was going to unpack everything she had learned and unravel this clusterfuck.

****

Jen had spent the best part of the night and most of her day caffeinated and digging through the depths of the internet, and she thought she might have something. She had found talk of someone called "The Executioner" at play. She wasn't entirely sure who he was and how he connected to all of this, but it had indeed been implied that the murders looked very much like his handy work. She had waded through a mountain of filth just to get this far, and she was far from finished in her search.

"Why are some people so bloody disgusting?" She asked herself aloud, looking at the screen with distaste.

Who was this Executioner and how did he fit into all of this? If he was the killer, and it was implied his services were highly valued and sought after by those who travelled in dark circles, then who was his employer? Who had hired him and why had he accepted the contract? By all accounts he was very selective about his clients. Why had he chosen to involve himself in this one? "That's a bloody good question," she muttered in frustration.

She had no answers to these questions, and she had only one route to travel if she was going to find out. She would have to try and follow the money.

Unfortunately, that first meant she'd have to find his previous clients; in fact, she was going to have to use any means necessary to try and find just one thread that could give her a link to this person.

She may have to call in sick, she could be at this a while. It was going to take time to find the right deviant to give her the information she needed, and they weren't going to do that without her giving them some reason to do so. She needed to find just the right carrot to dangle, and she needed to find just the right scumbag to lure. Then and only then she might have a chance at this executioner. She was going to need more caffeine if she was going to put her life at risk hunting down a hired hitman.

"I can sleep when I'm dead," she mumbled ruefully.

****

It had taken a few days for Alec to get here but he'd finally arrived and was starting his new position in the MCU tomorrow. It had taken some wheedling on his old Super's part, considering how the last transfer they'd taken from his old unit had panned out, however his Super had insisted that nobody within the unit knew Dev better and if they wanted to get to the bottom of it all, they would do so quicker with his help. It would seem there had been some developments after the arrest, which had persuaded his soon to be superintendent to reconsider his request, though he had yet to discover exactly what that development had been.

He hadn't had time to check in with Stephen since he had been organising things so he could make his way at the earliest opportunity, and he'd also figured he would be busy dealing with Dev's release; or at least he hoped he had. Either way, come morning he was going to wade into this shitstorm and hope he could pull his friend out from the centre of it.

"Fucking idiots," Alec uttered, wondering what kind of shitshow they were running down here.

He then considered how he had become aware that his friend was in trouble. He had received a tip off from the mysterious Kelly. How did she fit into this equation? What did she gain from divulging this information?

He didn't know her motives and frankly, he found it hard to care considering she had done him a huge favour; he owed Dev this, and this woman had given him the opportunity to even the score. But, he found her interest in his boy more than a little concerning. She was a piece of this puzzle, of that he was sure, however since she didn't seem to have nefarious intentions towards them, he decided that her motives were not the priority here.

"What does it matter why?" he wondered aloud, shrugging to himself.

His top priority was to prove that Dev hadn't done this. When he had apprised himself of the case and focused his attention on catching the bastard responsible, maybe then he could figure out her role in all of this. Until then he had a hero complex to assuage and work to do.

Chapter Two

August 13th, 2014

Superintendent Jan Wright expected the DCI to be by to give her an update on DI Devlin Doyle. They were waiting for the psychologist to finish the evaluation so they could ascertain the kind of mental illness with which they were dealing.

She'd been on the force a long time and it had been her ability to read people and know how to assess their capabilities that had made her successful in her position. She was shrewd and ran a tight ship, and it was for these very reasons, she wasn't convinced of DI Doyle's guilt. It was too convenient, too neat and, whilst she couldn't deny he was dealing with some serious issues, she didn't think it was in line with the officer's character to have committed these crimes.

"I haven't worked this long in law enforcement without learning a thing or two," she muttered.

The timing of his arrival was also suspicious. She had discreetly discussed this with the Super in London, and they'd both agreed something was off about it all. However, he still needed to be treated the same as any other person of interest. If the media were to discover that not only was a detective a suspect, but that a detective who was investigating the very crime he was accused of was also being given preferential treatment or shown leniency, it would be a PR nightmare. As much as it pained her to subject Devlin to this, especially when he was already reeling from injustices she couldn't even begin to fathom, it had to be done this way; more so because of what he was.

Once they'd had him evaluated and done what they needed to, they could resume their investigation and investigate the other persons of interest in this case, because the person who had committed these crimes had the capability to set this up, and she would stake her career on it that DI Doyle wasn't their perp. The door swung open and Richard entered, walking purposefully into her office followed by the psychologist Dr Jean Winters.

"Good afternoon, Dr Winters, I'm glad to have you here helping us on this case. We find ourselves in a precarious position and we are lucky you were on hand to offer your professional opinion," Jan greeted.

"I'm glad to be of assistance," she returned.

"Please take a seat. As you can imagine, we're keen to get this cleared up as quickly as we can," Jan stated, waving in the direction of a chair opposite her.

"I understand. Firstly, I feel it only fair to tell you that the evaluation I am presenting is not a complete study, therefore it's only an initial assessment. It would take months to determine a patient's exact mental state or illness and offer a proper diagnosis. What I can tell you is my thoughts based on what I have managed to glimpse during this preliminary assessment. Devlin by his own admission is suffering from a variety of symptoms, twice during our interaction he entered an unresponsive state. It is my opinion this occurred when we discussed something that caused him severe emotional distress on a subconscious level."

"What does that indicate?" Jan asked.

"I believe he is suffering from *"flashbacks,"* he was unresponsive and had physical reactions such as: sweating, rapidly increased breathing, clenching fists, etcetera. When he returned to a conscious state of awareness he continued as though no time had passed, unaware there had been a time lapse. He also mentioned he had been suffering with nightmares recently, something he hadn't suffered from since childhood, and they appear to have occurred regularly this past week or so." Jean recounted.

"What kind of nightmares?" Jan inquired.

"I will get to that. I asked him about his childhood from the age he could recall, and his answers indicated he may have also been suffering with dissociation. I find it interesting though, that when I made mention of his time here since his relocation, he appeared more engaged with the people he works with now. It could be that confronting his past on a subconscious level at least, has lessened his dissociation while exasperating the nightmares and causing flashbacks. I do believe that with proper counselling on a regular basis he may be able to rid himself of these issues to a manageable degree," Jean recommended.

"Should he be found innocent, we will look into that," Jan assured her.

"He also mentioned that he had remembered a memory from the time before he had suffered from amnesia. Whilst he hasn't remembered everything, it is possible that memories will gradually resurface over time, and he may regain his lost memories. I saw no signs indicating that he is suffering from dissociative identity disorder, though over a period of assessment it is possible that might be the case, a full diagnosis can't be given without further analysis. It is my opinion that it is more likely to be PTSD," Jean surmised.

"Aren't people who suffer with that usually a little more confrontational or aggressive?" Jan asked with a frown.

"He shows no signs of the aggression that can sometimes be a symptom which, considering the severity of the crimes, I find unusual. I am not convinced he is the person responsible. That kind of violence usually has characteristics that I have yet to see displayed in Devlin. Overall, my advice is to have him meet regularly with a counsellor or therapist and have them help him deal with his issues so they can be managed better to avoid them becoming progressively worse," she concluded.

"Should it be determined later that he does in fact suffer from D.I.D. would that mean the likelihood he committed these crimes is higher?" the DCI asked.

"Despite how this illness is portrayed in the media, not everyone who suffers from the disorder is a violent offender capable of murder," Jean replied, waspishly, "in fact many are victims of trauma and in order to function, they develop what is termed as a *"protector"* personality, this allows them to live without having to deal with the trauma on a daily basis that may otherwise incapacitate them. However, I do not believe this is the case as far as Devlin is concerned, currently I am tentatively leaning toward PTSD." Jan sighed with relief. That was a positive outcome. Police suffered from PTSD with unfortunate regularity, it was a consequence of the profession.

Although it was rarely diagnosed and most dealt with it without seeking help, often due to the stigma that they were somehow seen as less for being human and finding the scenes they dealt with traumatic. They could arrange for him to have medical help and if it turned out, as she suspected, that he was innocent they could put it behind them by insisting he see a professional and be cleared for duty.

"In your opinion, is he our killer?" Jan asked.

"I can't be a hundred percent sure, even if I explored his case and completed a more thorough analysis. I don't think he is. The person responsible would be a psychopath and there are extremely specific indicators in their behaviour that thus far is not apparent in Devlin's demeanour," Jean answered.

"So, what signs would we be looking for?" Jan enquired, hoping it may help to have a profile of sorts.

"They would lack empathy or remorse, be manipulative and enjoy hurting others. They'd likely have an inability to distinguish right from wrong, and wouldn't fit into society easily as they would behave in a manner that conflicts with the social *"norm."* They'd lie often, likely have a criminal record in their past or have a link to crime in some way, have no regard for safety or responsibility and be quick to anger and display more than a little arrogance," Jean rattled off without hesitation.

"Thank you, you have been most helpful. One more thing, should Devlin prove to be innocent, would it be possible to arrange for you to help him in the future? Since you have already built a rapport and begun to assess him. Possibly arrange regular sessions. Assuming he isn't our perpetrator, and he is cleared of suspicion, he is an officer we wouldn't like to lose," Jan said.

"Stephen, his legal representative, has already spoken to me on this subject and I will make the necessary arrangements to have him added to my regular client base," she confirmed.

"Thank you again, you've been most informative. If we could ask you to send us a report of your assessment for our records that would be most useful," Jan enquired.

"That won't be a problem, I will get it to you without delay. It was nice to have met you," Jean replied, standing to take her leave, and offering a hand for Jan to shake, "I will be in touch."

"Have a good day and I will be sure to contact you if we need your services in the future," Jan finished, taking the proffered hand and shaking it.

With that the DCI escorted the doctor from the room, leaving Jan to consider all she had learned. She found solace from the assessment and felt as though her suspicions had been confirmed. DI Doyle was not their killer, he was their killer's "patsy." That meant that their perpetrator had an intimate knowledge of Devlin's past as Keir Whelan, which narrowed the suspect pool down nicely. Armed with the doctor's outline of the character profile and the short list of suspects who knew of Dev's real identity, they would have fewer suspects. Now they just had to find them and prove it.

****

Stephen had received a message about the assessment and rushed to the station. Jean had wanted to talk to him alone, so that Dev's assessment wasn't hindered in any way by outside influences or expectations. Which was how he came to be sat outside. A tall, wiry looking officer approached; his sandy blond hair pushed back as though he had raked his fingers through it. "Do you want some coffee? Or a tea perhaps if that's your bag. Bag? Like a tea bag?" he joked lamely, seeming only to make the joke to break the ice but not really feeling it.

"I wouldn't say no, it's been busy at work and this case has been trying to say the least," Stephen admitted.

"I'm DS Matt Ainsworth, so you know. I'm really hoping Dev isn't guilty and I wouldn't mind some help in proving that. We aren't Dev's enemies in this, we do however have a duty to see that the law is upheld. Do you understand what I'm saying?" Matt stated, the implication that they could use each other's assistance was clear in his words and tone.

"I do. I will be doing everything in my power to see that he is released and cleared of this, so we can agree so long as our goals align. Should at any time that prove not to be the case however, you should know I won't be pulling any punches, metaphorically speaking of course. Do you understand?" Stephen fired back, not missing a beat.

"In that case, this may be the start of a beautiful friendship," Matt teased, leading him toward the canteen, "Now let's see about that drink, shall we?"

After being given a less than stellar coffee and a contact number from the DS, "should he find himself in need of assistance," he'd returned to his post. On arriving, he found Superintendent Jan Wright waiting, the DCI stood gazing around, impatience clear in his posture.

"I'm sorry, were you looking for me?" Stephen asked, "Your DS offered me coffee and honestly, I needed a boost."

"Yes. Hello Mr Doyle, I was hoping we could have a discussion with Devlin and yourself," Jan answered, offering him a polite smile, "shall we?"

"After you," Stephen agreed.

They entered the room where Dev was being held and he looked up warily as they did. Stephen shot him a look of reassurance and his posture lost some of its tension. Stephen took a seat next to him while the two officers sat opposite.

"Devlin, DCI Head and I are here to discuss the process we will be following from here. Now, we will not be charging you. After much deliberation we believe there is not substantial evidence to do so at this time. You are still a person of interest and therefore it would be in your best interests to remain local and be on hand should we need to re-evaluate this stance. We will be keeping your warrant card and placing you on suspension, unfortunately that's procedure in situations such as this. Therefore, you will not have access to the system or your fellow officers until the matter is resolved and the case concluded. Do you understand?" the Super informed him.

"Aye ma'am, I understand," Dev answered.

"Good. I'm glad. Now I want to be sure that you take particular care to understand my next instruction, you are to avoid anything pertaining to this case and let the team deal with it. Are we clear?" she said, watching him closely.

"Aye, I hear you," Dev acknowledged, but this time some of the sincerity from before was missing. Stephen took that to mean he may not be taking that particular warning under advisement.

"In that case, you are free to go, I will have your release processed and your belongings returned to you. Might I suggest you use this time to focus your attention on seeking regular counsel from Dr Winters? I believe your representative has made arrangements on your behalf," Jan remarked, giving a more subtle warning to Dev not to take matters into his own hands.

"Thank you, ma'am," Dev responded, his face unreadable.

As the officers departed from the room, a message beeped on Stephen's phone. He pulled it out to check it and Dev looked at him in question.

"They're here," he said simply.

****

Wren heard the buzzing around the incident room, and she wasn't sure she believed it; Dev was being released. She hurried along to see for herself, and arrived just in time to see Dev and his brother step in her direction. She'd not considered what she might say to him, only felt the compulsive need to see him free. As they stood, each in the other's path, there was a moment of awkwardness one might expect given the circumstances. They eyed each other warily in silence, a myriad of emotions passing between them, both unsure of which they should settle on.

"Dev..." Wren began, finally settling on guilt.

"Save it, Angel," he replied, sarcasm dripping off the pet-name as he brushed past her. His brother's usual stoicism left his face as he gazed at her with curiosity. Dev left the station, not bothering to check if his brother followed.

"Give it time. I'm sorry, I don't believe I know your name..." Stephen said, looking at her expectantly.

"Serenity, though most people call me Wren," she offered quietly, still perplexed at Dev's coldness.

"But not my brother though, he doesn't call you that, does he?" Stephen mused, more to himself.

"No..." Wren replied flatly, "not your brother."

"Hmmm…" Stephen muttered, deep in thought, before turning to catch up to his brother.

Wren stood in the foyer, feeling more than a little foolish. What had she really been expecting? She stared helplessly at the two men as they strode to a vehicle before slowly turning away, a numbness settling over her. When she returned to the incident room, Matt waited expectantly.

"Well? Is it true?" he asked when she offered no reply to the question he wanted answered.

"It would appear so," Wren answered, with no emotion in her voice.

"So, that means we have to go back to the drawing board...or the big board in our case," Matt surmised.

"He's still a person of interest," Wren corrected, "he's just not our only one. I just wish Jen was here, we could use her help. She'd already begun trying to track down Kelly Whelan and we could definitely use her help digging through Mary McNamara's life with a fine-tooth comb. There might not be any evidence she is linked, but that woman sets off my radar. I don't believe that bullshit she was selling that she had only just learned her husband was a crook, she may have caught me off guard throwing Dev under the bus that way and it certainly had the effect she was hoping for. If I could arrest people from vibes alone, she'd top my list," she stated, sighing. Matt nodded then frowned.

"Aren't you going to be late?" Matt asked suddenly, as though the thought had just occurred to him.

"Huh?" she murmured, distracted by her thoughts of Mary.

"For the pathologist?" Matt reminded her.

"Oh shit!" Wren exclaimed, rushing towards the exit before doubling back for her keys and making a hasty retreat for the door.

She arrived twenty minutes late. Dr Jodie Malone stood eating, using the delay wisely and stuffing a piece of pasty in her mouth. Upon seeing Wren's arrival, she hastily tried to swallow her mouthful and when that proved too hard, the big bite not chewed enough to fully digest it, she mumbled through it.

"Sorry, I thought you forgot."

"I did and it's fine, finish your food, I kept you waiting, only fair I take a turn," Wren replied, a wry smile pulling at her mouth.

Once Jodie had polished off the pastry and picked up her drink, taking a swallow to wash it down, she indicated for Wren to follow her and stopped before a door. She pulled on a mask and offered one to Wren, who took it gratefully. The smell was never something to look forward to; it didn't matter what you did, whether you wore a mask or not, it lingered long after you got your first whiff and stayed cloying up the cavity in your face long after you left. No amount of deodorant or cologne would erase it. The foul odour clung to life in contrast to its source. Having the bodies refrigerated did slow the decomposition process some, yet not enough to stop the process or the smell. Jodie pulled a small tub from her pocket and Wren saw a small pot of VapoRub in her hand.

She offered it to Wren and said, "Might take the edge off." Wren nodded, taking a small dab, and putting it under her nose and replacing her mask.

The strength of the menthol concoction hit her hard and she could feel its potency racing along the pathways connecting the nose, mouth and throat as it spread, the sting of it burning at her eyes a little. If nothing else it cleared her head, she thought. Jodie had taken the time she had done this to open the door and they entered. On the other side Jodie pulled some gloves on and they approached the two metal tables on wheels, covered with sheets, the outline of the bodies beneath them unmistakable which Wren presumed to be their victims.

"I sent the preliminary report to the station when you didn't show, I wasn't sure you were going to make it," she began, "Cause of death for Jack McNamara was beheading, though I think it was a close call. If that hadn't been the cause then he would likely have bled out after having his penis removed from his body," she stated.

"I'm sorry, what?" Wren gasped with surprise.

"Oh...You didn't know that, right, I'll back up. It is my opinion the two were stripped of their clothes and restrained while unconscious," she pulled back the cover of one to reveal the body of Jack McNamara, his head now returned to its original home, though whether or not it had been reattached or just rested in place Wren couldn't ascertain. "I have taken samples for toxicology to examine. I believe that they were injected with some kind of sedative, they both have similar looking marks on their neck indicative of an injection," she pointed to the mark on Jack's neck and Wren nodded.

"I found no signs of a struggle, no tissue under the nails or anything that may indicate they'd had some kind of struggle with the killer. I did find marks on the wrists and ankles that showed they did struggle whilst restrained though," she once again showed Wren the area she was addressing and Wren saw the bruising and marks she mentioned, "by the abrasions we found and some small samples I collected and sent off, I would be inclined to say they were tied with rope. If we had managed to get the rope, we may have been able to pull DNA from it, but as the sample was small all it would tell us is what they were tied with," she explained.

"So, they were sedated, stripped, tied and then they woke up and struggled with their restraints before the murderer removed his...they lopped off his...part...while he was unconscious," Wren reiterated, awkwardly.

"Almost but no, it was removed while he was conscious." She indicated lower and pointed to several marks around where the penis would have been, "See these marks? I believe that the killer made several attempts to cut it off but Jack likely wasn't inclined to allow this easily, he struggled so the cuts here and here," she pointed to the places she addressed, "are what I believed to be his attempts to do the deed while Jack fought against it. Since he was restrained eventually the killer finally hit his target and as you can see..." she made a whoosh and thump sound, while using her hand she mimed out the effects to accompany them, giving Wren a thorough yet unnecessary understanding of what followed.

"That's...unpleasant." Wren remarked, at a loss for a better description.

"Yes, that does seem likely," Jodie concurred.

"Okay so you said he didn't bleed out," Wren prompted, not wanting to linger on that subject.

"You'd think he would, but no, I mean he would've eventually but he had his head chopped off before that came to pass," Jodie told her, then continued, "he was cleaned up and redressed in the costume the killer put him in. The decapitation was more obvious than his castration so was only noticed upon examination after the clothing was removed. The forensic evidence from the crime scene will likely support my theory," Jodie explained.

"Okay, so Jilly's cause of death was also decapitation, I'm assuming she didn't get castrated, so was Jilly's a straightforward decapitation?" Wren asked, wincing at the idea that she could consider any kind of decapitation straight forward.

"Unfortunately, Jilly had problems of her own. She died before her beheading," she said, moving to the second table and uncovering Jilly's remains pointing to a long cut that ran from between the alley of her breasts and ended down in her pelvic region.

"What the hell?" Wren's eyebrows lifted in surprise as her eyes widened.

"She was cut with a very sharp knife, looking at the wound I would be inclined to say it was a fixed blade, a bowie knife. Easy to control, not likely to bend under duress or break off, then her womb was removed," Jodie informed her.

"What? Removed? How?" Wren spluttered out the questions in short succession.

"Cut out, with the same blade, in fact all of the injuries sustained beside the severing of their heads appear to have been done with the same blade. Also, I don't know if this will be important or not, she had recently had a surgical procedure. It would appear she had an ectopic pregnancy that needed to be removed. Now, there is a time period in the initial stages where being injected with methotrexate will stop the tissue from growing and prevent it rupturing, however it would appear in her case that time had passed. She had a laparoscopy performed. It is hard to say if this relates to her death or is just a coincidence, however it never hurts to know these things in the event it becomes relevant later," she remarked.

"So, she was cut open and had her womb removed and had recently had an ectopic pregnancy. Anything else?" Wren enquired; not entirely sure she wanted the answer.

"The cause of death in her case was the incision made to remove her womb; she was decapitated postmortem. We also found the penis in her oesophagus," Jodie told her.

"Seriously? Was that before or after she was beheaded?" Wren asked, wrinkling her nose with distaste.

"After, otherwise we may have had to spend longer digging through the scene for the two halves, it is unlikely it would have been pushed far enough down her throat if it had been before, it wouldn't have avoided a second chopping if that were true," she remarked as though considering it.

"Well, that's a comforting thought," Wren muttered sarcastically.

"The time of death remains as stated in the report I have sent. The toxicology report may be slightly longer coming back, there is a backlog with so many things being processed in the last week or so," Jodie stated.

"Is that all?" Wren asked hopefully.

"Is that all? Wasn't that enough?" Jodie asked, looking at her in amusement.

"Oh yeah, more than enough," Wren agreed, adding emphasis to the word more, to stress the point, "Thank you for your time, sorry I kept you waiting."

"No worries, it was probably a good thing I finally found time to eat something," she returned.

After covering the two bodies, she followed Wren from the room and bid her farewell as she left the building. Wren wasn't sure how all the information she'd been given would help, but writing it onto the big board may spark some ideas. Either way it was time she returned to the station.

Chapter Three

Dev was still annoyed when he reached the vehicle. He stopped and waited for Stephen to move his ass, shifting his weight from foot to foot impatiently, his agitation clear.

"It's not her fault, you know," Stephen said gently, "It's the job, I know deep down you know that and you're hurt she didn't fight your corner, but she was in a corner of her own. Trapped in it by her duty. She has to follow where the evidence takes her and if the roles were reversed, no matter how much you delude yourself into believing differently, you would have done the same thing," he preached, "you are usually so reasonable about things, ever the peacemaker. I find it intriguing that you are suddenly being led by your emotions and not logic in this. What about that particular officer, I wonder, is causing this deviation of character, brother?" He smirked and looked at him expectantly. Dev scowled in return and then chose to ignore him as though he had said nothing.

"Nothing to say for yourself, brother? How unlike you." He chuckled wryly.

"Feck off," Dev muttered, only serving to increase Stephen's smug smirk.

"I suppose it's for the best, we don't really have time for a brotherly chitchat, we have guests arriving," Stephen replied.

Dev frowned at that before realisation dawned on him. "What did you do?" he asked suspiciously.

"I sent out a distress signal, and Dev mate, make no mistake you are in distress," Stephen answered shiftily.

However, Dev wasn't fooled and groaned, "you called them, didn't you?"

"I did," Stephen confirmed, not even a bit sorry, "you may not believe it, but they are your family. Whether you choose to believe it or not doesn't change the facts. You don't get to decide how others choose to view you, that's not how it works. I gave them a heads up, but I didn't put a gun to their heads and demand they show up, they chose to come, just as I did. So, suck it up buttercup and try to look a little more grateful," he scolded.

Dev looked sheepish and nodded with as much graciousness as he could muster, which frankly, needed some work given his mood. He couldn't say he wanted this but at least they had his back. His thoughts briefly returned to Wren, but he pushed them away. He wasn't ready to deal with them yet, apparently he had a family reunion to attend.

Upon their arrival, the "guests" fell over each other to make themselves known, Dev had always been the quietest of their number and the others were...not.

"Well, well, well, if it isn't the prodigal brother," Chris began slapping him on the back affectionately, "I hear you have finally found yourself in a spot of bother mate. A little late in the day for a teenage rebellion, but you always were a late bloomer," he joked.

Dev raised an eyebrow before replying, "It wasn't that I bloomed late, it was that you were always freakishly large."

Raven rolled her eyes at the two of them before entering the fray, "you never call, you never write. One might think you are trying to pretend you don't know us," she bit out sharply, then chuckled at Dev's guilty expression.

"Itsybit, still hacking into places you shouldn't?" Dev asked tutting at her.

"I did that one time!" she exclaimed and at Dev's knowing look, she shrugged and smiled mischievously, "Okay, I got *caught* one time."

"Aye, that's what I thought," Dev laughed.

"Just the two of you?" Stephen asked, yet didn't seem as surprised as he might.

"Gabe is currently *"otherwise engaged,"* on a job, but sends his regrets and a message I can only presume you will understand. He said *"tell Stephen I am doing all I can from my end."* Care to enlighten us?" Chris replied, narrowing his eyes with suspicion as though he might be able to read Stephen's thoughts if he looked closely enough.

"I'm afraid not," Stephen answered mysteriously, "it would ruin the surprise."

"Room for one more?" A voice came from the open doorway behind the arrivals.

"Alec?" Dev said in confusion.

"None other. Never did like to miss a party," he teased.

"Looks like we have quite a gathering going," Stephen said.

"It's great to see you all, truly, however is somebody going to let me in on the purpose for your arrival?" Dev enquired, not at all convinced something untoward wasn't afoot.

"We are going to be your team," Stephen supplied.

"I'm not allowed to work this case, you were there, you heard the Super tell me that exact thing," Dev chided.

"I know you, brother, we all do. No amount of warning is going to stop you from finding the underlying cause of this. You were already hunting them; they made it personal. Their mistake, undoubtedly, because now you will be like a bloodhound. You will not stop until you have found them, and you'll be even more relentless than before," Stephen replied, knowingly, "So here we are, you may have lost your *"law-abiding friends"* but we are better," Stephen finished.

"I resent that implication, I am still his law-abiding friend," Alec chimed in, feigning hurt.

"Chris' misspent youth means he has ears on the ground in a world you can't begin to get into with your job title," Stephen explained, "Raven's role here speaks for itself. Not much can transpire on a computer that she can't get to and of course we have *"eyes on the inside"* courtesy of Alec, and I will be working to keep you all out of prison."

"Oh aye? What pray tell is my role in this band of merry men?" Dev asked.

"You, brother, have the pleasure of trying to keep us all in line. Lucky bastard!" Stephen winked at him, then laughed at the look of horror on Dev's face.

"Holy Mary, mother of God!" Dev groaned, "What did I do to deserve this?"

"Trying to go it alone was what landed you in the slammer, Dev. We are here to see you don't make that mistake a second time," Stephen answered, "Now. Where do you want us to begin?"

****

Keri watched the gathering and merriment from afar. She found herself both a little jealous and a little glad that her brother had people he could count on. She considered for a moment if there might be room for a little one before recalling that she had other priorities in this game of cat and mouse. Later she might, hopefully, have a spot in her brother's gang of misfits, she suspected she would fit better than he did. However she had a snake problem to take care of first and unfortunately, her mother was waiting and she wasn't known for her patience. She gave one last wistful look at the house before standing tall and heading off to meet with her wicked fake mother.

"Where in the name of God have you been?" Mary hissed as she arrived. A few unfamiliar faces stood amongst the remaining "old-timers". It would appear her mother had been "recruiting".

"Are you allowed to say his name aloud? Doesn't Satan have to repent if he speaks the Lord's name?" Keri jested.

"This is not a laughing matter! They have released him!" Mary seethed.

"Released who, Mother?" Keri asked, innocently.

"The detective that I set up to take the fall for your father's murder of course!" she said, looking at her as though she were an imbecile.

"So? Find a new patsy. What does it matter?" Keri asked, knowing the answer, but also knowing her mother would let the matter drop so she could continue to keep her "secrets."

"It matters because I can't seem to find out *why* they released him," she answered through clenched teeth. "The investigating team has closed ranks and are keeping that information to themselves, meaning my source is unable to give me the answers I need. If he is released and they do not charge him, then that means that they will continue to poke around where I do not wish them to. This is vexing to say the least. If I do not know why he was released, then I cannot rectify their error and give them what they need to reconsider. Honestly, am I the only person with a brain?"

"What do you suggest, Mother?" Keri asked, sarcastically.

"I suggest that we find a way to *persuade* the source that it would be in his best interests to try a little fucking harder, that is what I suggest!" she said, stomping her foot in a fit of temper. The men drew back slightly, wary of what a mood like that could mean.

"I'm assuming that you have a plan?" Keri replied, and the men stepped a little closer again, waiting with anticipation for her answer.

"I do," she said, a smile finally appearing on her face.

After listening to what her mother had decreed, she kept her face passive and played along, keeping her composure, and doing what she needed to so that her mother didn't suspect her part in all this. She showered her mother with false praise for her brilliance and her mother's smugness and arrogance meant that she found her admiration fitting and didn't suspect Keri's deceit.

Keri wasn't sure if she was going to be able to stop this madness, but she hoped with everything she had, she could in some way prevent it from happening. Her mother had always been cunning and mean but this was a new level of insanity. Power had only strengthened her delusion that she was the ultimate villain, untouchable to all those that challenged her. For all those involved she hoped that her mother was proved wrong. Leaving her mother's house, she speed-dialled a number and waited.

 "Keri-blossom!" the voice answered sweetly.

 "My heart, I need you to do something for me and I need you to do it quickly..." she began.

****

  Jen had been playing a game of bluff for some time now, she had offered herself up as a "prize"; her "real self," not the fake person she was currently pretending to be. They had gone back and forth for a day or two and she felt like she might finally be making some headway. The monster on the other end of the conversation was extremely interested in acquiring her as a "toy" to be used at his bidding, it would seem that the idea of having an "uptight police bitch" at his mercy appealed to his sadistic tendencies.

  She nearly had what she needed, just a few more pushes and she'd be there. She had made it clear she would be willing to have herself delivered as payment if he could return the favour by explaining how to get in the same circles as the Executioner. Feeding him some bullshit about acquiring his services so he could have his bitch wife dealt with. She waited anxiously for the reply and the moments seemed to pass in slow motion. Finally, a reply came, and she read it with excitement.

"Got you, you bitch," Jen said excitedly and re-read the message just to be sure. "If you wish to deal with the Executioner, you first have to get the approval of his bitch, Mary."

She raced to the door, dialled Wren's number but it went to voicemail. So, she left a message, "Wren, it's me. I'm coming in. I have something you need to see, I'm on my way."

As she hastened to her car, she opened the door and sat down, buzzing with anticipation of the piece to the puzzle she had uncovered and then she realised something too late. The door had been open without her unlocking it. Before she could react, something was pressed into her neck and fear trickled down her spine as realisation hit her.

"It would seem you and the Executioner have made an appointment," the voice said, and a cloth covered her mouth...chloroform... her last thoughts were that, if she had to die, she wished she had at least managed to get the information to the team first.

****

Dev needed some air. As nice as it was having his family around him again after all these years, he needed some space. Family... He found it strange that for the first time he considered them as such. On some subconscious level he'd been aware of the family he'd once had. The memory there but locked away. Knowing this now made his reluctance to accept a new one more understandable, it came from a place of fear. Fear of suffering more loss and his unwillingness to accept any more pain.

Now though, it would seem the fog had lifted and he had finally accepted their role in his life. His brothers and his sister. His sister... it occurred to him then that somewhere out there he had a real sister, was she still out there somewhere? Had he forgotten her and left her to suffer a fate worse than death? Or had she died too. If he hadn't lost his memory, could he have saved her? Was she the person out there exacting revenge on the "victims" he'd been investigating?

"Where is she?" he wondered aloud, sadness in his muttered question.

He'd not had a lot of time to process the truth of his past properly yet, he'd accepted it as the truth but between his arrest and Wren's betrayal he had been focused on his situation rather than the actuality of his real identity. This was the first time he'd been alone, truly alone since he'd found out and he found himself analysing it. Not from the standpoint of the prospect of being a killer; but as the victim of the crimes committed against himself and his long-forgotten family.

The police hadn't played him the video that had been taken into evidence. They had been advised against showing it to him by the psychologist for fear it may be a trigger, causing untold anguish and harm to his mental health and possibly causing a physical reaction that may have put officers at risk of physical harm. Since the full extent of his PTSD was not yet diagnosed comprehensively, they had agreed. He found himself curious though, convinced not knowing might be more harmful and drive him insane with the possibilities of what might've been on it instead.

"I should be allowed to watch a video that I'm the fecking star of," Dev murmured bitterly.

Wandering into a nearby park, he sat down on a bench there, his thoughts turning to the one memory that had resurfaced. The last memory of his father. Thinking back now, he had always had a gut feeling he'd been better off not remembering and it turned out, he had a worthy cause for that. He then wondered how it had come about that he had been mistakenly assumed dead; his identity being mixed up with that of the traveller boy who had died in his stead. He felt an array of feelings rise in his chest, each fighting for a place and attention in his thoughts and suddenly he felt overwhelmed. His breaths came fast and ragged, his tongue felt too big for his mouth, as his throat felt as though it was closing and air couldn't seem to pass through it, his heart raced furiously, and panic made him consider if he were having a heart attack.

"Excuse me?" A voice that sounded far away, came out of nowhere. He looked up and the blurry sight of a blonde woman swam in front of his eyes as she crouched down to his level. Amidst his struggle to breathe, he vaguely heard her giving him a stern command to take deep breaths. His gaze locked on her shoulders as they rose up as she breathed in slowly, then fell again as she released it. Emulating her actions, he found himself doing as she directed in a cool, calm but firm voice. His vision regained focus, and the feeling of suffocation ebbed away and finally receded. As he relaxed, he looked at her with curiosity.

"You were having a panic attack," she told him with a certainty that made him feel strangely reassured.

"How did you–?" he started.

"I'm a doctor," she said simply.

He nodded, that made sense. He looked at her once again and a strange sense of familiarity had him pausing, he narrowed his gaze, eying her with suspicion before asking, warily, "Have we met?"

"I was the doctor who treated you when you were brought in not long ago," she replied, "perhaps between your bouts of unconsciousness you had moments of lucidity," she answered smoothly, showing no signs of deceit. Dev nodded and relaxed.

"Thank you for helping, I thought for a moment there that I was having a heart attack," he told her, laughing at the absurdity of it.

"It's not a problem, I have a brother who suffers from them, he has PTSD and gets nightmares too… I miss him sometimes, I wish we were closer," she confided, sadly.

Dev went quiet at this, wondering if he really wanted to know any more on that subject, the parallels making him uncomfortable.

"I should be getting along now but here," she handed him a piece of paper with a number neatly scribed on it, he hadn't seen her write it but took it anyway not wanting to seem rude after she had aided him, "should you need any medical assistance or need to talk to an objective ear, then give me a call and I'll listen, okay?" Then she stood up, gave his arm a squeeze and left as suddenly as she had appeared. He sat a few moments in a daze when a hand landed on his shoulder.

"Are you finished brooding, brother?" Stephen enquired.

"Aye," Dev answered, giving one final lingering look at the direction the woman had left in, before turning to head back to Stephen's home.

****

Keri watched from her hiding spot, knowing that she shouldn't have done that but seeing his fear and distress had been too much for her to bear. She watched as his defence attorney and foster brother led him away from the park and she sighed. She hadn't lied; now that she had found him again, she found that she wanted to know her brother.

They were both survivors of a brutal past, only he could understand her as she understood him. She longed to leave this place and take him far away from all that had been stolen from them here and start again as a real family, but she knew that wouldn't happen while their aunt, her surrogate mother, still had breath in her body. With even more reason to see this concluded she left and rang Cameron. When he answered she asked him, "did you get it done?"

"Keri-blossom you wound me, I will deliver anything you ask of me..." he replied, dramatically.

"Thank you, my heart. I will be sure to reward you in kind," she told him smiling.

Chapter Four

Wren made it all the way back to the incident room when her phone pinged with a message on her answerphone. She pressed to listen, and Jen's voice spoke excitedly on the other end. Guess she was feeling better judging by the sound of her eager, happy tone. As she listened, she frowned and checked the time. Her phone had been off whilst she had been with the pathologist, and it had been an hour since the message had been left. She did the maths in her head of Jen's travel time and looked around the room, but saw no sign of her having been there. Ash was on the phone near the back end of the room, and she waited for him to finish his call before addressing him.

"Have you seen Jen?" she asked.

"Isn't she sick?" he returned, his confusion clear on his face.

"She rang me, left a message. It would seem she was feeling better, and she was making her way in. That was an hour ago," she explained, before reaching for her phone and replaying the message on speakerphone so he could hear it.

"That's odd because I've been here the entire time. Unless she came while I was making coffee, but then why wouldn't she check the canteen? Maybe her car broke down or something and she got waylaid," he offered, trying to keep a level head and think logically.

"We should check it out. Have a drive to her home? If her car didn't start, she might be there," he tried again.

"Then why didn't she let us know that she was still coming but had been delayed?" Wren countered.

"Maybe she's on the phone with someone arranging to get it fixed?" Ash considered, uncertainty creeping in.

"I've rung her. It goes straight to voicemail each time, she isn't answering. We should go and check on her just in case," Wren said adamantly, worried about Jen, "by the sound of her message she had information and people with information have not fared well during this case."

****

Alec arrived at his new station and found it surprisingly quiet. That made him slightly concerned, they knew he was coming, right? He waited a few minutes looking around for signs of life, maybe there had been another murder and he'd missed them or another case, maybe they went out for lunch.

"Sorry for the delay, DS Morgan," the DCI said as he rushed over to greet him, "It would appear my officers have vacated the premises for a spell, so I had to come down to collect you. What with Devlin currently out of commission and Jen out sick, we are a little short-handed with the others in the wind."

"No problem, I understand," he replied politely, relieved he could stop running scenarios through his head.

"So, tell me, how acquainted are you with the *"Brother John"* case?" the DCI asked innocently, a knowing look on his face.

Alec cast his mind back to Dev's wall of chaos and while he hadn't had much time to study it in depth and take it all in, he felt he had a fairly good handle on the ins and outs of it.

"I'd say I have a working knowledge of it, not a complete and detailed account," Alec answered, honestly.

"That's a good start, follow me and while my officers do whatever it is they decided was important enough to jump ship, let me see if I can get you fully up to speed," he said, amiably.

He walked him through to the incident room and over to the big board full of case information, not entirely different from the one he had left behind that was taking up residence on Dev's wall. The DCI began going over the case as it had unravelled the week prior to his arrival. Alec listened attentively, silently drawing conclusions from the new pieces he learned as they came up and added them to the pieces he had ascertained from before Dev's arrest and from the time spent with the "Doyle Delinquents" not long before.

Next the DCI began going over the persons of interest they'd had over the course of the case. As it had developed many had been removed as their deaths had joined the victim's numbers. He wasn't surprised to see his friend's name listed at the top of the most recent additions, his recent arrest still fresh and had made him the prime suspect for a time. Mary McNamara was also listed in that particular list. He wasn't sure when she had been added, with Devlin's arrest he hadn't had much opportunity to add the most recent details to his own wall. That was when his ears pricked at something the DCI had been saying and he froze.

"Repeat that last name," he said with urgency.

"Sorry?" the DCI asked, confused.

Alec's mind whirled, trying to recall Dev's account of the case, he had not told him her name. He'd referred to Mary as his "aunt" and said they'd had no luck finding his sister.

"The name! What was the name?" Alec all but shouted.

"The Whelan girl?" The DCI enquired, clarifying his question, his own gaze unsure as though he wasn't clear on what all the fuss was about.

"Yes, I need to be sure that you said what I think you said!" Alec pressed, alarm making him prickly.

"Kelly? Kelly Whelan. What on earth is wrong with you?" the DCI asked, wariness making him give him a once over, watching him closely as he waited for an explanation.

"Kelly," Alec repeated, dumbfounded, "If I'm not mistaken and I may be wrong, but I believe not only is Miss Whelan very much alive, but she is also not really missing, just not found," he informed the senior officer, enigmatically.

"Speak up, boy," The DCI said, his tone sharp, "whatever you think you must add, spit it out already. I have neither the time nor the patience for guessing games and evasive answers."

"I can't be sure, but I think I received a call from the infamous Kelly herself," Alec finally divulged.

The DCI's posture straightened, and he went still, he eyed Alec with suspicion and spoke through gritted teeth, "I think you had better tell me what you know, son."

Alec told him, only leaving out Stephen's involvement and the unauthorised investigation being run on the side. He did, however, tell him what he considered to be relevant.

"She rang you. Do you have a number we could trace?" he asked Alec quickly.

"No, it was withheld," Alec replied.

"Did you get a trace on it?" the DCI continued, hopefully though knowing it was highly unlikely.

"I was not expecting to need to, she hadn't called before and hasn't since," Alec answered.

"So, no contact since that one call?" the DCI returned.

"None," Alec informed him.

"Do you think she might?" The DCI asked his questions, coming with such quick fire speed Alec was barely keeping up with them.

"I don't know," Alec admitted.

"How did she come to have your number?" he pressed.

"Again, I don't have any answer for you," Alec answered patiently.

"Okay, so we don't actually have much more except that means she's at least in the country, she's alive and she is a suspect who *isn't* trying to frame Dev but help him." He paused to think this over, "so she might not be the killer but she knows he isn't?" he suggested, more to himself than to Alec, "or is she an accomplice and are they killing together?" He was floating the ideas aloud, sounding it out as he processed this added information, trying to see how it fit in with what they already knew and what it meant.

"I'm quite sure Dev is unaware she is alive. I only just worked it out for myself, and you are the only person who knows she rang me," Alec contradicted.

"So how does she know he's not guilty?" the DCI frowned in puzzlement.

"She's watching him!" Alec suddenly exclaimed, realisation and alarm flooding him.

"Jesus!" the DCI concurred, "You may be right."

****

Wren and Ash pulled up to Jen's place. Getting out of their car they looked around, spotting her car beside the curb out front. They approached the front door warily, nothing seemed amiss. Reaching out Wren pressed the bell. It rang loudly and they waited. Jen would normally answer with her voice, she had the system set up to do it, since she was often in the middle of some technical thing or another on her computer. However, there was no answer. They looked at each other in confusion. Her car was here but she wasn't. What did it mean?

Ash left Wren's side to walk to the car, Wren pressed the bell a second time and waited. Turning to watch as Ash assessed the vehicle, he made a face and reached for the door and without any resistance he found it opened. He looked at Wren, worried now, his forehead creased as he stated unnecessarily, "It's open."

Wren moved away from the front door to join him at the car, pulling on gloves as she went. Ash, noticing her actions, reached into his own pocket and mimicked her. Wren popped her head inside the car and took a long look around and then stopped her gaze settling on something. She leaned down and found a scrap of torn clothing and what looked like blood spotting it. Her assessment of it left her fearing the worst.

If she didn't know any better, she would think that Jen had scraped herself as she'd been dragged from her vehicle. Whether it was worry and paranoia that had her jumping to this conclusion or experience she wasn't certain, but what she did know was that Jen had been heading to the station. She'd found something she deemed important enough to get excited over and she had neither shown up at the station or made it any further than her vehicle which had been left unlocked, indicating she had entered it as the torn cloth suggested.

She shifted her weight onto her back foot and leaned back out of the vehicle reaching this time for her phone. She needed to call this in, they had an officer missing. As she spoke on the phone and gave the Super the news, Ash continued to look inside the vehicle through every window, gazing intently from different viewpoints without further disturbing it in fear he may taint any trace evidence that might be there.

"I can't see any sign of bleeding, Wren," he announced, "no sign of a struggle either."

"No... so, what are we thinking? Someone was waiting for her inside the vehicle, and she was drugged? Like the others?" Wren asked.

"I don't think that would be a long stretch," Ash agreed.

"So, she is still alive, we have time to find her?" Wren asked, fear mixing with hope and a little desperation thrown in.

"Christ, I hope so," Ash answered with fervour.

"Me too," Wren replied, quietly.

****

Alec and the DCI were still thinking about all they had discovered when the Super gave them the news. They'd barely had time to come to terms with one revelation before they had landed themselves amongst another. An officer was missing, a suspected kidnapping and she'd had information on the case. This was not looking at all good for officer DC Cartwright. As they assembled a backup team together to head out, Alec took a moment to take out his phone and drop Stephen a message. He couldn't be seen to be feeding information to Dev, but Stephen would relay the news. He typed quickly. "Kelly Whelan is alive. She was the person who called to tip me off. Might be watching Dev. Jen Cartwright is missing. Can't talk now. Keep your eyes open." He pressed send and got into gear.

They had just arrived at Jen Cartwright's home when his phone rang in his pocket. He looked at it and the withheld number flashed up on the screen. The DCI looked at him and must've noticed the odd look on his face. He approached Alec and they moved off to the side.

"Is it her?" the DCI asked.

"I'm not sure, the number is withheld," Alec replied.

"Answer it," the DCI instructed.

"Hello?" Alec answered cautiously.

"Tell them Jen Cartwright is dead. You have a leak, tell them she's dead. It's important," Kelly Whelan said and then the line went dead.

"Well?" The DCI asked, waiting for him to speak. "Was it her?" Alec nodded, still processing the short call. "What are you waiting for? What did she say?" He whispered to Alec angrily.

"She said, tell them Jen Cartwright is dead," he repeated.

"What?" the DCI said, his face going grey and his eyes going wide.

"She said tell them—" Alec began to repeat again.

"I heard what you said, boy!" the DCI snapped, "Is it true?"

"I can't imagine why she'd lie, that's not the same as knowing it's true though," Alec responded.

The DCI seemed to shrink before his eyes, his body deflating like an untied balloon. He whispered to Alec again, "no, keep the calls between us for now, not that you received them but who is making them, just until we figure out what the hell is going on." Alec nodded.

"For what it's worth, I'm sorry." Alec said just as quietly.

"Me too, son, me too," the DCI replied flatly.

Alec took a moment to process the call. They had a leak. Was Jen Cartwright really dead? He couldn't be sure. He did hope he'd done the right thing, keeping the leak part to himself. If there was, he hadn't been here long enough to know who to trust. Was Jen's death part of some bigger picture and did it involve flushing out the leak? He couldn't be sure of anything; he would need to get to Stephen's place as soon as he finished for the day.

He couldn't be seen at Dev's home, but Stephen would see that they were apprised of the new situation, his friend and his family couldn't be the leak therefore they were safe to work this out with. Other than them he didn't know. That was the thing about moles. They hid until they were lured out into the open.

As he reassured himself that this was the right course of action, he noticed a tall, white-haired woman barging her way toward him. She moved with noticeable anger flashing in her eerie violet eyes and Alec braced himself for the arrival of what could only be Dev's "Angel", Serenity Jones.

"Who the fuck are you?" she spat.

"DS Morgan," he said simply.

"The DCI informs me you received an anonymous call? He tells me they said that Jen is dead?" she hissed.

"Yes," he said, not knowing what else to say. She pushed at his chest roughly, before continuing her tirade.

"Let's get something really clear. I don't know you. I don't trust you. You appear out of nowhere, it's your first day on the case and you're receiving calls telling you that one of our officers, my friend, is dead? Why would they tell you? Seems a little convenient to me. I'd go as far as to say downright suspicious. I'm fucking watching you, make no mistake. Secondly, until I find Jen's cold, dead corpse, SHE-IS-A-LIVE," she emphasised each syllable with a shove, "are we clear?"

"I believe so," Alec answered and found himself smirking despite his best intentions. Yes, he could see why Dev was so enamoured with the DI. She was a spitfire and his polar opposite, tempestuous to his stoic. He'd bet they'd make a formidable duo.

"Something fucking funny? What about this do you find so bloody amusing DS Morgan?" she raged, fury flaming her pale, alabaster skin.

That wiped the smirk from his face. He recalled the hugely inappropriate circumstances he was currently in and realised his amusement and admiration for the woman was poorly timed at best.

"I'm sorry, that was in poor taste, however I forgot myself. I was thinking that I understood why Dev liked you so much," he answered honestly.

Her face fell at that, his use of past tense seeming to deliver a blow he hadn't intended. The wind taken from her sails, she sucked in a gasping breath at the mention of Dev. After she got over the initial shock, she narrowed her eyes, her anger had dwindled however her suspicion had not.

"Who *exactly* are you, DS Morgan?" she asked again. This time expecting a more detailed offering.

"Alec Morgan, I'm from the London Met," he informed her.

"You know Dev," she stated, her grasp of the situation as accurate as he'd expected.

"I do, he's a good man," Alec replied. His implication with that statement almost sounded like he'd passed a judgement of his own, without saying it directly.

"I thought so too," Wren said quietly.

"Perhaps you should've trusted your gut more and your doubt a little less," Alec chided, showing no more mercy in his assessment of her than she had with hers of him.

"I really don't think you have any grounds to point fingers here, DS Morgan. You are the person who declares death without a medical degree and no corpse, after all," she sneered, his well-aimed shot hitting its mark and making her defensive and snappy.

"I didn't say she was dead; I just relayed the message. You know what they say about shooting the messenger?" he asked, taking another potshot.

"I believe they suggest that we don't shoot them, yet I wonder DS Morgan, if they'd had you as the messenger in that instance, would they perhaps have reconsidered," she fired back.

"Touché DI Jones," he replied, a hint of admiration to his voice. "I had better see where DCI Head wants me, wouldn't look good slacking on my first day," he added as he began to turn to make a move to bow out. He paused when she addressed him again, this time with a softer tone, not one of anger.

"How is he?" she enquired, a healthy dose of guilt painting her face.

He looked at her and assessed her more closely before replying. "He has come through far worse, and he has never been one to hold onto a grudge. He's relentless, yes, but forgiving. You hurt him, intentionally or not, it doesn't really matter. He'll get over it," he assured her, then turned and walked away.

Wren got herself back together. Jen might be dead. Dev's hurt feelings were the least of her problems. She found herself praying that Alec's informant had it very wrong. She wasn't sure she would be able to cope with her friend no longer in the world. Sweet, sassy and loyal to a fault, yes, the world couldn't be right without the likes of Jen Cartwright in it. She swallowed back the pain, skirting the edges of her mind and used it to become focused. No body, no certainty. With that she continued to where the forensic team waited.

Chapter Five

Stephen had received Alec's message and looked at it in surprise. He read it and re-read it more than a few times. It was a lot to unpack, Kelly Whelan was alive. She was who had alerted him to Dev's arrest, essentially calling in the calvary. That alone would be enough to have him contemplating this new development for a good long while. Add in the fact that a detective was now missing, and he knew he needed to get himself over to Dev's without delay.

He packed up a few necessities into his briefcase and left to go to his car. He wasn't entirely sure how Dev was going to take the latest information; it would seem this Pandora's box had a surprising depth to it that wasn't visible from an initial glance.

"Will we even find the underlying cause of it," he wondered aloud.

He finally pulled up to Dev's place and after parking up, approached the door to knock. Almost immediately the door opened, and he came face to face with the dark skinned, sweaty chest of Chris. He craned his neck up to look at his face, his neck complaining at the unusual movement. Being 6 ft 1 he didn't spend an awful lot of time gazing up, but Chris Doyle was a bulldozer of a man. At a whopping 6 ft. 8 and with his wide build it would be impossible to try and pass him in the narrow hallway, so he waited for him to move down it to allow him entrance.

"Morning, Baby Shark," Chris taunted. Chris had dubbed him with this nickname not a year ago. With his gigantic frame there were few who could match him in size and with Stephen being the youngest in their number, he had been the baby of their foster family. Add to that his chosen profession and the charming children's song released the year previous, he'd decided it was the perfect name for him. Stephen was just grateful he had long since tired of sending him the ridiculous variations of adults dressing up singing the song, walking beside their car. He'd received them sometimes three times a day in the beginning. He'd been irritated in particular when he found himself unconsciously humming it at random times throughout the day. Some days he had sworn he'd heard the "do do's" in his sleep.

If he never heard that blasted song again it would be too soon. He often wondered how the staff in children's nurseries didn't go insane or perhaps they did, he considered. He realised then that he hadn't answered Chris getting lost in his thoughts of singing shark families. Chris was looking down on him, his grin wide and delight shining in his eyes.

"You were singing it in your head, weren't you?" he needled.

"Fuck you, man," Stephen snapped.

"You were, weren't you?" he laughed, turning around, whistling the tune as he walked down the hallway.

"Stop that! Stop it right now or by all that's good and holy, we will be adding your name to the victims on that wall," Stephen bit out.

Chris, unfazed, turned into the living room, the sound of his booming laughter echoing down the hall behind him.

Stephen took a moment to pray for patience, he forgot how incredibly aggravating his siblings could be. As he walked the distance of the hall and entered the room beyond, he caught sight of Raven digging the "pokey finger of Death," between the muscle and sinew of Chris' arm.

It was a well-known fact between them that Raven's bony, index finger caused more effective pain than a slap directly to the face. No one really knew how she managed it, but she had a gift for finding the most sensitive spot on anyone's arm and poking it to cause a significant amount of pain.

"OW! Quit it!" Chris said, scowling, rubbing the sore spot on his arm. "Why did you poke me, Death!"

"You know that song winds him up, we aren't here for your entertainment. This is serious and don't call me Death!" she scolded, emphatically poking him again.

"Mother—!" Chris winced before he could finish swearing, as another well timed poke got him in the arm. He scooped her up, holding her above his head as though she weighed nothing, her body nearly pressed to the ceiling.

"Put me down!" she shouted, flailing uselessly as Chris chuckled.

"You know I don't think I will," he replied smugly.

"I'm warning you—" she began.

"A threat from Death?" Chris exclaimed, in a mock scared tone, "That's serious."

"What the feck is going on? Will you three stop playing the maggot," Dev spoke with a calm, warning tone that brooked no argument. Immediately everyone scrambled to attention. Stephen wasn't entirely sure why Dev had this effect on them, he just had a natural gift for command. That had given them the structure they'd been missing in their youth and even as adults they still did as he bade.

Despite Chris' size, Stephen's irritability, Raven's talons and Gabe's deviousness, Dev had somehow always been able to restore order to their chaos. He was their safety net, always calm and in control; he naturally soothed their wounded souls without much more than a well-placed look.

"Thank you," he said quietly as the room became peaceful once more.

"Now can someone tell me what all this fuss is about?" "He was winding Stephen up," Raven said, sulkily.

"She poked me!" Chris countered.

"You picked me up over your head—" Raven started but Dev held up his hand in a stop command to halt the bickering and they both fell silent. He looked at Stephen.

"I have news I'm not really sure you're going to like and I'm trying to figure out the best way to tell you," Stephen admitted like he was a child, admitting to some bad behaviour, even though he hadn't actually done anything wrong.

The two siblings behind them, stopped pulling faces at one another and fixed their eyes on him.

"Open your mouth and tell me, it's easy. Try it," Dev said evenly, his stoicism unmoved by his previous words.

"I got a message from Alec. He is in the middle of something, so he didn't tell me much but what he did manage to relay, well it wasn't comforting," Stephen hedged.

"What was the message?" Dev asked, his tone implying he should stop dithering and get to the point.

"It says Kelly Whelan is alive. She was the person that called to tip me off. Might be watching Dev. Jen Cartwright is missing. Can't talk now. Keep your eyes open," he read aloud before putting his phone back into his pocket.

Dev tilted his head as though considering the information, then said, "Okay. Missing is not dead. It's not good but better than being dead. My sister is alive. I honestly don't know what to feel about that right now but again: living is better than being dead," he paused for a moment and winced, likely thinking of what she may have been through since he had last seen her and added, "maybe."

"Are you okay?" Raven asked gently, giving his arm a hug.

"Whether I am or not, it doesn't change the facts. This needs to end, we can unpack everything once we get to the root of all this madness," he said, calmly, as cool as he always was. Until he wasn't. His eyes seemed to glaze over all of a sudden. Stephen, having already witnessed this particular display, immediately indicated Chris and Raven should move away. Chris grabbed Raven's arm and tugged on it in order to expedite her movement.

Dev snatched her arm, his eyes locked on Chris with a fierceness that made the giant man flinch, even though he could likely snap Dev like a twig.

"Let her go! She's my sister! You let her be!" Dev shouted with a snarl.

Chris looked at his other siblings with uncertainty. His natural inclination made him clutch Raven's arm tighter. Dev looked ready to charge him and Raven tugged on her arm. Chris looked down at her and she cleared her throat.

"Let me go, Chris," her voice tinged with emotion.

Chris nodded, shaken by Dev's uncharacteristic ferocity. Dev pulled Raven behind him and squared up to the two men in front of them. His body was tense, and waves of rage emanated from him as he eyed them both with the intensity of his fury and they were both stunned. Chris looked to Stephen, a look of helplessness on his face and Stephen held his hands up in surrender and backed away.

Dev turned his attention to Chris. Taking in his size he seemed unperturbed, his agitation not waning. He stood his ground, seeming to brace for a fight. Chris mimicked Stephen's actions and backed off. When Chris joined Stephen, Dev's shoulders seemed to drop a little and he calmed.

He turned to look at Raven then, seeing her but not really seeing her. Her slight frame was huddled behind him, she clasped her knees to her chest making herself small as though she might not be seen if she did. Her black locks fell around her face, hiding it from their view. Dev knelt towards her, lowering himself slowly to the floor before pulling her into his lap and holding her. She looked up at him, her hair parting away from her face as she did.

"Oh Dev," she said, quietly.

He looked at her in confusion before wrapping her in his arms protectively and stroking her hair. Whispering to her, promising to do all he could to keep her safe. The two men watched them, their own murky pasts haunting them in unison. Chris seemed to soften, looking at Dev almost wistfully. It was as if he wished he'd had someone when he had been younger that had shown him even a tenth of that sort of love on display before them. Raven hugged him back, her eyes full of unshed tears.

"I really love you, brother," she whispered.

"I love you too," he returned, kissing the top of her ebony tresses.

As they curled together, Dev's glassy eyes began to droop and with Raven locked safely in his embrace he fell asleep.

"I'm glad they are dead," Chris stated vehemently, his tone hard and unforgiving, "I hope they burn to their very souls in pits of hellfire."

Stephen nodded, looking toward their brother and sister, Raven stroked the hair from out of a sleeping Dev's eyes, before easing away from him. She crossed the room to them and a glint in her eye warned Stephen she was with them every step of the way.

"We need to get to work. Dev needs us," she muttered and then sat determinedly at her screen without another word.

****

Mary McNamara looked at Keri as she arrived.

"Is it done? Is she dead?" she asked.

"Aye, she's gone," Keri replied, with no emotion on her face.

Mary smiled, "Good girl, now go and do something useful, I have a call to make."

She waved her hand dismissively at her daughter, Keri, who in return gave her a bored look and shrugged before leaving the room. Mary picked up her phone and called her little mole friend.

"H.. Hello," the voice stuttered on the other end.

"Reece, darling. How are you?" she began casually, her icy tone leaving no room for doubt she did not in any way care how he was.

I don't know anything; they aren't saying much—" he started to make his usual excuse, but she cut him off.

"DC Cartwright is dead, Reece. Consider that your final warning, get me my answers or next time, it will be you on the missing person's list. Have I made myself clear?" she demanded.

"Yes, Mrs McNamara but how?" he began hesitantly.

"I believe there is now a vacancy in the Major Crimes Unit, is there not?" She couldn't make her meaning much clearer, she really did have to do all the thinking for these imbeciles.

"Yes, I suppose there is," he replied.

"I will see that you find yourself in a position to fill that deficit," she informed him, "will that make it easier?"

"Yes, I'm sure it will," he answered, swallowing nervously.

"Then do get back to me, darling, lovely to chat but I must dash, things to do and all that. Goodbye Reece," she finished, ending the call without needing a reply from him. Perhaps he might have more luck actually doing what she required.

****

Keri listened from the hallway and was glad she had. She now had a first name for the little spy in the station. She was going to need to warn them, however she couldn't tip her mother off. She was going to need to consider how she could let them know without garnering suspicion from her.

She left their new headquarters. Mary had moved their operation to a more discreet location and had decided it would be wise if she didn't return to her residence for the time being. With Keir out of the limelight and that light shining in other directions, she wanted to be away from the immediate area.

She got to her car and nodded in the direction of one of her mother's new recruits. What was his name now? Mick? Mickey? Michael? She couldn't recall. He peered at her from under a hoodie and she wondered what direction her mother intended to take the business if her men didn't even dress the part? Or maybe he was guarding the perimeter and she wanted something a little more subtle that the regular hoodlums wouldn't notice.

She stopped thinking about him, he wasn't all that important in the grand scheme of things after all. Driving to her own home she arrived, and was out of the car and up the path as quick as her feet could carry her. As soon as she turned the key in the lock and entered, she was ambushed by her fiancé, Cameron.

"You are home Keri-blossom!" he exclaimed, "and not a moment too soon I might add. See?" he said. Leaning into her and indicating a swelling forming on the side of his head. "I have a boo-boo."

"What happened?" she asked with incredulity.

"She walloped me. She is feisty, I thought she was still out for the count, and she used that to take advantage and club me over the head, I think you'd like her. Now doctor... How are you going to make me feel better?" he flirted, pulling a sad face.

"Aww Cam, the doctor will make it all better," she soothed, playing along, "First though, show me to our guest."

"Fine," he huffed, "my injury can wait I suppose."

Cam led her along the hallway and, when they reached the furthest door, he took a key from his pocket unlocking the door. They took the stairs down into the basement and she swept her gaze over the area and rested it on the restrained form of DC Jen Cartwright.

"Good evening, detective. It is a pleasure to finally meet you," she said, smiling warmly.

The DC looked at her like she had not just lost her marbles but sent them scattering across the floor willingly.

"You have got to be fucking kidding me, doc. You?" she snapped.

"I'm afraid so," Keri admitted, delighted she had remembered her.

"Why?" Jen asked.

"Because, my little Jenny friend, you poked your tippy-tappy fingers into something bad and the chippy-choppy man wanted to kill you," she replied, chuckling.

"So why aren't I dead?" She queried.

"Because Jenny friend, I got to you first and for all intents and purposes, well at least to all of the outside world, you are dead. Only the people in this room know that you are very much alive," Keri explained.

"That doesn't really answer the question, you know that, right?" Jen said, rolling her eyes.

"No, I don't suppose it does, does it?" Keri agreed, "You were to die. If I hadn't jumped in and *"arranged"* your *"death"* you would be playing nursery rhyme games instead. So, here's the skinny; you are dead. You have to stay dead, or you will be really dead. That means you are now team *"dark side"* in the help Dev campaign. You can aid us in our efforts, in your new basement home, to deal with my evil fake mother. Or you can take an exceptionally long basement vacation, which will be considerably longer without you helping us and will likely mean you outstay your welcome a little. Or death that's an option too, not by us you understand, you made The Executioner's list of playthings. So, what do you say?" she teased.

"Stay here, stay here longer, or die. Not exactly top-notch choices, are they?" Jen said sarcastically, "Why would I deign to help you might I ask?"

"Because, my little Jenny friend. We are on the same side, admittedly our team is not quite so...pure and holy, yet your enemy is my enemy and so on and so forth," Keri replied.

"Why would you help Dev? How does that benefit you?" Jen questioned suspiciously.

"That is the question of the hour, isn't it?" Keri cajoled playfully, "the answer is simple. Let me introduce myself... Keri McNamara formerly known as Kelly Whelan, surprise!"

"Kelly Whelan? I have been searching for your ass for weeks!" Jen exclaimed, then frowned, "Are you telling me I wasted hour upon hour dredging up trafficking records for nothing?"

"I'm afraid so, Jenny friend," Keri acknowledged, shaking her head in regret, "however, happy news is you've found me! Ta-da!" Keri clapped her hands together feigning excitement, "Yay you! Is it everything you hoped it would be?"

"Yay...I'm in wonderland with the bloody mad hatter," Jen responded glibly and with not nearly as much enthusiasm.

"So?" Keri asked.

"So, what?" Jen repeated confused.

"Are you coming to the dark side? We don't currently have cookies, but I know a guy," Keri joked.

"I'm not sure I really have much of a choice, I'd like to go home sometime this year," Jen grumbled.

"Ooh, burn! You wound me, Jenny friend. Now, would you like some tea? We have much to discuss," Keri stated, "Cameron, my heart? Be my dear and fetch some tea for our guest."

"I'm your humble servant, my little Keri-blossom," Cameron shot back with a wink.

"I may have just puked in my mouth a little bit," Jen said, scrunching her nose up with distaste.

"Aww, Jenny friend, I like you," Keri smiled, waggling her finger at her like a naughty child, "now let's get down to business."

Chapter Six

August 14th, 2014

Reece Carter had finally made it to the incident room. After he had spoken to the DCI and given a marvellous speech about how he knew they were short-handed and had an interest in joining the MCU. That his brother had worked in it and he wanted to be a part of the team so he could help them catch the killer who had abducted one of their own, and he'd been temporarily reassigned here.

He looked at his brother Ashley as he talked with the officers, he had yet to spot his arrival and he surveyed his brother with quiet spite. He was the younger of the two siblings and had always been the "golden child" he thought hatefully. Despite being younger, Ashley had been promoted higher than he had and become a part of one of the most prestigious departments within the force, while he himself had been passed over.

Well, he had finally made the team and his parents could kiss his ass. Maybe now he wouldn't have to listen to them crow about how their "baby" was a detective, while he got "Oh Reece, he's an officer too," the demeaning add on, only serving to heighten his resentment all the more.

As though his brother could feel his eyes penetrating into his back like daggers he began to turn, and Reece's mask slipped into place without missing a beat.

"Hello Baby Bird, miss me?" he said with false friendliness, completely at odds with his thoughts from moments before.

"I wish you wouldn't call me that here. What are you doing here?" he asked in surprise, grasping him and patting his shoulder in a man hug.

"You appear to be short of hands and I have two. I offered my assistance with one DI on suspension and a DC on the missing person's list. I wanted to help. So, I asked for a temporary reassignment, plus I haven't seen much of my baby brother recently," he said smiling, not quite pulling off affectionate and feeling more like a grinning shark.

"Is that right?" Ash replied in amusement, "Well don't linger in the doorway like a creeper, Reece's Pieces. Join the party, I'll introduce you to the team."

"That would be incredibly useful, Ash. Makes a pleasant change," he said playfully, making it sound like a joke rather than the truth, "after you've done that, you can catch me up on the case, I'm just dying to get stuck in."

He trailed his brother across the room and while he followed his cues and did all he could to slip into the team dynamics, he allowed his mind to wander to what he had to get done. He required information and he needed it quickly, Mary McNamara was not a patient lady.

After being introduced around the team he began to tire of the pleasantries and wandered over to the big board, looking at DI Doyle's name on the person of interest part.

"So, Baby Bird, explain to me why we haven't charged the DI for the murders?"

****

Alec had ended up finishing his shift in the early hours of the morning, he hadn't started work as early as the others and so had been on the graveyard shift. When he had realised the time, he decided that the rest of what he had to tell the Doyles could save for a more appropriate hour, before he headed to the hotel he was currently staying in. Since he'd moved here in a rush, he had been residing there until he could organise a more permanent living arrangement.

Thanks to working so late the night before, he hadn't woken up until 11am, but still had a few hours to spare before his next shift and he needed to catch Stephen up. Grabbing his phone Alec called his number.

"Good morning, Alec. Long time no hear," Stephen answered, reproachfully.

"Yeah, sorry about that I was working late...or early I suppose. I couldn't call you. I will explain why when I see you. Speaking of which, don't suppose you can spare me some time before I have to go to work?" he asked hopefully.

"I do actually have a job but since Dev is now part of that job, I suppose I can do a home visit," he replied.

"Do you remember where I'm staying?" Alec enquired.

"I do, shall we say thirty minutes to an hour? I just have some things to get finished first," Stephen asked.

"See you then, I'm going to hit the shower while I wait," Alec agreed.

They ended the call and Alec looked towards his ensuite bathroom; he better get a move on. Thirty-five minutes later he was sitting eating toast and drinking coffee when Stephen knocked on the door. He rose to open it and allow him entry. Stephen walked in briskly, saw his breakfast on the table and groaned, looking hopefully at Alec.

"Don't suppose you have any of that going spare?" I haven't had time to eat yet," he asked cheekily.

"Yeah, the plate in the middle is yours, I'll get you a coffee." Alec said and headed into the kitchenette to put on the kettle before returning and getting his own cup deciding a top up wouldn't be a bad idea.

On his return he found Stephen had demolished his own food and he reached for the coffee, swallowing his mouthful before taking a big gulp.

"Do you always eat like that? You'll give yourself indigestion," Alec commented.

"I grew up in a home with four other foster children, you eat fast, or you don't eat. Have you seen Chris, a guy that size puts it away, let me tell you," Stephen informed him.

"So, there were five of you? Where's the fifth Doyle? Couldn't he make it to the reunion?" Alec asked, curiously.

"He is otherwise engaged at this time, I have him working on a different angle," Stephen hedged, "So what have you got for me?"

Alec noted his hasty change of subject but allowed it, they had other things to discuss that were of greater importance.

"I've done something and I am in two minds about whether or not I have done the right thing. Though I suppose I can still rectify it, but I need an opinion, someone who I can trust and at work I don't know who that is," Alec rambled.

"Alec, stop thinking out loud and tell me what we are dealing with," Stephen said, unable to follow the incoherent jumble of words.

"When I was given an overview of the case, the name Kelly Whelan came up. Until then Dev had only referred to her as his sister, I wasn't aware of her name. The call I told you about; the tip telling me Dev had been arrested. The name she gave was Kelly, I believe it to be Kelly Whelan," he began.

"Kelly Whelan, Dev's sister? She's alive?" Stephen interjected.

"Let me finish before we dissect that, I got another call today. We attended DC Cartright's residence when the call from her came. The DCI and myself had already discussed her involvement and he was with me when the call came, same as before withheld number. He told me to answer it and I did. After he asked what she'd said, I told him she had told me DC Cartwright was dead. Here's where it gets dicey, she did say that but there was more. She said, "tell them Dc Cartwright is dead. You have a leak, tell them it's important," then she hung up. She didn't explain or say anything more, just that. I didn't tell anyone else the rest. I'm new, she didn't give me a name, just said there was a leak. I didn't know who I could trust if she was even telling the truth. I know that it can't be Dev and none of you work there. I couldn't tell anyone in case she knows something I don't, which seems likely since I only just got involved," he finished his explanation and looked to Stephen, patiently waiting for his take on the matter. He didn't answer right away, instead he looked deep in thought.

So Alec prompted, "Should I have told the DCI? He told me to keep the identity of the caller to myself until we figured out how she fit but is he the leak? I just don't know, I needed perspective before making any sudden decisions."

"This is a whole lot of messed up, I'm not sure that I have an answer for you either. There is only one person that can possibly give you some insight into the station without the risk of them being this leak, assuming it exists and isn't some game to mess with the investigation, a wild goose chase if you will. We need to speak to Dev. He may not have been there long, but he's been working with them longer, he'll have some idea of who's who. I'll talk to him and tomorrow we can decide how true the information is or if you are being spoon fed," he advised, "until then you are fresh eyes on this, you won't have any preconceived notions about them, you are likely the most objective person to root out a leak. Keep an eye open and look closely at the players. It might be that you'll see something that their familiarity with them misses."

"If it isn't true this could blow up in my face," Alec stated, his worry clouding his face.

"If it is and the killer is being fed information, we may never catch them and that comes with its own consequences. The question is what do you consider more important? Avoiding getting a dressing down and a reprimand, possibly removed from the team, perhaps losing your job or is saving the lives of future victims and finding justice for those fallen at their hand? Perhaps somebody you care about a colleague, or an innocent person may be next. Jen Cartwright has already vanished; at this time, I am unaware of any wrongdoing on her part. That, my friend, is a decision solely in your own hands," Stephen challenged.

"If I hadn't already considered that possibility you wouldn't be here," Alec reminded him.

"Then it would seem you didn't really need my opinion, you had already made the decision, you just wanted tea and sympathy," he teased.

"Hey! I gave *you* the tea and toast if you recall, you cheeky bugger!" Alec scoffed with belligerence.

"That you did, now I have a DI to speak to, so if we are all done here?" he said.

"Yeah, go on, clear off," Alec returned.

"Speak soon and let me know if you get any more calls," Stephen shot back, vacating his seat at the table, and going to the door.

"I think I can manage that," Alec said wryly.

"And Alec. Be careful, people with information seem to have misfortune befall them in this case," Stephen offered a warning as he crossed the threshold.

****

Mary hung up the call and she was not happy with what her mole friend had told her. Someone had scuppered her well thought out plan, somebody with easy access to her residence and an exceptionally good knowledge of it. She pondered that for a moment and the answer came to her. The household staff. They were the only ones she could think of with that kind of access, which weren't already dead.

It was unlikely to be the men, the longer serving employees were either dead or not given access to the residence, only the business. The newer staff didn't have enough access to find her hidey hole. Keri was living with Cameron and rarely came when called, and was more than a little lazy and self-serving, she'd never shown any inclination to explore the house, opting instead to spend most of her time here trying to leave it. That left the household staff by default.

Jack had been the one to recruit them, needing to know exactly the type of people being given access to their home. John, Jerry, and Janet. He'd always said it was useful for them all to share an initial that way if he called them J, he would never need to recall their name. If he had just been able to keep his dick in his pants maybe their marriage could've worked out long into their golden years.

"So, John, Jerry, or Janet? Who is the deceiver?" Mary mused aloud.

Who of the three had decided to step out of turn and get above their pay grade? Maybe one of the three were used by Jack to spy on her, she had of course had her own spy, Jilly's housekeeper had been easily lured with the chance of some extra money. Had Jack been lining someone's pocket for his own information and had that pay become a deficit since his murder? It wouldn't be so unlikely. Not also unthinkable that the housekeeper had been giving an entirely separate set of services on the sly. Lord knows her husband had a wandering eye.

Jerry had come over from Ireland with Jack and had a long-standing arrangement with him, could he be the rat? Or the mouse…Mary smiled to herself; she knew what to do. She picked up her phone and dialled Cain, he would be so upset if she had all the fun.

****

Keri received the call from her mother. While they had set Jen up in the basement no expense had been spared, to deck it out with all she had declared she needed. It had been decided that she would aid them until it was safe for her to return home, despite Jen's reservations the matter really did need to be settled and after Keri had apprised her of what they were up against, Jen got straight to work.

She suspected Jen almost relished the idea of having the freedom, under duress of course, to get her claws into Mary. It would be the perfect excuse should she uncover something that could be used against her if she had obtained the illegal information at the behest of her kidnappers. Though Keri hoped she could find some way to avoid them being arrested on the grounds they had done so to preserve life and foil a murder. She wasn't certain, but perhaps Keir's legal friend might assist them, since they had saved his foster brother from the same fate.

"Quid pro quo, Clarice," Keri said beneath her breath then chuckled.

She had been summoned to a location, one Keri had not heard mention of its existence before. But she had been instructed to meet with Mary and honestly, something about that set her nerves on edge. She didn't care for surprises, especially when Mary was the one delivering them. However, to not go would likely draw more suspicion than doing as she asked. So, she packed a weapon and set off to find out what her mother needed her for now.

When she arrived, she found The Executioner waiting to receive her. She tensed and had a decidedly bad feeling about it, but he offered her a slightly crazed smile and spoke.

"Welcome to the party, princess," he said with amusement, a slightly mad looking glint in his eye, "it is a rare thing to get to share my art as the process is in development, I'm quite looking forward to it."

"I can see that," she said coolly, feigning interest, "however I haven't been given a programme of tonight's entertainment."

"Don't worry that pretty little head about it, I have it all arranged, it's going to be quite a show," he crowed.

He led her inside and her mother moved to greet her, she too seemed happier than Keri was comfortable with. It was really quite disconcerting.

"Keri darling, just in time, now that you have finally joined our number and have proven yourself by taking care of our little police delay, I felt you would appreciate being a part of this. A small show of thanks for your assistance if you will. It will be good to show you the nitty gritty of our little empire, your father kept you from it for too long, believing Cameron as the man, would pick up the grunt work but that is no longer the case. As I have proven, women are as capable if not more so of having what it takes in this business. As my successor it seems only fitting you get the proper training. This time we'll show you how it is done, next time you can take the reins, so to speak," Mary divulged, though Keri wasn't entirely certain what was going on.

"Show me how to do what?" Keri asked warily.

"You see, Keri darling, some people in our business can sometimes come unstuck by greedy, jealous, or duplicitous employees. Think of it as being royalty. Sometimes as rulers, you need to deal with traitors. Those who commit treason must be dealt with, so others know not to follow their path. Come with me," Mary finished and directed her into a different area.

It was large and at the centre she noticed three large wooden structures. As she neared she saw three familiar faces each attached to their own individual structure. Other than one lone chair and the structures, the area was completely empty. Keri felt a sinking in her gut but did not allow the distress to show on her face, she needed to keep her cover, or she would likely be joining them, she wasn't sure what their supposed crime was, but it would do no good to reveal herself. She surveyed the scene, noting the piles of kindling at the base of each and had a sneaky suspicion she knew what might occur, but she said nothing and waited for her mother to continue.

"Take a seat darling," Mary invited, indicating the lone chair in front, "And watch as the pros work."

Keri did as she was instructed and sat in an almost dream-like state as she waited for it to begin.

Mary turned to address the three tied to their wooden prisons, gags over their mouths, bound tightly and unable to defend themselves.

"John, Jerry, and Janet. You stand accused of treason, today I have been informed that somebody in my household took from my home evidence that may have been detrimental to my reign. In doing so, they ensured the release of a prisoner I had declared to be guilty, and he is now walking free, leaving me under suspicion instead.

"What say you?" she paused, cupping a hand to her ear, before laughing, "Oh, that's right you can't speak. Never mind, you have all been found guilty. Well one of you is guilty and since I can't allow any room for error and single out the guilty party, part of your punishment is that you will also cause the death of two, likely innocent, people." Mary declared as fear crossed the staff's features.

"I don't mean to interrupt mother," Keri said, "can I ask what they gave them? If I am to learn, should I need to know what they did to earn their punishment?"

"Very good, dear, learning already. They took some collectibles I had stored, specifically trophies I had taken in my battle with the King, and sent them, using a rare model church my own father gave me as a small child, to the police. This meant that they released DI Doyle and decided there was still a perpetrator on the loose, directly disobeying my judgement as ruler and causing undue harm to my continual reign," Mary explained, "now where was I? Ah yes, you are guilty, and the punishment is death."

"Long live the Queen!" The executioner cheered from the side and approached bowing before her. She preened at his attention and gave him a wicked smile. Keri paled but said nothing.

"I wonder, since I have such a captive audience, if any of you are aware of the origins of the rhyme three blind mice? No? Let me tell you. The rhyme's original lyrics were, "three blind mice, three blind mice, Dame Iulian, Dame Iulian, the miller and his merry olde wife, shee scrapt her tripe licke thou the knife" of course it has been long since updated now. It is suspected this rhyme depicts the death of three Protestant Bishops. Queen Mary was catholic, and they "blindly" followed the King's religion despite his reign being over. Mary didn't like this. So, she sentenced them to death. I believe historians refer to the incident as "the burning of the Oxford Street Martyrs."

"So this is a history lesson too? Oh joy," Keri quipped dryly.

"Don't interrupt darling. Now where was I…Oh yes. Two of the three steadfastly refused to recant their Protestantism and were immediately sentenced to death. One did recant and signed documents avowing himself catholic, however he was forced to watch the first two being burned at the stake and not a year later met the same end." Mary summarised. The three household staff began to struggle against their bonds to no avail.

"You, my disobedient little mice, will be suffering the same punishment and whilst there was no actual account of blinding that was recorded, I think it might be a fun twist to add it in, for the new nursery rhyme readers' enjoyment. Blind them darling," Mary instructed the executioner.

He used a blade and in the longest, most excruciating moment of her life, Keri watched with as much control as she could muster, to not react as the executioner used it to dislodge their eyeballs, offering the blade to Mary after each successful removal. She smiled widely and licked the bloody blade, in some weird ritual that bypassed Keri's understanding of it completely. As the screams finally faded and the three terrified victims were left once more, the executioner grabbed a bag and placed it around Jerry's neck.

"You my man, get the honour of playing Nicholas Ridley, this here is gunpowder. Your fire is not going to burn quite as fast as the two others, accuracy is key in a re-enactment after all. If you should tire of slowly burning, I would suggest you follow his example, based on accounts given and shove your face into the flames to end yourself a little faster," he told him, the crazy smile spreading, his delight at recounting that tidbit almost more than Keri could stand.

"Won't they be able to identify them? If they are found?" Keri asked suddenly, wondering if she could dissuade them from this course and encourage them a shot to the head would be better instead.

"Keri darling, so short sighted and a total buzzkill. We have removed their teeth, look closer. They have no fingers, on the off chance they have any flesh left when this is done it will be difficult to identify them, I assure you. We have a camera set up so we can enjoy the performance further on a monitor after we have to vacate the premises. It would be quite the anti-climax if we missed the climax, wouldn't it? All in all, the likelihood of identifying them is small, however when they came to work in our employ, they were given new identities, we didn't want them being traced back to us if we had ever needed to dispose of them.

"Now Keri, let's watch the fires being lit, it will be like those bonfire nights we used to go to when you were young, just like old times," Mary informed her, undeterred by Keri's attempt at reason.

The stakes were lit, and one by one they sparked to life, the three helpless victims made attempts to evade the flames as they grew beneath them. Jerry's fire as promised burned slower, and she watched in horror as the muffled screams began from the first victim to feel flames.

"Come now darlings," Mary called to Keri and the executioner, "it is time to watch the show from a less conspicuous position." And with that they left the three damned souls to their fiery fate.

Keri cast one more look in their direction as they went, apologising to them silently, for her part in their death. They were, after all, her scapegoats. Receiving the punishment in her stead, for her "crime." She was led away from the scene, despite the gags around their mouths she could hear their dulled screams of pain from outside. She tried to tune it out and broke away from the madness of the couple before her.

In history, there were depictions of criminal couples, Myra Hindley and Ian Brady, Bonnie Parker and Clyde Champion Barrow, Fred and Rosemary West and more besides. She wondered to herself as she watched the two together, how anyone could have missed the signs of sheer evil. How did they manage to hide in everyday society without people feeling the evil radiating from them?

She felt it now, watching as they giggled like naughty children, flirting and excitable. It was as they were going to the seaside not leaving people burning alive, it was complete and utter, unrepentant insanity. Another thing to consider, if they were the next criminal couple, where did that now leave her? After contemplating her answer, she realised it was simple; she was in way over her head, swimming against the current and if she didn't get the hell out soon, she would likely be ripped apart by the sharks in the water.

"See you soon, darling. I can't wait for it to be your turn," Mary called as though this was some kind of messed up graduation celebration.

"Goodbye Mother." Keri said evenly.

She reached her car and got in, breathing her first real breath since she'd arrived. She was glad to not have been squeezed into a small, enclosed space with the two monsters now getting into their own vehicle. She prayed that this particular venture would end swiftly. She wasn't sure how much longer she could bear their company. She needed to get away from them at the earliest opportunity and double her efforts before they finally saw through her, and she became the next target.

Chapter Seven

When Stephen divulged the latest information to Dev, he and his siblings watched warily, wondering if he might have another "episode." However, as he showed no signs of shifting to his glassy eyed stare, he let the breath he'd been holding go, only now realising he'd been holding it. Dev appeared to be contemplating what Alec had passed along but made no move to speak. As several more moments passed by in silence, Stephen finally lost patience and spoke first.

"So, brother? What is your take on it? I told Alec you would likely have a clearer answer to his dilemma than myself, since you have been working alongside them, albeit for a brief time," Stephen prompted.

"The suggestion of a leak has come up before, Angel hinted at the possibility and I told her not to borrow trouble until there was cause to do so." At the use of Wren's pet name, Dev's face clouded over, and the siblings once again studied him cautiously. Dev noticed their attention and snapped at them, "will you all stop looking at me like I'm a bomb that might go off!"

"Sorry," they all mumbled in unison, shifting uncomfortably. Dev refocused and continued.

"I believe Kelly is telling the truth. I do think there is a leak, but I don't think they are on the team I worked with. I would scratch Angel out entirely. For one reason, she already suggested it as a possibility. The second reason is because she is so damn "by the book" that she wouldn't demean herself by being a mole," he said, an edge of bitterness making the last part sound sharper than he'd likely intended. "Alec can trust her, or at least trust she isn't the leak."

"So, Serenity isn't likely," Stephen interrupted, reminding Dev to stay on point and not allow the grievance he had with the DI to distract him.

"No, it isn't her," Dev replied begrudgingly, "I would also rule out DC Jen Cartwright based on the fact that she's missing and if not already dead then seriously in the line of fire. I don't believe it's Matt Ainsworth either. He plays the maggot but he's pretty solid when he needs to be and he is a pretty cheery guy. Just doesn't really strike me as the type but that's more a gut feeling I don't have any particular reasoning for making that assumption. Ash Carter... If I'm honest, Ash is the one I know least about. He doesn't say much, he's quiet, a bit of a dark horse truth be told. The others are all quite forthcoming and exuberant, Ash he's more serious than the others," Dev paused to think about him as the leak, before dismissing the idea. "He was pretty gutted by Rosa Salvador's death though, doesn't seem like he would've been if he was the leak."

"Okay, so not your direct team. Can you think of someone else?" Raven asked this time, "if you give me a list of possibilities, I may be able to track the in-going and out-goings in their bank accounts, see if there are any questionable transactions, do a general background check and dig deeper if it warrants it."

"The DCI not wanting the team to know Kelly is the caller, that's a little suspicious," Chris offered.

"Aye but if he were the leak, wouldn't he have leaked that information? If Kelly is somehow tangled up in this mess, that might be quite the reveal. Or do you suppose he has done that? Is she going to be our next victim?" Dev asked, not to hide his concern.

Stephen supposed that despite her involvement in the case, she was still his sister who he'd assumed was dead and had reappeared, likely it would be quite a discomfort to think she might die before he found her again. Maybe Dev had begun to remember her a little.

"So, for argument's sake, let's run checks on all three, Matt, Ash and Richard," Raven suggested. At Dev's frown she continued, "You didn't immediately clear them, you just justified why they were unlikely. Something made you hesitate from completely taking them off the table. Trust your gut and if you can't, I will," Raven finished.

"Anyone else we should add to that list?" Stephen interjected.

"I haven't had much cause to deal with the rest of them. I haven't been there long enough to really get to know many people outside of my own corner, beside the Superintendent that is. However I would put money on it not being her. She has nothing to gain from leaking information, I would say the opposite is true. Having a leak looks bad, that fact aside she is also straight to the point, no nonsense and treats her staff like family. A leak would not only be disappointing to her, but it would also make her life harder, not easier," Dev replied.

"Not exactly all that insightful are you, Dev mate?" Chris chuckled, joining in the discussion.

"Feck off," Dev retorted.

"Perhaps Alec could use Serenity's insight? She's been there a while, so she would have a better idea of who might fit the bill. If you're sure she isn't the leak and she has already considered it might be a possibility, he may be able to convince her to help him smoke them out," Stephen mused.

Dev scowled at that suggestion and Chris crowed in delight. "Not a fan of that idea, Devvy boy?" he cajoled, "Is that because you are a green-eyed monster or is there a valid reason that you dislike the suggestion?"

"You're an eejit. He could try though she isn't exactly the most approachable or the most trusting individual, she would be suspicious and less likely to participate if anything. Though if he were to use Jen Cartwright's missing status to his advantage and suggest that finding the mole would lead to information on the killer and of course her whereabouts? It would make for suitable motivation, she may be persuaded by that. He would have to approach with caution though, like a spooked horse if he is too full on, she will kick him in the balls," Dev chuckled at the thought.

"Would it be worth a try though," Raven asked.

"If he, by some miracle, managed to get her on board? Aye. She is pretty gung-ho, she will go at it like a pit-bull," Dev admitted.

"So that's settled. Raven will begin looking at the suspected leaks, starting with the three remaining on your team, after that if she doesn't find what she's looking for then she can branch out. Alec can try and lure Serenity on side and attempt to find out more from the inside," Stephen summarised.

"What am I supposed to do?" Chris pouted.

"You can try and dig up some dirt on Mary McNamara from your "contacts". Since Dev isn't the killer and it looks as though Kelly is helping us, that leaves a pretty big spotlight aiming her way," Stephen surmised.

"Aye, since I've not met Kelly," Dev began frowning at that statement and choosing to rephrase it, "since I don't recall much of her, I can't say what her motives are. Mary however, I've met her and there is something not right about that one. Though I'm probably biased, from the way she told me my identity, but something about her whole vibe, tells me she enjoyed causing me harm," Dev concluded.

"So, she's our prime suspect?" Raven asked, at Dev's nod of assent, she continued, "I'll dig a little deeper on her too."

"Also..." Dev started, but stopped as though unsure before shrugging to himself, seemingly having an internal discussion that had the others looking at him as though he weren't quite the full ticket.

"Also...?" Chris prompted, amusement dancing in his eyes.

"I'm not sure if you can do this," Dev began again.

"Just ask already!" Raven ordered.

"Jen was taken. Why? She's the tech whizz, if she were taken, what did she find?" Dev explained, following his train of thought he asked, "could we somehow find out what she was looking into?"

"Not without a place to start. I'd need to know more; I wonder if they've looked at her computer? Or if it was even there?" Raven mused.

"If Alec manages to get Serenity involved, maybe he could bring it up?" Chris suggested.

"He has to convince her first," Dev scoffed, "maybe, and that is a big maybe, if he can somehow talk her into it, we can discuss that eventuality. Until then let's stick with what we do have."

"Okay, so start digging into what we have, later look into retracing Jen's steps," Stephen instructed.

They all looked to Dev for his direction, and he nodded. "Aye, let's get to work then, shall we?"

****

Keri was both furious and unnerved. After enduring an uncomfortable amount of time in her mother's company, not to mention her creepy as fuck boyfriend, she was beyond done. Reece, whoever he was, had to go. He had nearly fucked her over and he had definitely screwed John, Jerry, and Janet. He'd made Keri's afternoon entirely unpleasant, and was a threat that needed removing, because if she didn't remove him soon, he may get his teeth into something that would have her own head on the chopping block.

It was dog eat dog here and Keri intended to be the dog with the biggest teeth and the meanest disposition. She needed to weed out that rat and fast. To do that though, she was going to have to take a risk. If it paid off, she would be able to breathe easy, at least for a while. If it didn't there would be consequences.

"What's one more risk?" Keri mused wryly.

First, she was going to need to identify him, she had his first name, but she was going to need to do some digging to put a face to the name. She could get Jen to give her a hand, she worked there and if she didn't know him then she would be the best person to find out. Once that was done, she was going to need to figure out how to make him disappear without upsetting the apple cart.

She would need to think on that but not for too long. While she worked that part out Jen could get busy on the who, hopefully by the time they had that she would be able to take care of the how. It wasn't going to be easy; she knew that but then lately what had been? Every time she made a plan it seemed there was a snag or some thread that led to more misfortune. It might be wise if she relocated for the time being. Set up the operation somewhere away from her home. If this went awry, not being where they expected her to be might afford them the time they could very well need to save their lives.

"Just fit a house move between trying to foil a madwoman. Not a bloody problem," she grumbled.

She'd known from the moment she'd realised that Mary and her lover were responsible for the recent murder spree, that she would be putting her life at risk trying to stop it, today she'd had a front row seat to what to expect if she failed and knowing it was one thing, but seeing it burning before your eyes was entirely different.

The reality was far worse and while she had considered that she could take her account to the station and go about giving evidence in the traditional sense, in Mary's case this wouldn't be enough, they needed proper proof. She had to get proof beyond any doubt that she had been responsible for these crimes. Anything less than that and she would fall through the cracks and find a way to be released. Keri knew that to be true, she had seen them evade the law for over two decades. She had to be arrested without doubt or die, anything less than these options and she would burn them all to the ground in her wake.

****

DC Ash Carter watched his brother flit around the incident room. He studied him discreetly as he went over and over the board with a thoroughness he had never seen him devote to anything unless it benefitted himself. He scrutinised his brother from afar as he spoke to officers who came and went at length, almost to the point of interrogation, which was unusual of itself because he wasn't a particularly sociable person as a rule.

Ash loved his brother, but he could admit, if only to himself, that he didn't really like him all that much. Usually self-absorbed, more than a little whiny and a bit of a brat if things didn't go his way, he was showing a suspicious amount of interest in the team around them. If he was being completely honest, he also thought his brother was lazy.

"He wants all of the praise without any of the work," Ash muttered.

In Ash's opinion, the reason he had remained so long unpromoted and not recognised for his work or in his life generally, was because he never made a conscious effort to do anything more than the bare minimum required whilst expecting maximum acknowledgement for doing even that. For that reason, this newly discovered need to lend a hand and his support for the unit while they had an officer missing, was out of character and had Ash more than a little puzzled.

He was in general more of a solitary figure, preferring his own company or that of his own small group of friends. He'd never to Ash's knowledge made any attempt to ingratiate himself with his own colleagues or blend in with his team. Ash himself was quiet in nature. When they'd been growing up his older brother, used to having the sole attention of his parents before Ash's arrival, would become sullen and moody if too much focus had been on Ash and not himself. There were many temper tantrums and displays of outrage that had tested his poor parents' limits, often leaving everyone involved drained, weary and at their wits end, not entirely sure what to do with such behaviour.

As a result, Ash had become more reserved, quiet, and modest about any accomplishments he might achieve, preferring to keep a low profile. He had learned that by doing so this had balanced the family dynamic and for the most part restored harmony; he worked hard, kept his head down and did his part, without fanfare or need for recognition. He had actually been a little relieved when he'd moved out of the family home and he'd had more room, free to be himself without having to worry how his actions might offend his brother's sensitivities. However, when his brother had chosen to follow him into his profession of choice, he'd had little option but to try and remain in the background and not allow himself to draw too much notice.

"Brothers. Nothing but a pain in the ass," Ash grumbled.

Ash wasn't sure where this new and improved Reece had come from, or what he expected to gain from this newfound desire to be useful, but Ash was going to find out. He hated that he had cause to distrust his own brother, but he did, nonetheless. He was up to something, Ash was sure of it, he just hoped that whatever it was, it wouldn't reflect poorly on his own character. He longed for a time when he wasn't tarred by the same brush, when his brother pulled a stunt that others met with disapproval.

Oftentimes he got lumped in, without justification for doing so by his peers, friends and sometimes even his own family. It got old quickly. He would have to keep a close eye on his big brother, with luck he may be able to nip it in the bud before it had time to blossom into a toxin that ruined the good standing he had within the unit.

****

Dev and his siblings had been busy. Chris had headed out to "meet up with some friends.". Dev wasn't sure who these friends might be, and it was probably for the best that he never found out. At one time, in Chris' past, he had joined a motorcycle club. In his misspent youth, he'd been drawn to the promise of family and kinship that Dev understood but didn't have any interest in himself. Chris' size and longing for some kind of unity had made him a good prospect and as such Dev had found that he and Chris had grown apart, both heading in different directions.

Dev had chosen justice and order while Chris' preference had been the lure of freedom and finding camaraderie. Despite the fact that it was rarely mentioned now, the motorcycle clubs were still going strong. Often a combination of ex-military and people with troubled pasts, Chris had slotted into the lifestyle with ease. After many years of living that life, something had changed for Chris. He never spoke of his choice to leave it behind him, bringing it up never ended well either. All they had been able to ascertain was that it no longer held the appeal it once had.

"Because he never saw fit to explain," Dev mused.

Since then, Chris had spent his time, aimlessly drifting from one place to another. One minute he would be the life and soul of the party, taking a new town by storm, next the wind would change, and he set his sights on new horizons. With this new nomadic way of life, the distance between them had only widened further, creating a chasm neither seemed to know how to breach. Dev didn't know which "friends" Chris sought out, but he knew that if there was information to be found Chris would likely be the first to hear about it.

Raven had stayed here with Dev while Chris went off in his search for answers, she spent her time searching and digging through various checks while Dev fed her what he knew and logged anything she found to their profiles, looking through each, searching for signs they may be the leak. Raven had begun her search with Wren. Even though Dev had insisted that it would be a waste of their time.

"In order to make it unbiased she needs to be included in the search. If she isn't the mole, chances are it won't take up all that much time," she'd argued. Which as she suggested, it hadn't. Satisfied she was not their leak, Raven had moved on. Dev however found the entire process incredibly uncomfortable. He didn't like the murky feeling he felt of having information on his team that hadn't been offered by them willingly, more so in Wren's case.

He shouldn't care, closing this case was personal and finding this person was vital to their task to resolve it. If she had taken the time to do the same for him, looking into the likelihood of his guilt before making accusations, they wouldn't be at odds now. Still, he couldn't shake the uneasy feeling of sticking his nose in matters that weren't his business. Strange given the profession he'd chosen; however, he hadn't ever had cause to look at his own colleagues before.

"I fecking hate bent cops," Dev mumbled. "Makes me paranoid."

"Did you say something," Raven asked without taking her eyes from the screen.

"Nothing, just thinking aloud," he replied.

"Can you maybe do it in your head? I'm trying to work here," she teased.

He watched Raven continue her work and some of his discomfort eased. He had always found Raven to be the easiest of their number to get along with, he couldn't really say why. He supposed being of slight build and female he'd been less stressed by her company. As a child, he'd been more cautious in the company of men, often wary and suspicious. He couldn't be in their company for long before he found himself getting claustrophobic and feeling the need to get away from them as soon as he could physically manage it. At the time, he'd not understood why he'd felt this way, just accepted it as the truth. Now with his past being slowly revealed to him, he found he had a greater understanding of his reservations.

While Raven had always been slight of build, she made up for her size with her attitude. She had always been seen as the "odd" one, the gothic style she embraced, her long black hair and thick goth make-up making her seem a little like an extra from a horror movie. It wasn't a style he was personally in favour of, however on her it was cute and fitted her perfectly right down to her given name, as though she was born for it.

Super smart and with a curiosity for knowledge, she had often found herself as fodder for other kids to pick on. She'd once hacked the school computer system to change Gabe's grade on an assignment he had failed to turn in because he hadn't completed it, he'd instead been focusing his efforts on tracking the movements of a group of bullies, who had cornered Raven at school the day before, trapping her in a janitor's closet in the dark.

Raven had a fear of dark, enclosed spaces; none of them knew why and it was an unwritten rule that they didn't ask. She had suffered for many hours, later being located by Dev himself, in a state of sheer terror, trembling and incoherent, in obvious distress.

"Assholes," he muttered as he recalled it.

"You're doing it again," Raven admonished.

"Sorry," Dev said sheepishly. If he continued talking to himself they may actually think he was crazy.

His thoughts drifted back to the day he'd been remembering.

Dev had been furious; Gabe had calmed Dev assuring him that he would see it was dealt with. He'd never told them exactly how he had done it, but he had systematically caused as much trouble and chaos for the individuals as he could arrange. Ensuring each had been punished until Gabe was satisfied, they had suffered the consequences of their own actions.

Dev wondered now about Gabe's current whereabouts. Stephen had been cagey about what had kept his other foster sibling from the "reunion" they had going on. Stephen had however reassured him that had he been able, he too would be there doing what he could to help. Gabe had always been the enigma of the group. Smart as a whip, though not in the academic sense that Raven excelled in, his being more of the tactical persuasion.

He had amazing recall and often saw how situations would unfold long before anyone else even knew there was a situation. Dev hadn't been at all surprised when he had joined the army. Unsurprised, but more than a little pissed by his decision to abandon them for greener pastures. Dev wasn't entirely sure what he did for a living now, he'd always been secretive. Dev had focused on his own burgeoning career, still a little hurt by Gabe's choices. They'd lost touch and Dev had never really given his next career path much thought.

"Secretive bastard," Dev grumbled.

If Gabe wanted you aware then he would tell you, otherwise you accepted he was not in the mood for sharing. Whatever it was he was doing now, Dev had no doubt he did it well. Gabe didn't know how to do things any other way.

"Seriously? Again?" Raven tutted impatiently.

"What do you expect? I've been watching you tap on a keyboard for an age," Dev retorted.

"Genius takes time, Devvy," she fired back, giving him a middle finger salute before continuing.

That left Stephen. Stephen had always been the one who kept tabs on things, made sure that there was a line left open so they could come and go as they pleased but never fell too far apart. Mostly he spent his time corralling the siblings out of various run-ins with the law and reminding them all that they had each other if the need should arise. Stephen had been a lawyer long before he had become one. Dev had never really needed his assistance in that sense, he'd mostly been the good boy of the bunch, until now anyway.

  Stephen was stubborn and argumentative, despite the fact that all of them shied away from forming ties with people. Each with their own reasons behind their trust issues, Stephen could guilt them and persuade them into playing happy families even when they weren't inclined to do so. Dev in particular, butted heads with Stephen. His hardship in accepting his foster family as family often frustrated Stephen, who countered his efforts by insistently calling him "brother" at every given opportunity. No matter how distant Dev became, how much time passed between them, Stephen always reeled them all back in eventually, patiently waiting for them to come around. Dev couldn't recall the last time Stephen had called him by his given name.

"I heard that huff. Do you always think this loud?" Raven sniped and Dev rolled his eyes.

  He paused to survey the room, wondering what exactly his younger brother was doing. He'd received a call a while ago and left to answer it. This wasn't wholly unusual with the nature of his job, he often had to deal with confidential calls and meetings with clients, so it wasn't uncommon for him to do so, however he had been some time now. Curiously, he looked from his window to the street outside and found his brother there. He watched as Stephen nodded as he spoke to the person on the other end. Dev smiled with amusement, finding this entertaining when the person clearly couldn't see him nodding through the phone.

Stephen appeared to sense his perusal, as though through some sixth sense. He turned in the direction of the window and eyed Dev through it, lifting one brow in question and holding up one finger to inform him without words that he was nearly done. Once he had wrapped up the call, he headed back inside and wasted no time in addressing them.

"I have something. Raven, I want you to dig up all you can find on a hitman for hire, using the moniker "The Executioner" and do it as discreetly as you can, ItsyBit," Stephen cautioned, ignoring Raven's flash of annoyance at her childhood nickname.

"Who is this Executioner and what does he have to do with this case?" Dev asked.

"According to my source, he is quite tightly linked with Mary McNamara. Has been seen with her here and there. There is some speculation that they are lovers and even more that she is using him as an enforcer, ensuring that the employees toe the line since she has taken over their *"family business"* in Jack's stead," Stephen reported.

"And where are we getting this speculation from?" Dev pressed.

"I'm afraid I can't tell you that, only that the information is sound, and the source is trustworthy," Stephen replied.

"I wonder how *"trustworthy"* a source he can be, that he is in a position to pass along information on

Mary McNamara and her supposed hitman lover," Dev scoffed, unconvinced by the reliability of this source.

"Believe me when I say, you can trust that this source is solid," Stephen insisted, unmoved by Dev's suspicion. Dev eyed Stephen and took in his stance. He seemed pretty confident that he was right about this. If Stephen was that sure, chances are he had compelling cause to believe what he had been told. He didn't know who had called Stephen, but if he trusted them, Dev supposed he could give them the benefit of the doubt. He may not trust the source, but he did trust Stephen to do what was best for him and for the case. Nodding, he accepted it and tried not to overthink it too hard. If it paid off, all was well and good. If it didn't, all they would be wasting was time.

"I guess it couldn't hurt to look into it, we aren't exactly getting anywhere quickly with what we have at the moment. Are we?" Dev conceded.

"In that case, I'll get on that now," Raven said from behind her monitor.

Dev groaned as she began a new search leaving him to watch as the process started all over again.

Chapter Eight

Alec had received a call not long before his shift was due to start. Dev had told him what they were in the process of doing as far as looking into the team went. He had agreed that he did believe there was a leak. Stephen had at that point intervened and had explained that it had been decided that Serenity was unlikely to be their mole, Dev had disclosed that she too had mentioned the chance that there may be one not too long ago.

"You are going to need to try and get her on side," Dev told him.

"You have got to be fucking joking? She doesn't like me!" Alec had protested.

"Wren doesn't much like anyone she doesn't know. She is, however, a good detective. She'll come around," Dev tried to assure him.

Alec wasn't on board with their suggestion he share his information with her, he was unsure it was wise to take the risk of trusting someone who already didn't trust him. However, he couldn't deny that she didn't appear to fit the bill as far as the leak was concerned. Her fury at her friend's current situation made him fairly sure of that. She wouldn't put her friend in harm's way like that if she were. That being said, he didn't agree that she would work with him on this. He just didn't see them going around arm in arm like the best of friends, playing "whack a mole" in tandem. Nope. He did not like his chances as far as that idea went, not at all.

He would be more inclined to believe she would dole out an ass-whooping before marching into the

Superintendent's office and reporting this information, which would blow their chances of catching them. Ensuring they went to ground and covered their tracks before they could learn their identity. The more he thought about it, the less he liked it, and he said as much.

However, he underestimated Stephen's gift in the art of persuasion.

"None of us know the officers at the station well enough to discern if they are capable of being the leak. Serenity does. She knows the people far better and has more motivation than we do to find the underlying cause of it; her friend is missing, and her life is in danger. Wren won't want to miss an opportunity to find out information from someone who likely knows the real killer's identity and what has become of Jen Cartwright," he reasoned.

Alec still wasn't sold on the idea, but he had begrudgingly agreed that it would take less time if they had a better insight into the officers working there. So here he stood not an hour later, trying to decide on the best way to approach her and bring the subject up without drawing attention from the mole and risk them realising they were being hunted.

After another hour passed, which in part was due to lack of opportunity and also the fact that she wasn't exactly sending out friendly vibes, he still hadn't figured out the answer to that question. It was for this reason, when he turned around and found her approaching him, he hadn't been expecting her question.

"What is it?" she asked, looking at him expectantly for a reply.

"I beg your pardon?" Alec said in surprise.

"For the last hour, on repeat, you have at various intervals, looked at me all skittish, looked away like you want to run and hide, then you bit your lip like you are trying not to say something. So, what is it? If you have something to say then do it already, you are starting to creep me out," she snapped.

"Oh. Sorry," he replied, lamely.

She rolled her eyes and decided on a different approach. "Do you or do you not have something to say to me?" she tried.

"I might," he stalled, feeling less confident about this plan with every second that passed.

"Ok," she sighed, "talk."

"I can't talk. Not here," Alec hedged looking around them, making sure they weren't drawing attention.

"Why not?" Wren asked.

"If I told you that, then it would contradict what I just said, which was that I couldn't talk here," Alec sniped.

"Fine," she huffed. Then turned away. Alec, assuming he had royally messed up, hung his head. He'd been assigned one task to do, and he'd blown it.

"Hey guys?" Wren addressed the three men a short distance away, "I need caffeine and if I'm honest, my stomach is angry with me. Moreno's?" she smiled sweetly, an action that so completely changed her face, Alec was immediately entranced, which of itself was more than a little disconcerting.

"Wren, I could kiss you! I've been dying over here but I didn't want to be the one to bring it up. You know I will always say yes to a breakfast from Moreno's cafe," Matt answered dramatically.

"Steady on there, Matt, I'll go and grab us something. The greenhorn hasn't got all that much to offer at the moment, he can tag along and give me a hand, might as well make himself useful," she quipped, the jibe hitting its mark in a clean, cutting shot to his pride. However, he was so relieved she was giving him a chance, he took the low blow on the chin.

"Come along greenhorn, coffee is calling my name," she said stiffly, sweeping from the room leaving him to trail after her like a damn puppy dog.

They didn't speak as they left the building. Without looking back at him she indicated the direction of her car and strode toward it. When they got inside, they put on their seatbelts, and she pulled out and away from the station.

"Now, greenhorn, what is your deal?" Wren asked in an icy tone.

"Look, I don't want to seem paranoid—" Wren cut him off.

"You know who starts a sentence like that? Paranoid people," she said sharply.

"Fine. I would prefer if we took this conversation somewhere quiet, where there is no chance that someone can't have listening devices planted," he whispered, sounding even to his own ears, like some crazy conspiracy theorist.

"Okayyy," Wren replied, dragging the last syllable out, implying he wasn't alone in that assessment.

When they finally pulled up and exited the car, she led him into a quiet area of a pretty, picturesque park. She sat down on a nearby bench, surveying their surroundings before landing her gaze on him, piercing him with her intensity. He shifted uncomfortably and looked away.

"Let's hear it, greenhorn. I swear if after all this dramatic cloak and dagger bullshit, I don't hear something important that explains the weird shit you're pulling, I will not be held responsible for what happens next!" she hissed, the threat behind her words clear.

"Where do I start? Ok there are two things. The first is that the anonymous calls I've been receiving are from a woman calling herself Kelly," he stated, pausing to watch her reaction. If she took this badly, he could always leave out the next part.

"Calls? Plural?" she asked first, the question was not the one he had been anticipating.

"Yes. Two to be precise," he told her.

"What was the first call in regard to?" she queried; this time he was expecting the question.

"It was to inform me that Dev had been arrested. That he was innocent and needed our help," he recounted.

She seemed surprised by this revelation and then after allowing herself a moment to let his answer sink in, she got to the question he'd assumed would be first.

"Kelly? As in Kelly Whelan? She's alive?"

"I believe so," he confirmed.

"Why do you think it's her?" Wren continued her line of inquiry.

"I can't be one hundred percent; she only gave the name Kelly. When your DCI mentioned her name, I was pretty surprised. That's when I made the connection," he answered.

"So, the DCI knows? Yet he didn't tell us? Why?" Wren wondered aloud, her confusion plain on her face.

"It was just before we were informed of DC Cartwright's disappearance. He wanted time to consider what this meant and allow you all time to focus on your friend," Alec offered by way of an explanation.

"Okay. So, what was the second thing?" she asked, abruptly switching topics.

"Now I want you to know I'm not entirely on board with giving you this information," he began, "however, Stephen was most insistent that I tell you, he seems to think we need your assistance."

"Stephen? As in Stephen Doyle? Dev's defence attorney, brother, whatever he is?" Wren rambled.

"Yes. Dev told him that you could be trusted. He said that you'd said yourself it might be possible—"

"Dev said that? That I could be trusted?" Wren repeated interrupting, her eyes wide with shock and something else that Alec couldn't put his finger on.

"He did," Alec said patiently.

"Sorry, what were you saying?" she pressed, remembering he had been in the middle of explaining.

"When I got the call yesterday, I relayed the message given. However, I wasn't entirely forthcoming," Alec started hesitantly.

Wren immediately stiffened beside him and any ground he had gained with the mention of Dev's faith in her being trustworthy, was lost when he made that last admission. She narrowed her eyes at him and looked at him with suspicion.

"What part of it were you not forthcoming about exactly?" She asked slowly, pinning him with a laser, violet glare.

"The message she gave was to tell them DC Cartwright was dead—" Wren cut him off yet again.

"You told us that yesterday," she stated coldly.

"I know that" Alec replied, losing his patience a little before continuing, "but that wasn't the entire message. She said, tell them DC Cartwright is dead. You have a leak, tell them, it's important."

"We have a leak, tell them it's important? Which part is important? The *"Jen being dead"* part or the leak part?" Wren asked.

"I'm not sure," Alec answered honestly.

"We have a leak. So, you didn't relay the whole message and followed the DCI's instructions to not mention Kelly. Not because he asked you to, but because you weren't sure if she was telling the truth, and you couldn't take the chance it was true. That would expose her and put her life at risk. Also, it would let the leak know that someone was onto them so they would go to ground," Wren guessed.

"Yes!" Alec exclaimed, relieved that she understood his dilemma.

"So, you took that information to Dev because he couldn't be the leak," she correctly assumed.

Alec nodded, happy she seemed to be following along and not outright dismissing his claims.

"He told you; the leak couldn't be me because I had already suggested there could be one," Wren continued, breaking the information down as she processed it out loud.

"Yes," Alec agreed.

"So, does that mean there is a chance Jen is still alive? Was it a ruse of some kind to root out the leak?" she asked, suddenly looking hopeful.

"I don't want to get your hopes up, but it is a possibility, yes," Alec conceded.

Wren released the breath she had been holding as she'd waited for his answer and sat back, unsure of what to do with the new intel.

"So, Kelly is still alive. Jen could be alive, there's a leak and Dev thinks that I might be better to assist you in finding this mole because I've been here longer and have a better chance of identifying them. I'm assuming the reason for this is that through the mole you may be able to use them to identify the killer. Which means that Dev knows they will likely know who the killer is." Wren mused more for herself than for Alec, "following that logic, if he is after the identity of the killer... Oh God! He didn't do it. He's innocent," she whispered.

"I don't want to be that guy who says *"I told you so"* but..." Alec teased.

"We need to leave now. We need to get the coffee quickly and head back. If we are gone too long, the mole might get suspicious and that might compromise us. Let me think about it and I'll catch up with you later when I've had time to think," she decided.

"In that case we had better get a move on," Alec agreed, feeling a measure of relief that it had gone better than he'd expected.

****

Wren had spent the rest of her shift feeling claustrophobic, as though the walls were closing in and there was no way to get out. Trying not to act any different, yet feeling such intense paranoia that she could not get her head into gear and concentrate on the case. Which in turn made her behaviour different, making her even more paranoid she was giving herself away. It was a vicious circle, one that she had spent the day running the circumference of like an athlete on a training track. It was exhausting being that on edge the entire time.

"You doing okay?" Matt asked, eyeing her with a look that said he wasn't sure what her deal was.

"I'm just worried about Jen," Wren explained, which in part was true. It was a plausible enough reason for her tension and Matt nodded, though the concern seemed to remain. Plausible if you weren't leaking information to a serial killer. However, if she was this paranoid, it was safe to assume that the culprit might be in a similar state of hyper-awareness, maybe even more so. Would they look deeper, see her anxiety, and suspect the worst?

"You need to work on your poker face," Alec whispered surreptitiously.

"I'm doing my best, but I am not used to holding shit back from my team," Wren hissed back.

If this wasn't bad enough, she was reading into even the smallest of details. Matt had asked more than once if she was okay; was it really out of concern or was he the mole? Ash seemed to be distant and distracted; was he trying to avoid drawing attention for nefarious reasons? Reece was new, he was asking a lot of questions; how many questions was too many questions? Was his interest with good intentions or because he needed to keep a killer in the loop? The entire day had been a clusterfuck.

On top of all of that, Alec was coping with it all much easier than she was, which had only managed to add irritation to the spiralling emotions she was trying to contain. She found herself not wanting to aid her colleagues to uncover more in their attempt to find their killer and possibly Jen, solely with the worry that any progress made may be used against them if it were reported back. Possibly endangering her friend's life, and subsequently hurting the investigation more.

"I need to get the hell out of here," Wren grumbled and Alec nudged her pointedly, only serving to put her back up even further.

She wasn't built for this double agent bullshit. Her best shot at looking at this objectively was removing herself from the toxicity of the environment in question. She all but counted down the minutes of every hour that passed and when Matt finally suggested they stop for the day, she was relieved. She nodded to Alec who would be here longer, since his shift had begun after theirs, before making a swift exit. Desperate in her need to get out of there and get some air, needing to leave the viper's nest she had created in her head.

t was like venom had discoloured her entire workplace: what should be a safety zone, where they should be finding solutions, had become the epicentre of the very problem. Suspicion crept slowly into her mind, spreading, and entering all of the hidden crevices, like venom might infect the outer membrane of capillary vessels, causing internal bleeding. Her heart felt like it was bleeding out. The thought that one of her friends, one of her colleagues may be responsible for this betrayal, making the injury painful and bleeding without the chance of clotting to stem the flow.

"Hold it together just a little bit more," she told herself.

Similar "symptoms" occurred then. There was a nauseous feeling in the pit of her stomach. She felt drained and lethargic from the weight of knowing one of them was working against them. She felt as though her mind was swelling inside her head, the venom still eating away at her, even though she had left the area where they were being attacked from.

She was struggling for breath, each pull of air was an effort to drag into her lungs. In all, the strain of it was attacking her as surely as venom might affect the bitten area, causing necrosis and killing off the infected area surrounding the wound. What was it that they suggested would help to treat a snake bite effectively? *Identifying the snake that bit you*, she thought, answering her own internal question. Suddenly she knew what she needed, who she needed to survive this attack on her senses.

****

They knew who the leak was. Keri wanted to fist pump the air but one thought stopped her. Knowing who it was and actually plugging the leak were not the same thing. In fact, they were two very separate problems with the second being the greater issue of the two. Until that was taken care of, the first was an empty victory at best.

"Reece Carter," Jen repeated, still reeling from the shock of it, "do you think Ash knows? I think they're close, at least, I assumed...Is he in on it?"

"I can't be sure," Keri answered, "I sincerely hope not, or we have another problem. Perhaps we should be sure, we don't want to chop off the head of a snake for another one to grow back in its place and bite us in the ass."

"I don't want to think he is, but I can't be sure," Jen said, still clearly distressed by the whole idea.

"So, what now?" Cam asked, "do we take him out?" Jen gasped, "we don't fucking *"Take them out"* not while I'm involved, we unmask him...them…him."

"Hmm..." Keri murmured. This was the question. What to do? What to do? If she told Alec, would they arrest him? Without proof it would be hard to keep him detained and her mother would almost certainly be alerted. She would ask questions. If they killed him, he would be out of their way but it would still arouse her mother's suspicion and add to that the likelihood they would also end up in prison, unless they killed Jen, which she would rather not do since she had grown quite fond of her Jenny friend. She would likely implicate them in his demise on her return to her life if they succeeded in ending her mother's reign of terror.

No, she was going to need a better solution to her dilemma. Perhaps she could lure him into somehow revealing himself. That would have the benefit of making him her mother's problem and keep their involvement in his removal concealed, but how would they achieve this? Maybe she could rattle him enough that he would get sloppy, let his own paranoia expose him. That was a thought…

Kissing Cameron on the cheek she headed to leave, as Jen looked at her with something close to worry or concern. She should ease their troubled minds.

"Don't worry, I think I have a better plan."

"Are you going to share?" Jen called behind her.

"No time. Don't worry so much Jenny friend. You will get frown lines," Keri replied cheerfully before exiting the building.

Chapter Nine

Dev and his two remaining siblings had worked together as quickly as they could to uncover as much information on "The Executioner" as they could find. After several hours of digging, they had found little more than speculation and urban legends. Tales of his exploits, while plentiful, had little substance and almost no fact to corroborate them. He was little more than the criminal world's very own version of the "Bogeyman", a tale that seemed invented to keep criminals towing the line by their employers. It was as frustrating as it was disturbing, they had a few admittedly grim accounts that held some small chance of resembling truth, the odd cases that bore resemblance to the graphic and embellished stories Raven had dug through. They shared some similarities but nothing close enough to substantiate those claims, no real evidence to back them and no further clue to the true identity of this "mythical" monster.

He raked his hand through his hair and pushed it back out of his eyes and looked at the information wall he had created. It had spider-webbed its way across the large length, seeming to have a life of its own, so complex and intricate that even he had trouble keeping track of the links. A secondary section had been added to the first, this one for the sole purpose of racking information on likely leads for their leak. With so many distinct aspects to try and keep track of, trying to find a clear path to follow was becoming increasingly challenging.

"This is quite an intricate little rabbit hole," Raven stated as she followed his gaze.

"Aye. It is certainly a fecking pain in the ass," Dev replied with a sigh.

A knock at the door pulled him away from his thoughts and had him studying it with curiosity. It had been some time since they'd been in contact with Chris so it would likely be him returning. It was far too early to be Alec who was still completing his stint at work. He stepped towards it and opened it, not bothering to waste time making pleasantries with his brother, eager to get back to the wall. Without even looking he began to head back down the hall casually calling behind him.

"Come in already. I'll catch you up, then you can tell us what you've found."

When silence followed, he frowned, looking back at the door still ajar, no sign that Chris intended to enter. He walked back toward it, opening it wider and froze in his tracks.

"Dev?" Wren said quietly. Her hesitation and awkwardness were clear for anyone to see.

They faced off, caught in an uncomfortable stalemate. Neither really knew how to bridge the gap, making no move to end it.

"What's the hold up?" Stephen asked, stepping into the hallway behind him. Seeing the pair, he looked between the two, studying them before a smile split his face, "You going to let the girl in, Brother? I know it's been a while, but it's usually considered polite to invite guests in and offer them a drink," he teased, attempting to ease the tension.

Dev blinked and stepped back before following Stephen's cue and indicating that Wren should come in. She nodded, accepting his silent invitation. She entered the living room and Dev caught the slight flinch as she did, before she shook it off as though it never happened. As he wondered what had given her cause to do so, he followed her line of sight and felt a slight spike of satisfaction, before feeling a little ashamed of it.

"I don't believe you've met our ItsyBit. This is Raven," he introduced quietly.

"Raven is another of our foster clan," Stephen rushed to add, intentionally clarifying the petite, dark haired woman's place in their number, "Raven this is Serenity Jones."

"Oh, I know," Raven smiled smugly, "computer nerd, remember? You think I didn't look her up?"

Wren looked a little alarmed at her bold statement and some of her fire, sparked in her violet eyes. "Should I have returned the favour?" Wren bit out.

"Probably," Raven admitted, smirking now, mischief twinkling in her blue-grey eyes.

Wren let out a burst of laughter, taking Dev by surprise. The tension in her body seemed to ease and Dev studied her properly for the first time since she'd entered. She looked tired, stressed, and worn down. This case was taking its toll on everyone, but seeing her natural spirit dampened by the dirt they were digging through made him soften towards her. She wasn't unaffected by this; she was suffering too.

"Pull up a chair," Dev offered evenly and Wren's laughter died as she immediately remembered the awkwardness hanging between them.

Perhaps Stephen had been right, she'd had a responsibility to do her job. Should he blame her for doing it? It was after all the reason she was here now, her sense of justice and her belief in righting wrongs had led her to his door despite the fact that she shouldn't be here. The same way those very values had meant she'd been duty bound to arrest him. Could he really continue to hold that against her?

Would he have felt the same way if it had been another suspect? The simple answer was no. He had taken it personally, but it hadn't been personal in the eyes of the law. He'd allowed his hurt to colour his judgement, he himself valued those same qualities, shouldn't he accept that the law must be followed even if he were the one who stood accused? Just because it wasn't true it shouldn't mean he should get a pass; nobody should be exempt from scrutiny. He had been more than a little harsh on Angel.

He realised then that the room had grown quiet while he had been lost in thought. Wren now studied him warily, Raven was looking between the two of them from behind Wren, fanning herself in a gesture that was meant to mock him. That made him blink back to life and roll his eyes at her, while Stephen smirked.

"Back with us, Brother?" he chuckled.

"Feck off," Dev said, some of his good humour returning, though he chose not to look too deeply at the reason for that.

"Aww," Raven interjected, unable to resist the chance to get in on the fun, "they are adorbsicle aren't they?"

"A what?" Dev said, frowning.

"Adorbsicle. Adorable and sweet like popsicles too," Raven replied cheekily.

"Bejesus Christ!" Dev spat, disgusted, "I would ask you to please refrain from ever using that as a word again."

"Oh Dev, on those grounds alone I'm adding it as my word of the week!" she crowed in delight.

While Dev prayed for patience, ignoring his sister's threat in hope that being unresponsive to her bid to get a rise out of him she might forget about it before long. "I'll put the kettle on, catch her up," he said, looking at Stephen and at his nod, he left the room.

Wren uncomfortably stared at the wall and tried hard to appear like she was absorbed in the compilation of information she was looking at in hoping to avoid having to face the stares of Dev's siblings behind her. In doing so, she noticed something. Something she had not seen on their own big board at work. Unable to stop herself from asking, she asked, "Who is The Executioner?"

"Ah, I see it now. There's that pit-bull Dev alluded to earlier. Let me show you where we are in this crazy set up," Stephen offered.

While Dev was making the drinks, Stephen gave a brief overview of their own investigation and Wren felt the horrible, suffocating feeling of before beginning to dissipate and her usual motivation return. It was as though the fresh air cleared away the polluted, toxic cloud she'd had hovering over her at work and infused her with a cleaner supply, allowing her to breathe.

"Drinks are ready." Dev's deep Irish brogue came from behind her, and the hairs rose along her arms, making her shiver and goosebumps break out along her skin. Her senses heightened for an entirely different reason than before.

"Thank you," she murmured quietly, avoiding eye contact so he couldn't see the effect he was having on her.

"My pleasure, Angel," he whispered.

Her heart stuttered at the use of the pet-name, not in anger this time. Instead his sexy baritone sent her pulse racing.

"You two need to dial that back a few notches," Raven quipped, "you're giving me the feels and I'm not sure my heart can take it."

"You'll get over it, ItsyBit," Dev shot back, tousling her hair.

Raven scowled, smoothing down her dark, silky locks and flipped him off. Dev tsked at her in mock admonishment and winked at her, making Raven startle in surprise.

"That's new," she mused to herself, giving Dev a look that said she wasn't sure what to do with this version of him.

"So," Dev interrupted, clearly calling order without saying more than one syllable, "are we all caught up?"

"I believe we are," Stephen answered.

"Welcome to our little team of horrors," Dev said to Wren, grinning, "now how about we find ourselves a mole."

****

Keri spied Reece at the bar, she studied him a moment before slowly making her approach. She'd been monitoring his movements since she'd left earlier. She's also noticed something interesting indeed. The brothers did not seem as close as Jen had led her to believe. Jen had assumed it to be the case, however Keri's more discerning eye spied trouble in the family paradise. When Reece thought nobody was watching she saw hatred. Almost unperceivable to the eyes of someone less observant. Keri saw it though, recognised the look after years of dealing with her wicked, fake mother. That wasn't all. She had also seen Ashley studying his brother; his gaze also held a familiar look too. Suspicion. *Oh, this would do nicely*, she thought.

Now though, Reece had finished his shift and was propping up the bar, the exertion of pasting that fake smile on for most of the day had clearly taken its toll judging by the scowl on his face. She strolled over languidly, evoking her mother's persona and preparing to use it on her prey.

"Good evening, Reece darling. Mother sends her regards," she greeted with a frosty smile. She watched fear creep into his eyes.

"Keri? H..how lovely to see you," he stuttered.

"Of course it is, darling," she stated, as though that fact was unquestionable and obvious.

"What can I do for you?" he asked hesitantly.

"Oh, nothing darling, just checking in. Mother thought us incredibly rude, leaving it so long between visits," she said with saccharine sweetness.

"I haven't heard anything new yet, it's only been a day since—"

"Now, darling, you forget yourself. We don't discuss business in the open," she tutted, reproachfully.

"Oh," he replied, letting the rest of the sentence drop.

"Though, I have to say it must be nice working so close with your family. Your brother and you must be awfully close, watching you today he couldn't seem to keep his eyes from his big brother. Does he suffer from a touch of hero-worship? He must really look up to you," she said, innocently.

"H..he does? Yes, of course he does," Reece said, trying to sound more convincing when he failed the first time. A small crease had appeared in his forehead.

There it was, Keri thought, the seed being planted. Having done what she had come to do, she gave him a final, assessing look before allowing her lips to curl in a slow, unnerving smile.

"Do have a pleasant evening, darling, must dash. Things to do, people to see..." she emphasised the last word drawing it out, the threat implied. Overall, he wasn't going to be that hard to put on edge. He wasn't exactly made of tough stuff, in fact she wondered how he had even made the cut as an officer. Seemed to her they had not been as fussy as they perhaps should've been. With that she left and stepped into the cool, summer breeze, feeling more than a little smug. Yes. She might just win this round.

****

August 15th, 2014

Wren woke up feeling unusually warm and with a strange feeling of safety that she didn't quite understand, until she felt the warm breath at the nape of her neck. Her eyes opened wide in surprise and the collage of information on Dev's living room wall stared back at her. She felt the weight of an arm slung over her waist and as she tried to recall exactly how she'd ended up in this position, she remembered working with the siblings to identify the leak and her eyes beginning to droop. She then vaguely recalled Dev pulling her down onto the oversized couch and telling her to have a cat nap. While Dev and Stephen had continued to talk in low, hushed voices, the steady clacking of keys in the background as Raven scoured online, was oddly soothing. She began to drift off and had been half asleep when she'd felt Dev stroke her hair as he spoke, the combination of his deep voice and the soothing strokes finally sending her to sleep.

As she lay there now half-awake, she wondered how long she'd been sleeping. She could still hear Raven's steady rhythm on the keyboard, she shifted her head slightly to assess the situation. She noted that Dev had somehow ended up behind her on the large sofa, his arm falling around her. She was resting back into him like a little spoon to his big one.

The sound of keys went quiet, and Wren looked up to see why. Her gaze met Raven's who must've noticed her rouse and paused in her work. Raven's black, painted lips twisted up into a mischievous grin before she made a finger heart and mouthed "Adorbsicle," and Wren scowled as she felt her cheeks heat with embarrassment.

"Morning Angel," Dev rasped, his voice husky from sleep. The vibration of the sound sent shivers down her spine and her stomach clenched, not unlike how it felt when she went down a down drop on a rollercoaster.

"Hi!" she squeaked, her embarrassment only increasing at the sound of the ridiculous noise that had come from her mouth. She heard him chuckle behind her and a soft brush of lips press against the nape of her neck, sending small sparks of sensation along her skin and along her nerve endings.

Wrapping her up in his arms he lifted her weight effortlessly, righting them both to a sitting position before giving her a playful shoulder barge, dopey grin and offering her a hot drink.

"Some toast wouldn't go amiss either, Devvy," Raven interjected, fluttering her thick, black lashes at him, and pouting her lips, pleading with him for sustenance.

"Aye, I could manage some toast, might even have a crumpet going if you fancy one," he offered.

"I don't share, Dev, and that's a pretty derogatory term for women these days," she joked, tongue in cheek.

"Stop that! I was trying to be nice, but you've ruined it now. I recant my offer, you don't deserve crumpets," he scolded.

Raven looked a little crestfallen at that and went back on the offensive, quickly switching back to pleading and pouting. Wren couldn't help the bark of laughter that slipped out. Dev's gaze swung to her, he clutched his heart dramatically and feigned hurt.

"You too, Angel? Ganging up on me already," he grumbled, and she couldn't hide the smile that spread over her face. He caught it, narrowing his eyes and surprising her by childishly sticking out his tongue before sweeping around and haughtily sauntering into the kitchen in the most ridiculous display she'd ever seen. She chuckled softly and shook her head and caught sight of Raven studying her like she might a dissected frog in a laboratory.

"Problem?" Wren challenged.

"Not a one," Raven replied, smiling enigmatically before turning her attention back to the monitor.

Wren took her cue and settled back into the surprisingly comfortable sofa before a thought dawned on her. "Shit!" she exclaimed, "What is the time?" She glanced around frantically searching for a clock or something that would tell her the time.

"Bless your little cotton top," Raven baited, "You're fine it's only 6am."

"Oh. Okay. Good," Wren said, choosing to ignore the "Cotton top" reference. It would only encourage her further if she acknowledged it, instead opting to snuggle back into the couch cushions while she waited for Dev to bring coffee.

****

Ash had made it into the incident room first. He didn't make it a habit to be the first here, often arriving after Jen, who was usually first. She either got here really early or never left, he was never quite sure. Today, he'd come a little earlier hoping to get a little peace and quiet and make up some coffee for himself and the others before the hustle and bustle of the other officers arriving crowded the canteen. He hadn't slept particularly well and wasn't yet ready for being crammed in.

"Hey there, Baby Bird," his brother greeted. He was glad he had his back to him, unable to hide his small smile falter on his face at the interruption of his peace. He fixed his smile back on and turned to greet him in return.

"A little early for you isn't it, Reece's Pieces? I didn't know you knew this time existed on your alarm clock," he replied, trying for humour. Judging by the look now plastered on his brother's face, it had fallen short of the mark.

"Any particular reason you've come in this early, Baby Bird? Trying to earn yourself some brownie points? Make the rest of us look bad while you collect gold stars?" he sneered, not quite able to hide his look of spite, letting the mask slip before fixing it back into place and smiling.

Ash gave him an assessing look, then shrugged allowing a cocky grin. "And if I am?" he taunted.

"Then good luck to you," Reece replied, feigning nonchalance but not quite selling it.

"Why thank you Reece's Pieces. Always nice to have your very own cheer squad," Ash quipped before turning back to make the coffee.

"Is one of those going spare?" Reece asked.

"Na... you're here early, you have time to get your own. Wouldn't want anyone accusing me of wanting a gold star for making coffee," Ash deadpanned, before taking the tray of cups and leaving his brother behind.

****

Matt stood at the entrance way to the incident room and could immediately sense the tension. For the most part, Matt portrayed himself as the joker of their pack. With so much darkness that came their way, he'd learned through years of experience the value of someone who could lighten the mood. Jen was also one of these people, she naturally came by her friendly, outgoing personality where Matt's had developed as a coping mechanism from his years on the Major Crimes Unit. He had a good ten years on the others and had more need than the others for some humour to help him get through the crimes they dealt with on a daily basis. It took its toll over time and if you didn't laugh, you'd get sucked in and dragged down from the weight of it all.

With Jen's disappearance Matt had felt the void her bubbly personality had left, and Ash's brother didn't come close to filling it. In fact, his presence seemed to only heighten the tension in the room, already strained by the heaviness of losing one of their own. While it held particularly true in Ash's case, he'd also marked a noticeable change in Wren's demeanour too. He knew Wren, and although Jen's disappearance would certainly have been a concern to her, it would also light a fire beneath her to relentlessly dig into the case and find her friend. However, she almost seemed reluctant to participate. Something was very wrong.

"Something funky is going down in funky town," Matt muttered, his gut had been telling him something was definitely amiss with this picture.

Now, observing the two brothers, who had yet to notice his arrival, he took in the picture he saw before him. Ash appeared to be steadfastly ignoring his brother, quiet and almost unmoving, as though hoping to blend into the wall. Reece, however, projected an entirely different image, one Matt didn't care for at all. What he saw was fury and loathing. He suspected Reece Carter's persona wasn't at all what he had been projecting to them yesterday. Maybe that was Wren's issue, she had a gift for sensing people's real intentions and perhaps she'd sensed something off about the brother, making her wary and preventing her from contributing as she might have otherwise.

Whatever it was, Matt didn't like how Reece's presence was affecting his team. Turning before they became aware of his arrival, he headed to the superintendent's office and knocked. Ordinarily there would be an officer posted outside her office to announce his arrival, but it was still early, and Linda wasn't due to start her shift yet.

"Come in," the super's voice called from within. He entered the office, closing the door behind him.

"Matt? Well, this is a surprise, what can I do for you today?" She asked.

"Reece Carter, that's why I'm here Ma'am," he stated simply.

"Is that so? If I'm honest I can't say I'm completely surprised. I had hoped his interest in supporting his brother's team was a sign he might be stepping up and becoming more of a team player. I assume I was wrong to hope. I'm not quite sure how two brothers can be so completely different," She mused.

"Ma'am with all due respect, I am not entirely convinced he's helping, I'd go so far as to say he's actually a hindrance," Matt informed her openly.

"Hmmm…I see. Perhaps we could find him something to do to occupy his time, something a little more in his wheelhouse. Some door-to-door enquiries perhaps? Is there a task you can recommend?" she enquired.

"You know we never did get around to speaking to the officers that dealt with the Liam Whelan case. He could trace those records and take a drive, to see if he can have a talk with the retired officers that dealt with it. He could see if there is any information that didn't make the official report that may prove of some use to us," Matt suggested, smiling now.

"You know that's an awfully clever idea. I think you may be right, that does seem like something he could do. I will speak to him personally, and task him with what might prove to be a vital piece of this puzzle," she assured him, a twinkle in her eye.

"Yes Ma'am, a very important task indeed," Matt agreed.

"Very well, return to the incident room and I'll have Linda call him through shortly, she'll be arriving soon," she directed. Matt turned to leave and stopped when she added, "Matt? Thank you..."

"Always a delight to pay you a visit Ma'am," he replied with a cheeky wink.

She smiled broadly and shooed him off, light-heartedly. As he left the office he felt a weight lift, perhaps now they might get some work done.

Chapter Ten

Reece was furious and more than a little worried. He had been summoned to the Super's office and tasked with a "special assignment" that had taken him away from the incident room, where he needed to be.

Keri had been right, though not about his brother's "hero-worship." He had been watching him. Clearly annoyed by his success at making the team, he had obviously set about trying to sabotage his new placement. He was going to get in his way, his jealousy making his position precarious. As he headed out to speak with some old-timers about some bullshit cold case, he took his phone out and rang Mary.

"Reece darling, calling back so soon?" Mary enquired coldly down the phone.

"I have a problem. My brother is on to me. He's making waves and that is not good for our interests," Reece stated, waiting for her reply.

"Indeed. Not good at all," Mary agreed, "Leave it with me."

When he hung up the phone he smiled smugly. *Well Baby Bird,* he thought, *you had a good run.*

****

Mary had summoned her daughter and waited for her to arrive. As she did, she addressed her consort.

"Cain, darling. I have a new muse for your work," she informed him, a hint of a smile curling her lips.

"Oh, your Highness. It would be my pleasure," he returned, bowing in jest. "Now, I don't believe you have met our new "masterpiece," and we have no time to prepare as we might. I've called Keri, she knows him and has been keeping a watch for me. She will arrange for you to get an "introduction," then you can take it from there," she explained.

"As you wish," he proclaimed.

A knock came at the door and Michael showed Keri inside. Giving Michael a nod, Keri watched as he exited and turned to Mary and her lover.

"Mother, you requested my presence?" She asked dutifully.

"Yes, darling, I have a job for you," she began.

****

Keri left her mother's company and didn't have much time to make arrangements. She hadn't expected her plan to see fruition quite so soon, and it had taken an unexpected turn and not quite what she had anticipated. She had expected her mother to cut her losses. This, however, wasn't what she'd had in mind at all. Yet if she was quick on her feet, she might yet be able to claw it back. She had until tonight to see that it turned out right. That was when her mother had assigned the "meet and greet." She had a lot to do and not much room for error. She headed to the station and pulled out her phone, making a short call.

"Hello?" The voice on the other end, asked warily.

"Are you working today, dearest? Do be quick now, it's important," she asked.

"Yes," he answered abruptly.

"Perhaps you might be a dear and go for a coffee run. Take that rather dashing Ashley with you," she suggested, before hanging up.

Immediately after, she placed another call. Cameron answered after no more than two rings.

"Keri-blossom, I have to say I am having some withdrawal symptoms. All of this *"do-gooder"* malarkey is rather hindering our alone time," he quipped.

"Aww, poor baby," she teased. "don't worry. If you complete this one little task for me, I shall make sure that I reward you tonight," she assured him.

"In that case, Keri-blossom? How can I be of service?" he asked.

****

Ash had been surprised and somewhat relieved on two counts today. The first being the sudden departure of his brother. He'd been asked to follow up on the cold case side of the investigation, sending him from the incident room for the day. This had lifted a weight from his mind, and he'd found himself relaxing. The second had been the offer from DS Morgan to head to Moreno's and splash for some coffee and rolls. He had then inclined his head and declared it might be better if he didn't wander around alone and requested Ash's company to help with the run. As they left the station and headed into the car park. Ash found himself asking.

"So, DS Morgan, any particular reason you requested my presence or was it just the luck of the draw?"

"I haven't really had much of a chance to get to know you yet," he began. "I obviously know Wren, and I have spent some time with Matt. Just yesterday, we discussed the case, with Reece out on assignment, I figured it was as good a time as any to make your acquaintance on a less official basis. You are not really as forthcoming as the others in your team."

Ash nodded; it made some sense. Being new to the team could be somewhat intimidating. It made it easier to find your feet on a one-to-one basis.

"So, Ash, how long have you been in the MCU?" Alec asked curiously, "You seem pretty young."

"Yes, I'm relatively new. I've been with the team about eight months now," Ash answered.

"I see, enjoying it?" Alec inquired.

"For the most part, though, this case has been challenging," he admitted.

"Yes, I can see why," Alec agreed, "it is a particularly nasty one."

"Yes, it is," Ash said simply.

They arrived at the coffee shop and before stepping inside. Ash caught sight of something interesting while surveying the area.

"Is that Cameron O'Reilly?" he asked stiffly.

Alec looked in the direction he was surveying and tensed too.

"So, it would seem. Stay here and I'll see if I can get closer. I'm new, he might not recognise me," Alec ordered.

Ash nodded. Alec discreetly made his way closer, his attention subtle but fixed on this strange development. With his own attention preoccupied, Ash didn't notice the small blonde doctor as she barrelled into him.

"Oh my God!" she gasped, her drink spilling onto the front of his jacket.

"I am so sorry I got paged and I wasn't watching where I was going," she said quickly, frantically patting at his jacket with a wad of tissues she'd pulled from the takeaway bag she was carrying, containing food.

"It's fine," he assured her, his brow furrowing in thought, "we've met, haven't we?"

"Yes, I do believe we have. I was the doctor on call when one of your officers was brought in," she replied, continuing, "I am so, so sorry."

"Doc, I'm OK. It mostly caught my jacket. Nothing to worry about," he soothed.

"Are you sure?" she asked hesitantly, giving him a once over as though not entirely convinced.

"I'm sure," he replied, smiling.

"In that case, sorry to have bothered you," she apologised again. "I don't mean to leave you in this state, but duty calls," she said, indicating her pager.

"No worries, you get off doc," he told her.

"Sorry again," she said before heading away from him.

He chuckled to himself before finding Alec looking toward him, a confused look on his face and saw Cameron O'Reilly leaving with a coffee in hand. Alec made his way back toward him and studied his wet jacket.

"What the hell happened to you?" He asked.

"A doctor from the hospital ran into me when she checked her pager, spilled her coffee on me," he said.

"Is that right?" Alec asked, amusement dancing in his voice, "Someone you know?"

"Not really, just the Doctor who happened to be on call when I was there not long ago," he explained.

"Was she pretty?" Alec teased.

"Not hard on the eyes, not really my type, though," he shrugged.

"Fair enough. Let's get some coffee," he said.

****

Keri waited at their agreed spot and Cameron strolled casually toward her, coffee in hand.

"Did you get what you need, Keri-blossom?" He asked.

"I believe so, my heart, I can't thank you enough," she said, kissing him soundly on the lips.

"That wasn't what you said earlier," he grumbled.

"That is true," she mused, "perhaps I can do something to take the edge off," she whispered low in his ear.

"Here?" he asked in surprise.

"There's nobody here. We are alone. It would be rude not to make use of the time," she said suggestively.

"Say no more, my love," Cameron said, his eyes suddenly predatorial. He tossed the coffee carelessly and scooped her up, pressing her against the wall, before taking her mouth in a hard, passionate kiss.

"Mm, good boy," she teased when they pulled apart a fraction. He bit her lip and she sighed.

A brief time later, after they had smoothed their clothes and regained their composure, she gave him a farewell kiss and sent him on his way. He whistled as he went, making her giggle at his ridiculousness before returning her focus back to the next task at hand. Once again pulling the burner phone from her pocket, she dialled the number she wanted.

"Hello?" A voice came in response.

"Hello, Terry. It is Terry, right? All these fresh faces, it's hard to keep track," she said.

"Miss McNamara?" he asked politely.

"Yes, dear, did you do as I asked?" she inquired.

"Yes, ma'am," he replied.

"Lovely. Now, where are you?" she queried.

He answered, giving her his location, she thanked him and told him she would join him shortly. This was a risky play, but she was unfortunately short of options.

****

Alec had returned with Ash to the incident room, carrying their spoils to a delighted whoop from Matt and a relieved look from Wren. He couldn't put his finger on why, but the environment seemed less reserved and more settled than it had the day before. He'd think more about that later when he had more time. He would also dissect the strange call that seemed to make no sense at all. He'd driven all the way to Moreno's. Bumped into Cameron O'Reilly, which was in itself odd, then returned here with no real idea what benefit it had served.

It was a mystery that seemed in line with the mysterious caller herself. Wren shot him a questioning look and he shook his head, almost unperceivable to the eye, to tell her now was not the time to broach it. She gave a slight chin lift in return, and Matt raised an eyebrow.

"Something wrong?" Alec asked in amusement.

"Not particularly, but since we've decided to talk using body language today, I felt left out," he quipped. Using the joker that he played to a tee, masking but not hiding the attentiveness of his sharp eyes as he studied the two detectives.

"I apologise. I'll try to communicate with words from here on out," Alec replied wryly.

"Good," Matt scolded, "I'm getting on a bit, and I can't be messing about playing guessing games. I don't know what's going on with young people these days, but I suggest you remember we're a team. Jen is counting on us, so I reckon we should get our shit together. Fall apart on your own time." With that, they got to work.

****

Dev and his merry band of misfits were working in twos. Chris had returned and through word-of-mouth corroborated Stephens' suggestion that The Executioner was important and linked to Mary McNamara. Now what they needed was proof. Stephen and Chris were working their way through the background of various police officers, prioritising those with close links to the case. There was a lot of staff, but they likely wouldn't look at the pile of unlikely suspects, unless they drew a blank on the likeliest. Raven and Wren had spent time arranging it into these sorted piles yesterday evening but hadn't managed to look through yet.

Dev and Raven were working on "The Executioner" trail. Sorting through their own prioritised pile of intel. They were taking the various cases they had found, matching them to similar criteria, trying to find one that might tie him to Mary. Until they could show indisputable proof that they were connected, they had nothing. By this point, they had firmly settled on Mary as their killer, or at the very least the person commissioning the killings. If the executioner was her lover, it made sense that the grunt work of the kills themselves were mostly executed by him. How involved Mary was in these deaths was unclear, but at the very least she was the person behind them. How Kelly Whelan fit into all of this was still a mystery.

"I think I've figured out the link," Raven said, unsure, "I can't find proof though, but from the general word on the street provided by Chris, matching the criteria to a case that links to Mary in a clear-cut way, I found only one so far, I haven't included the current murders, since there's no proof they are his work," she rambled.

"Which one, ItsyBit..?" Dev cut in.

"Your father's," she whispered, "you told us about your memory of this particular incident yourself. Whoever Chris spoke to give this account," she finished handing him a sheet of paper.

Dev read the notes Raven had taken as Chris had given various accounts of what he'd heard from his information gathering. Upon reading it, he called Chris. Chris strolled over, unhurried despite the bite to Dev's tone.

"Devvy boy! What can I do for you? Kinda busy over there, you know," he said.

"Who did you hear this from?" Dev asked.

Chris glanced at the paper, and his lips grew thin as he pressed them together as though wanting to keep quiet.

"It's important," Dev stressed, noting his hesitation.

"His testimony won't hold up in a court of law Dev, and he likely wouldn't show if it could," Chris admitted.

"If they found out he said this, he wouldn't get the chance to be called," Dev stated sharply, "they will kill him if they get wind of it."

Chris laughed. "I wouldn't worry about that, mate. He isn't exactly an angel himself. He knows people too."

"OK, so there is a link, he's involved, but the only proof is from an equally unreliable source who won't testify. Do I have that right?" Stephen interjected.

"Yep," Dev said, popping the 'p' at the end, his frustration clear. "This is a wild goose chase."

"Any luck on the mole?" Raven asked hopefully, changing the subject.

"We think, but can't prove, that it might be Ash's brother," Stephen said, sighing.

"Reece?" Dev asked. He hadn't met the guy, but Wren hadn't been too keen. She'd said he was a little too interested, whatever that meant.

"We think he's our best guess, which is all it is without proof. From the records that Raven pulled, and Wren's own opinion, he's lazy, not particularly popular, does sloppy work and only does something if it benefits himself. Yet he's turned up offering assistance in this case?" Stephen surmised, "it's the only person who makes any sense."

"Plus, with his brother on your team, he likely picked up a few rumours or passing comments made by Ash. He wouldn't have considered his brother would be using them as a source of information. Wren said after your arrest, they closed ranks, were told to keep quiet on the developments in case you had made any connections within the station. His source dried up and then a spot opened up. It's suspicious," Chris added.

"Give me his Deets, I'll run his accounts, see if we can't find signs of a deposit we can't account for," Raven suggested.

"Finally," Dev said, "about time we got somewhere."

****

Keri had already arranged the meet and greet. Now she just had one thing left to do personally, and with luck, she would pull this off. She approached Reece for the second time in two days. She once again studied him. After meeting his brother not so long ago, she noted they actually bore quite a resemblance. Not enough that someone who knew them well enough wouldn't figure it out, but close enough. It was a shame, really. That he had caused his brother so much trouble, Ash actually seemed to have the better character of the two brothers. She ordered a drink beside him and then addressed the distracted man when he hadn't noticed her arrival.

"Good afternoon, darling," she began, "we really should stop running into each other this way," she cooed, watching in amusement, as his complexion went pale.

"Keri, err, how nice to see you again," he said.

"Mother asked me to tell you the problem has been resolved," she told him.

Taking the drink the bartender had brought over to her, she slid something to him, leaning in close, and he looked at it. Opening it and smiling he nodded to her, then put it inside his jacket. She finished her drink in one swift motion. Then placed the glass on the bar and said, "you have a nice day now, darling," before stepping towards the exit and nodding to a man as they crossed paths on her way out. Going out into the sunshine, she had one final thing to do. However, she needed time to prepare, and she had a few hours to kill. She had Michael keeping an eye on things back at the station. He was her mother's man and assumed he was covering her while she took care of other arrangements. It was time to relieve him of his post.

Chapter Eleven

Wren felt as though the incident room seemed lighter today. After Matt putting his foot down, they got their act together and she found herself convinced that the four of them in the room now were unlikely to be the mole, but not enough to divulge that Dev's unsanctioned investigation seemed to be progressing further than their own. However, he had advantages that they didn't; he had Raven. With Jen out of the investigation, they'd had to muddle through as best they could without her.

They had borrowed another tech geek; however, he wasn't quite as used to their set up, which made him slower than Jen would have been. He also had help, it would appear. Between his foster siblings, his real sibling and his friend all feeding him source information, he had more incoming leads that their uniform hindered them from getting. Also, since they still had a leak and Alec and herself were not supposed to be allowing Dev involvement in the case, the information he had would have to stay secret until they could add it to their own board.

"Fucking mole," Wren grumbled.

She wouldn't be able to resume business as usual, at least until they found the rat. Which she hoped wouldn't take that long. Also, hands on deck were spread thinner here. While Dev was solely focusing his efforts on one case, their resources had to be shared among many, meaning they were progressing slower.

Overall, she found herself wishing she were working on the wall at Dev's and not here in the incident room. The only real benefit to being here was that she suspected Alec had more information than he could currently share and since they were unable to discuss it here, they were going to have to wait until they left for the day. As she had headed to the bathroom earlier, he'd slipped her a piece of paper. She had to remind herself to walk normally, but on pushing open the bathroom door, she rushed to an empty stall and opened it.

AFTER WORK. SAME PLACE AS BEFORE.

When the time had come to finally clock off, she had all but raced to her car. Matt had given her a funny look before asking.
 "Some place better to be?"
 "Any place, really," she teased back.
 Alec hadn't been far behind them, while Ash had offered to clear the cups before setting out, so he'd stayed behind. When she pulled into the park, she got out and waited impatiently for Alec to get there. He hadn't been far behind her, so she wasn't sure what was taking him so long. He finally appeared but she realised what the hold-up was.
 "So," Matt said angrily, "Which one of you is going to tell me what is going on?"

****

Ash had finally left the station. Getting into his vehicle, he drove home in silence, feeling like the day had gone a little better with his brother out of the room. Although there did seem to be a lingering, peculiar vibe at play, on the whole it had felt lighter.

Or maybe that was how he felt with his brother not there to make him tense. Arriving home, he entered and sighed with relief that he had some time alone to breathe. He enjoyed the quiet and found comfort in it. He was at ease in his own space. As he opened his fridge and took a gander at the sparse options in it, he had a sudden feeling of being watched. He wasn't sure what happened next, but the world went dark.

****

The executioner enjoyed his work. He enjoyed it a lot. Mary was his biggest fan and he loved her for that. As a hired killer, it was hard to find a woman who appreciated his talents. When she had instructed him to perform this execution, she had asked that he make a display of it. The Met Office in London had been handling the "Three Blind Mice" piece that he'd left displayed, but Mary had a few sources within several stations that she wanted to send a message to. That failure wasn't an option.

As he studied his latest work of art, he felt it certainly sent that message. However, something was missing. Then it came to him. Reaching into his bag of tools, he found what he was looking for. He then reached into his pocket for the item he'd found on his victim earlier. He smiled a wide, maniacal grin. Moving towards where he'd placed the head, he used the claw hammer and a nail he'd removed from his bag, then nailed the item to his head, right between the eyes. There, it was done. The perfect work of art. With that finished, he packed away carefully and set off into the night.

****

Matt sat in Dev's living room, staring incredulously at the walls. The vast amount of information strung together, spidering out in a web of deceit and lies, of murder and mayhem.

"I'll admit, I'm more than a little pissed off that your big board is cooler than ours," he joked lamely, studying it in fascination and curiosity, "I see that the therapy is going well."

"Speaking of which, Brother, Jean has been in touch and offered an appointment. Your sessions will begin from tomorrow," Stephen informed Dev, who pulled a face, Stephen dug his heels in and continued, "you will attend, Brother. If you don't, it might harm your defence should you be charged and also you need them. Don't pull that face. You can't deny you have issues. They need to be addressed so suck it up, Buttercup."

"So," Matt cut in, getting back on topic, "we have a leak, Dev is running a separate investigation, and he has his foster family aiding and abetting, with the help of officers that are supposed to be working on the actual board in the incident room, but can't in case they tip off the leak, does that about sum it up?"

"Add in the fact we're getting anonymous tip offs from Kelly Whelan and investigating a hitman with the moniker *"The Executioner"* and yes, that's about right," Alec corrected.

"OK, so to my understanding, the reason the MCU has defected to the delinquent team is because we don't want to risk Jen's life by feeding information to her captors. Do we know who it is yet or are we still working on that?" Matt asked.

"We believe that it's Reece Carter," Raven answered, "he fits, and looking at his account, he has been receiving payments for which we can't account. He's our current front runner."

"Do we have proof?" Matt queried.

"Not conclusive just yet, but it's looking likely," Stephen replied.

"And in the *"Brother John"* case, we suspect it's Mary McNamara?" Matt asked.

"With the help of her hit man lover, the Executioner," Chris interjected this time.

"Is that supposition, or do we have evidence?" Matt pressed.

"Circumstantial at best," Dev supplied, "but we're working on it."

"Alec and Wren are the only two at the station who know this?" Matt said.

"Plus, the *"Brady Bunch"* here," Alec quipped.

"And you," Wren added.

"So, on the current team, the only two in the dark now are Ash and Reece," Matt surmised.

"Yes," Dev and Alec said together.

"We don't know if Ash is unknowingly giving Reece information or if he knows, though I don't think he does," Wren explained.

"OK then, where do you want me?" Matt replied, standing, and moving closer to the board.

****

August 16th, 2014

The call came in the early hours of Saturday morning; sending Wren, Matt, and Alec all racing from Dev's to attend the scene. They'd ended up sleeping in the living room like the strangest sleepover Wren had ever been to. The siblings had taken the two bedrooms and Dev had pulled some blankets from an airing cupboard and tossed cushions at the two male officers, before pulling her towards the sofa for some rest. Reece and Ash had been on the earlier shift, which should have meant they would have had time to sleep a little and possibly pick up their investigation for a few hours before they were due to start their shift.

The first call had come when neither one had turned in. Wren had received it and told them she would be in as soon as she could. Then, not half an hour later, calls had come in for all three of them, each heading to a different room to speak without their voices overlapping. They had raced out into the early summer morning, all of them heading in the direction of Welwyn Parish Cemetery. Wren pulled up outside and found the DCI barking out orders to set up the perimeter. As Alec and Matt joined her, the DCI joined them.

"What's going on?" Wren asked.

"We have another one," the DCI said, though judging by his face, there was more to it than that.

"What else?" she asked.

"Sorry?" the DCI said, looking a little unsteady on his feet. "We think it's DC Carter," he admitted.

Wren gasped as various expletives came from the two men behind her.

"Ash or Reece?" Matt asked quietly, his face hopeful.

"Ash," the DCI informed them gently.

"Why?" Alec asked, his face ashen.

"If we knew that we wouldn't need you here, would we?" The DCI snapped harshly before wiping a hand over his face and looking repentant, "I'm sorry, that was uncalled for."

"Why do they think it's Ash?" Wren questioned.

"His warrant card is…nailed to his head," the DCI said slowly, as though choking out the words.

The four of them went quiet, no one knowing what more to say. After the silence had gone on for a while, Wren finally asked in a broken voice. "Who's with him?" As though he was still dying, not already passed, and she didn't want him to be alone.

"The Super is there," the DCI assured her.

Matt stepped forward and said quietly. "Can I go to her? Someone should be with her. It must be hard. It's one of her staff."

"No," the DCI said firmly, "I'll go, Wren, take over here. When the divisional surgeon arrives, send her back," he indicated the tent behind him.

This scene was different than a crime scene would normally be. It was usually a pretty serious affair. However, knowing it was one of their own added to the seriousness of the crime. No jokes were made to lighten the mood, the officers that attended were quiet and sombre out of respect for their fallen comrade. The divisional surgeon finally arrived. Katerina seemed to sense the mood and frowned as she walked towards Wren and Matt.

"Morning, the photographer and pathologist are not far behind me. What have we got? You know, beside a dead body."

"It's DC Ash Carter," Matt snapped, his usual good humour missing.

"Oh," she said softly, "Did you know him?"

"He's one of ours," Wren answered almost inaudibly, her throat feeling scratchy and tight.

"I'm sorry for your loss," she responded, dipping her head as she spoke before being ushered into the tent behind by the waiting DCI.

It wasn't long before she re-emerged and as she did, she made no attempt to speak, nodding to Carl, the photographer, who was waiting for his turn to enter the crime scene. Once she'd cleared the path, he disappeared inside. Doctor Jodie Malone joined them during this time and offered her condolences, having clearly been briefed by another officer before reaching them. It seemed likely to be Alec, who was currently overseeing the perimeter entrance until CID arrived to take over. As the photographer exited, the DCI nodded his head gravely for her to approach.

It was a few hours before they had been told they could head back to the station. Police officers had been assigned door to door calls and the SOCO team had begun to set up. Nobody had dared to ask for details. Wren herself had put it off, not ready to hear how her friend had been killed. She knew that eventually they would have to face it. However, now she just wanted to leave and block it out. They hadn't found Jen yet. Was there another scene out there waiting for them to attend? Was she going to have to solve another murder with another friend as a victim? She wasn't sure she could bear it. That was when another thought occurred to her. Where was Reece Carter?

****

Dev had received the call two hours after his colleagues had hastily made their way to the crime scene. Alec had been the one to break the news, and once they had got off the phone, he'd launched the coffee cup at the kitchen wall in a fit of rage, a torrent of expletives flowing from him as it smashed with an almighty shattering sound. Chris was the first to enter the room, the surprise on his face made Dev calmer but not any less furious.

"What the hell is going on here?" Stephen demanded. Dev couldn't answer, the sheer ferocity of his anger making him unable to form the words.

"I think he got bad news," Chris spoke in his stead and sarcasm dripped from his words as though mocking his brother's unnecessary question.

Raven entered silently, warily approaching Dev, checking to see he was with them and not having another flashback. When she stopped before him, she watched him, assessing his demeanour, trying to read it for an answer before launching herself at him in an unexpected hug. He made no move to accept it, still unable to make himself move, just stood immobile, and let her hug his stiff form.

They stayed that way for some time, Dev's mind reeling from the terrible news. He hadn't known Ash well, but he'd been a good man, too young to die and undeserving of the way he had gone. It hadn't been a quick death or a painless one. It had been brutal, cruel and it horrified Dev, making him hot with hatred and cold to the very bone at the thought of his suffering.

He finally forced himself to move as though in a trance, except he was completely aware of his surroundings. Unable to speak, he could think of no way to explain exactly why he was behaving the way he was, choosing instead to pick up a piece of card and write the new Intel down.

DC ASHLEY CARTER: VICTIM.
DECAPITATION
GENITAL MUTILATION
DISLOCATED THUMBS
BODY DISCOVERED ON GRAVE OF FLOWERS
BODY POSED WITH ARMS CROSSED
HEAD PLACED UPRIGHT ON DISPLAY
WARRANT CARD NAILED IN BETWEEN HIS EYES
POSSIBLE SIGNS OF MEDIEVIL TORTURE

Without making eye contact with his siblings, he stuck the card onto the wall in place with the other victims. Then stepped away, seating himself across from it on the settee and staring at the card, feeling numb.

"Oh no," Raven whispered as her hands flew to her mouth in shock, smothering the sound of dismay beneath them.

His two brothers said nothing, neither knowing what they could say. So, they stayed frozen in silent prayer for the detective Dev's team had lost. It was then that a memory hit him. Visions of Vincent Walker entering a room, a knife to his throat, squeezing his eyes closed and screaming, so much screaming. Then the world went dark.

When Dev came back to the room, he found Dr Jean Winters seated across from him. A chair had been pulled up for the settee and she was talking to Stephen, who was looking at him, with worry in his eyes.

"Do psychologists usually make house calls?" Dev wondered aloud.

At the sound of his voice, the two focused on him, and the doctor said pleasantly, "Good to see you again, Devlin. Your brother called me, he said you'd had a shock and you have been catatonic ever since."

"I have?" Dev asked.

"You've been just sitting there for an hour, brother," Stephen told him.

"I remembered something. It was Vincent Walker. He was hurting my mother, I think. I had a knife to my throat…" Dev trailed off, putting his hand to his throat as though feeling a phantom hand grasping him there. A shadow of the memory he'd recalled, lingering in his mind, foggy, like he dreamt it.

"It is likely the shock of losing a colleague has caused you to have an episode," Jean surmised, before glancing at Stephen, "Could you give us the room?" he nodded and left. "Now, where would you like us to begin?" she asked.

****

The incident room was quiet—with the DCI still on scene— the Superintendent, Jan Wright, was now standing at the front. There were many officers in the room waiting for her to speak, and while she looked more than a little tired, she rallied and straightened, preparing to speak. There was no need for her to quieten the room. They were all silent and waiting, no one having the desire to chit chat.

"It is a sad day today when a detective as young and promising as DC Ashley Carter dies in the line of duty. It is beyond comprehension. I know that many of you will be mourning his loss as you rightly should. His loss is a devastating blow to us all. However, we owe him justice. We owe him our dedication to seeing it delivered, just as he would offer it if another had fallen. Do not disappoint him or me." She delivered the words and watched as the officers felt them down to their souls, "now find whoever is responsible. We still have officers missing and I would like to see them return alive, so find them and those responsible so I can bring the weight of justice down upon them," she continued, "Lord, have mercy upon their souls, because when we catch them, I will not."

With that, she left the room, leaving the officers behind her to let the words sink in and resonate with them all.

Chapter Twelve

Dev and his three siblings had finally found the evidence they needed to prove Reece Carter had been receiving payments from an offshore account for a while now. It was paid in religiously at the same time, on the same date for as far back as the last year. What they hadn't been able to do was prove who had been paying him. With him now missing, Dev was no longer sure if it mattered. But Stephen insisted on continuing to dig. Should he be caught, they could prosecute him and see he was punished appropriately.

Many hours had passed of them relentlessly working before there was a knock on his door. When he found Wren there, looking lost and in clear distress, he ushered her inside. His siblings, catching his look as they entered, mumbled about going to get food and left. Now alone, Dev reached for her and pulled her into his body, wrapping her up in his arms and told her gently. "It's OK. You don't have to hold it in now. Let it go."

At his words, she released a heart wrenching sob, as he pressed her into his chest and told her how sorry he was. They stayed this way for some time, and when she finally pulled back, he wiped the tracks of her sadness from her face. In a quiet voice very unlike her own she asked if she could use his bathroom, he nodded and released her. Knowing she needed the time to re-centre herself and clean away the evidence of her grief before his siblings returned.

When she finally re-entered the room, they remained silent. He handed her a cup, he added a little sugar, and she pulled a face when she tasted it, but sipped it anyway, accepting her need for the drink. When she'd managed half a cup, she cast it aside and focused her attention on the wall. Catching sight of the new edition, she averted her gaze, instead focusing her attention on Reece Carter's updated information. Upon scanning the new intel, her eyes flashed with rage, her violet eyes not unlike lightning as they sparked with fury.

"That rat bastard!" she hissed through gritted teeth. "Did he do this? Did he cause Ash's death?"

"I think he had a hand in it, Aye," Dev admitted.

"That rat bastard!" Wren repeated.

There was a knock at the door and Dev left to answer it, finding himself a little relieved Wren's grief had been replaced with anger at Reece. He wasn't sure if he could bear to watch her sadness much more at the moment, his own, though not as sharp, was still weighing on him. When he opened the door, he got more than he bargained for.

"I found some strays," Chris told Dev, "they seemed to be deciding whether or not they should knock," he explained, indicating Wren's car. Matt and Alec looked at their feet.

"Where are Stephen and Raven?" Dev asked.

"Parking. It was a little crowded on the street," Chris shrugged, "I jumped out at Stephen's insistence. He didn't want your friends left outside to debate whether or not they were welcome."

Dev nodded and walked back in so they might follow. Chris waited at the door for the others. Wren glanced at them as they entered and when she looked at Matt, her anger made her visibly shake.

"He did this, Matt," she spat, pointing to the wall. "Reece fucking Carter helped murder his own brother!"

Matt moved silently to the wall to read where she pointed. When he'd studied it, the usually good-humoured detective's face became thunderous.

Alec's face remained passive, but Dev knew him. He was far from the calm he presented. If it hadn't been personal before, it was a declaration of war now, that every one of them were mentally signing themselves up for.

"Do we know where he is?" Matt asked, quietly seething.

"No," Dev answered simply, "but Raven is working on it."

Alec's phone rang. He looked at it, his face filled with suspicion. Dev snatched the phone from his hand and pressed to accept the call, incensed.

"Kelly? I believe it's time we had a family chat..." he raged.

"Kier?" she breathed, surprise evident in her voice.

"My name is Dev now," he told her coldly.

"Yes, I know," she replied.

"How are you involved in this?" he demanded. "If you were trying to help us, you failed. Ash is dead, Kelly, do you hear? A good man is dead. If you want to help, help us better," he shouted.

"All isn't as it seems. Keir darling. Have faith. The leak has been plugged." With that, the line went dead, and Dev growled with frustration. He stared at the phone before pulling his arm back forgetting himself, about to launch it in temper.

"Dev, I need that!" Alec warned, reminding him that the phone wasn't his to obliterate.

"What did she say?" Stephen asked, taking Dev by surprise. He hadn't noticed he'd entered the room. Calming, he related the conversation.

"The leak has been plugged. Well, that isn't ominous at all," Chris commented.

"Have faith?" Wren scoffed. "She isn't exactly leaving much room for that, is she taking the piss?"

"I don't want to get anyone's hopes up, but has anyone considered that if the leak has been plugged, that our victim might be Reece? How similar were they? To look at, I mean," Chris asked.

The group stalled at his words, looking amongst themselves. Wren pulled her phone from the pocket and dialled, praying, as she put it on loudspeaker so everyone could hear.

"Doctor Jodie Malone speaking. What can I do for you, Detective? If you were after my preliminary report, I'm afraid I can't quite deliver it. There are a few complications to iron out…" she hedged.

"By any chance is one of those complications anything to do with corroborating the identity?" Wren asked and held her breath, awaiting an answer.

"It is, detective," Jodie began, "I don't suppose you have something to add that might speed up that process."

"He broke his arm," Matt interjected quickly, hope began lighting his eyes, "It was a childhood injury. He had a scar. I asked him about it once."

The phone went quiet, the silence almost unbearable as the group awaited her findings.

"It would seem the warrant card does not match the victim," Jodie concluded, "before you begin to celebrate that happy news, is there somebody we have as an alternative option to speed things along?"

"We suspect it's Reece Carter," Alec supplied when the emotion was too much for Wren to offer a reply, "his brother."

"Very helpful. Thank you," Jodie returned, gratefully, "Anything else I can do for you, or can I continue?"

"No. You're a star. Thank you," Matt answered, his relief clear. The line was disconnected, and the room seemed to release a collective breath. Wren, in an uncontainable surge of joy, launched herself at Chris. With surprising finesse, she sprang upon him, wrapping herself around him and planting a kiss of sheer delight on his shocked face.

"Angel, I think you're scaring my brother," Dev chuckled, unable to contain his relief.

"I don't care!" she declared, giving him a second kiss on the cheek dramatically, the smacking sound intentionally loud for emphasis, playing up to her audience. As the room broke out in much needed laughter, Stephen cleared his throat loudly to get their attention.

"I don't mean to put a dampener on the jubilation. However, I feel the need to point out that if Reece Carter is the victim, then where is Ash?" he asked, reluctant to remind them of this issue but knowing that he must.

Chris helped Wren back to her feet, and she spun around to Stephen, her head tilted to one side, considering his question thoughtfully. "I don't know," she decided, choosing her next words carefully, "however, I will take missing over dead."

****

Keri put down the phone and frowned. "Help Better? Bloody cheek! If he had any idea of the shit I've put up with, the ungrateful sod," she grumbled. Walking out into the main room within their new location, she asked Cameron, "is he awake yet?"

"He's coming around, but I wouldn't say he's completely with it," he replied.

"Let's go now. If he's still a little drowsy, he might not kick up quite so much fuss over the unfortunate death of his brother," she decided.

"I'm sure when you explain the circumstances, he will take it a little better," Cam said.

"I wouldn't be too sure, my heart, Keir just bit my head off for saving his friend's life," she huffed.

"He doesn't actually know that Keri-Blossom, he thinks he's dead, remember?" Cam reminded her.

"Oh, of course he does. He said as much…still..." she whinged.

They headed to the reinforced door to the left and Cam unlocked it. On a mattress in the corner, Ash lay restrained, his eyes half open, he looked at them with confusion, as though not quite sure what he was seeing.

"Doc?" he said, sounding a little drunk.

"Yes, darling?" she answered.

"Where am I?" he asked. This time, his speech seemed a little more coherent.

"I'm going to explain. I will take questions at the end if you have any, but if you interrupt it will take a little longer. So, listen," she instructed. Then did her best to give him the tale, getting a little tired of retelling it for a second time. He didn't appear to take the news as well as her little Jenny friend had though. He was quiet and tense, seeming to fold in on himself.

"That was quite a lot to digest, I understand, so we'll leave you for now, to you know, let that sink in," she finished, not quite sure he was all that happy with the news. People were so ungrateful today. With that done, they left him to think over what they'd told him.

****

Ash was still a little unsteady, though he couldn't be sure if it were from his sedation or the news he'd been given. There had been a lot to take in. His brother was a leak. Who'd been feeding Mary information on their case. Likely using his own brother as a source to do it. If that wasn't enough of a blow, his brother hated him enough to arrange for him to be murdered. His brother had tried to have him killed. He let that thought wash over him and found he felt hurt. Hurt and betrayed. He may not have been fond of his brother, but he didn't wish him dead. Yet he was now. His brother was dead. By his own hand, sort of. He'd arranged his own death.

Ash laughed bitterly at that, though he was far from happy about it. Keri or Kelly, he supposed, had chosen not to go into details about how his brother had died. Whether, because she didn't know or out of respect for his feelings, he was unsure. He didn't trust her, though. While she was not completely evil, she was still aiding and abetting a serial killer. If she had chosen to go to the police, people might not be dead now. Or his brother may have got her killed. It was easy to judge when it wasn't you trying to dodge death, he supposed. She had saved his life and Jen's. Jen! Was she here too?

"Jen?" he called out.

"Ash?" A voice came, muffled through the wall. Relief filled him at her reply.

"Are you OK?" He asked.

"Am I OK? Oh Ash," Jen's voice said faintly. "I'm so sorry about your brother."

"Sorry that he's dead, or that he was a dirty, greedy asshole?" Ash bit out.

"A little of this, a little of that," she replied.

He smiled at that in spite of himself. "Yeah," he said. "Me too." After a pause, he asked. "So, what happens now?"

"We hope we survive, that Mary is caught, and the others are as lucky as we are," she answered, after a slight pause.

"Are we? Lucky, that is?" he wondered, truly not knowing.

"I think so. We're still here. If she wanted us dead, I think we wouldn't be," Jen said.

"What if that changes?" Ash countered.

"Then we lasted longer than we would have faced with the alternative option, and we will at least have each other at the end," she tried to reassure him.

"That might be the only thing about this that I find comforting," Ash admitted.

"I'm sending you a *"Jedi mind"* hug," she told him.

He pulled a confused face. "Dare I ask what a *"Jedi mind"* hug is?"

"Not a *"Star Wars"* fan, then?" she asked, tutting, "I thought I liked you. Now I just don't know."

"I've seen it," Ash corrected. "I'm just not sure what a *"Jedi mind"* hug is supposed to mean."

"I'm sending you a hug with my mind," Jen teased. "Can you feel it? Can you feel me all up in your head?"

Ash laughed. He hadn't expected to laugh again quite so soon, after all he had learned. Yet here he was laughing at Jen's ridiculous antics. He sobered before speaking.

"I missed you, Jen. Thanks for making me feel better."

"You are most welcome, Ash," she replied, and they fell silent once more. Ash might be trapped, yet somehow, he felt freer than he had in years.

****

Michael, Terry, and Paul were all in the warehouse moving stock for Mary McNamara. They were new and as such, were left to take care of the menial tasks.

"So, I know that Mary is the big boss now, but who do all the shipments go out to?" Terry asked.

"Fucked if I know," Michael muttered.

"She thinks she's the big boss," Paul laughed, "that's not the truth though. There's a bigger boss up in London. She may swan around here like she's the Queen of bloody England, but she's just a grunt to them, like we are to her," he sneered.

"I'd watch your mouth, Paul," Michael warned. "If you are going to last in this business, you may want to learn to keep your mouth shut and your eyes open."

"Yes, Michael," Mary said coldly from behind. "Very wise advice."

"I... I didn't—" Paul began. He didn't get to finish. Before he could say anymore, The Executioner had him by the throat, the blade pressed to it.

"Paul. Paul. Paul. I'm disappointed. Loose tongues are dangerous ones," she crooned in a singsong voice, a little crazed.

"What is your decree?" The Executioner asked.

"Take it from him," she declared.

"W... What?" Paul squeaked.

"Take. His. Tongue," she repeated. Pronouncing each word with sharp, cold clarity. As Paul was dragged away from the warehouse, his shrieks echoing behind him. Mary, leant closer to Michael. "I like you, Michael. Come and see me later. I believe I have a job better suited to a man of your wits," she ordered. Then left the area. The echoes of Paul's screams, silenced and they warily watched her leave.

"Not sure if that is a good or bad thing, mate." Terry said quietly. "The closer you get to that one, the more likely you are to end up dead, I reckon."

"Fortune favours the bold," Michael replied, "Or kills off the stupid. I guess we'll find out which one I turn out to be." Terry chuckled and they continued on with the task at hand.

Chapter Thirteen

August 17th, 2014

Superintendent Jan Wright called the three of them to her office the next morning. Wren entered, followed closely by Alec and Matt. The Superintendent indicated for the door to be closed.

"Right, which one of you is going to tell me what is going on?" she asked. The look she gave made it clear that she had a good idea of what it may be. They all waited in silence, not entirely sure what they should do.

"Very well, DI Jones, since you are the superior rank, why don't you start us off? Then, should they feel it necessary, they can add in their thoughts or additional information as they see fit." She turned her gaze upon Wren expectantly.

"Um," Wren hesitated.

"I tell you what, how about I give you a head start? Today I had a call from Doctor Jodie Malone to discuss her preliminary report. I was shocked to learn that Reece Carter is actually a victim, not Ashley Carter as originally suspected. If I couldn't be more surprised by this unexpected development, she informed me that she had only been able to ascertain that so quickly thanks to the help of the MCU team, who alerted her to the likelihood that the victim may have been incorrectly identified. This was a surprise to me, since it was the first, I'd heard that there was any doubt. So, then I asked myself a question. How did my officers come to this conclusion? I'm not sure, so why don't you enlighten me, DI Jones?" she said in a clipped voice.

Wren looked at her feet and began to explain. The jig was up. Along the way, Alec chimed in. Matt, who was relatively late to the party as far as the story went, said extraordinarily little, only adding in how he'd come by the information. When they had finished, the Super sat thoughtfully, considering all of what they had told her.

"So, is that everything?" She finally asked, giving each of them a look in turn to check for deceit, as they assured her it was.

"None of you are to mention DI Doyle's name in connection to anything you have learned from this unsanctioned investigation. It is not wholly unexpected that his defence attorney would want to build a solid case should he be charged, so I'll consider this information his attorney's attainment of evidence on behalf of his client to the best of my knowledge. I suggest you spend your time today finding the same information via a legally obtained route to support the information you will be adding to the big board in the incident room. I understand why you felt the need to contain it, but since the suspected leak is now dead, I expect to be kept updated to the full extent possible. Am I clear?" Her tone left no room for argument.

"Yes, ma'am," they chorused in unison.

"Get back to work, I want to find some evidence that ties Mary McNamara and this "Executioner" to these killings and I want them in my custody. Also, I would quite like my officers back alive, so find them," she finished, before dismissing them.

When she was sure they had gone, she picked up the phone and called Superintendent Andrew Panderman at the London Met Office.

"Hello?" the Superintendent's voice came across the phone.

"It's Jan Wright from Welwyn. I have news," she told him.

"Can't talk here," he said, his voice one of warning. "It's been a while since we had lunch. Perhaps we could arrange it, we can have a catch up," he suggested, his message clear.

"That would be delightful, Andrew, when are you free?" she replied.

"How about tomorrow? 1PM, OK for you?" he offered.

"Perfect, Andrew. Where would you like to have lunch?" She asked.

"How about we meet outside the station and take it from there?" Andrew replied.

"Very well. I'll see you then." Jan agreed.

"Always a pleasure to catch up, Jan," Andrew told her.

"Indeed. Enjoy the rest of your day and take care of yourself," she said simply, before replacing the handset.

"Curiouser and curiouser," she mused. It was quite the rabbit hole indeed.

****

Mary had been having a pretty pleasant morning until the call came in. She'd been surprised to see Alistair King's name flashing up on her screen.

"Hello, darling. I wasn't expecting a call?" she began, "the shipment should have arrived as I promised. Was there a problem?"

"No problem with the shipment Mary," Alistair told her, "you do have a problem though. My sources tell me that Reece Carter is dead. And we appear to have people poking into places where they should not be poking."

"Reece Carter isn't dead. I spoke to him not too long ago. It was his brother, Ash Carter who met an unfortunate end," she assured him.

"I'm sorry to be the bearer of unwelcome news, Mary but that is not the case. Ash Carter is missing but not dead as far as I'm aware," he replied, "It would seem someone nailed the warrant card belonging to Ash Carter to his brother's forehead. An unfortunate error, wouldn't you say?" Alistair contradicted.

"That can't be," she said in surprise. Cain had never failed her before. Her mind raced as she tried to assess where they had gone wrong.

"And that isn't all. Somebody in London is looking into the incident. The one you arranged to ensure Devlin Doyle's transfer. It would seem someone is convinced that it was a setup. Though we have yet to find the exact cause of this problem. Since they're not wrong, I would suggest clearing up that particular mess, finding them and seeing to it that they are dealt with. We wouldn't want your troubles spilling over into our business relationship, and we would hate to have to sever ties after all these years," he said pleasantly, the threat clearly implied by his tone.

"No, that would certainly be an inconvenience," Mary replied, "I shall take care of it immediately."

"See that you do, Mary or we'll take care of it for you. We can't be certain who may have to be punished for this breach of trust, if you fail," he warned.

"I understand," Mary said.

"Good. It was nice talking to you, Mary. I look forward to speaking to you soon," Alistair said before the line went dead.

"Well, this just won't do," Mary hissed through her teeth, "This will not do at all." She spent the next half an hour going over everything in her head. Replaying all that had happened and taking great pains to assess each action as they had occurred before she finally landed on the source of her problem.

"Michael dear, can you come here for a second? I have a job for you. Could you be so kind as to ask Connor and Cameron O'Reilly to join me tomorrow evening, if possible, I have some matters to discuss with them. If my daughter is available to join us, that would be splendid," she told him.

"Yes, Ma'am," said Michael, "I'll get on that right away."

"Good man," she said, smiling. Once he'd left the room, she dialled Cain.

"What can I do for you, My Lady," Cain said as he answered.

"I need you to use your talents and find out who in the London Met Office is digging into the incident that resulted in DI Devlin Doyle's transfer. There is a bit of a time crunch, darling. So if you could deal with it swiftly and see that they are dealt with, that would be much appreciated," she commanded and waited for his reply.

"How much time do I have?" he asked.

"Preferably within the next twenty-four hours, we have another little hiccup to address tomorrow evening," she informed him.

"I will see what I can do, Your Highness," he responded. "That is all I ask from you," Mary assured him, "and darling?"

"Yes, My Lady?" he replied.

"Make it hurt for me," she ordered sweetly.

"The pleasure will be all mine, I assure you," he said chuckling.

****

Andrew Panderman left his office and pulled out the burner phone he'd been using. He dialled the only number on it and waited, hopeful.

"Hello," the voice answered.

"Can you talk?" Andrew asked.

"Yes," the voice replied. He wasn't much of a talker, Andrew knew. "Do you have anything we can use?" Andrew asked.

"Not yet," the Voice answered.

"Damn it, have you found anything, any evidence connecting the two?" Andrew queried hopefully.

"Sorry, not yet, it will take time," the voice replied.

Andrew swore. "I have lunch to attend with Superintendent Jan Wright tomorrow. She wants to speak to me to catch up. She may have something to offer that might help, I think I may have found something that might lead me to the leak on this end but I'm not quite there yet. Keep working your end and hopefully we can take down the entire operation, not just a branch of the tree," he directed.

"I hear you. Just remember I have motives of my own. If I have to blow my cover, I won't hesitate," he reminded Andrew.

"I understand. Happy hunting." With that, the line went dead.

As he turned off the burner phone, he put it into his glove compartment. He put on his seat belt and drove through the London traffic at the pace of a snail, sighing with frustration. Nearly forty minutes later, he entered his home and took a harsh intake of breath at the sight that met him. His wife stood before him, her eyes wide, tears leaking from them. A gag across her mouth, sounds coming from her but with the cloth covering it, the words she tried to form were incomprehensible.

From behind him, a voice whispered. "Hi, honey, you're home."

****

August 18th, 2014

Chris sat in a bar and was waiting for his friend to turn up. He hadn't been here before, but he thrived in unfamiliar places. Phantom entered, and looked around, surveying the area. An old habit he'd picked up in the Army, Chris imagined. Phantom was tall, not on par with Chris himself, he had yet to meet someone who was, however he was far deadlier.

He was at one time a Royal Marine; he had also been the medic in his team. He was nicknamed Phantom for his ability to get in and out of places without being seen unless he chose to be, and if he chose to be seen then woe betide them. He had a quick mind and even faster reflexes, not someone with whom you would wish to pick a fight. He also had the tall dark and deadly look that women seemed to go gooey eyed over.

If Phantom wasn't so fucked up, he might actually notice the many looks he had drawn from the women in the bar, however, Chris knew that Phantom wasn't keen on being in crowds. He'd suffered from PTSD after an operation went South and his team had been sold down the river by their Superior. He, alone, had been the sole survivor. Crowds made him twitchy. He had long since dealt with his issues after being discharged, but he still had a tough time being "caged" in with strangers. He also had some issues with following orders, since the last orders he'd followed had ended so disastrously.

"Chris," he said.

"Phantom, did you find anything?" Chris asked.

"Word on the street is these are the names of the people collaborating with her," he replied.

"Thanks, man," Chris said, "consider our debt clear."

"No, my friend, that doesn't really come close to covering what I owe you. If it hadn't been for you, I don't know if I would be here," Phantom replied quietly. Chris had told him many times that he owed him nothing, each time Phantom replied the same.

"That's not true," Chris began.

"It is true," Phantom cut in.

"How have you been?" Chris asked, changing the subject.

"I won't say that I'm over it, that would be a lie. But I'm starting to accept that, for whatever reason, I'm supposed to have lived. If you can call what my life is, living," Phantom shrugged.

"You never know what's around the corner without the lows in life, we wouldn't truly appreciate the highs," Chris philosophised.

"When do the highs kick in because I'm still looking for them?" Phantom asked quizzically.

"It can't be all that bad," Chris said.

"It isn't bad, it's just nothing. Neither high nor low," Phantom replied.

"Dying won't improve it, though, nothing could improve if you're dead," Chris reasoned.

"Not hoping for death, I'm hoping for a reason to live," Phantom told him flatly.

"And I'm sure you'll find it," Chris assured him. Phantom said nothing, so Chris continued, "Thanks again for this."

"No problem, and Chris," Phantom began, "Keep a low profile, your old club has heard whispers you are back up this way. They've put the word out that they wouldn't mind mending fences and put the past to rest," he informed him.

Chris frowned at that. "There's nothing they could do to mend fences with me. They nearly caused her to die. My connection with them cost me everything."

Phantom nodded. They said their goodbyes, and Chris was left with the names Dev had asked for and an ache in his chest.

****

Keri was troubled. Her mother had summoned them to a meeting this evening. Cameron had told her it would be business, they had a new shipment arriving soon and with Jack gone, a meeting had been on the cards. But Keri had a bad feeling about it. There should be no cause to be concerned, Reese was dead, her mother would likely assume the rat had taken off after his brother's death. She couldn't see a reason for the feeling but had still told Cameron to rearrange, however he insisted that avoiding it entirely would probably make her more suspicious than not going with no real cause, other than her own gut feeling.

To try and make her feel better, he reminded her she would not be able to attend. Her mother knew she still had shifts at the hospital and Keri had a shift that night. It was her last one at that. But that didn't make her feel better either. Cameron and Connor would be at her mother's mercy without her to smooth the way. She was becoming increasingly unstable, and she knew that meant her volatile nature could cause her to decide at any time to find some disrespect to her reign if she chose, no matter if none had been intended or indeed existed. Cameron had laughed off her worry.

"I'm a big boy Keri-Blossom. I can hold my own," he'd scoffed.

He wasn't by any means a lightweight, he wouldn't go down easily, and he dismissed her concerns as paranoia. With all her cloak and dagger dealings, it was common to see threats everywhere when there were none to be found.

Still, no matter his argument, no matter how much sense he spoke to assure her, she couldn't rid herself of the feeling that something was off. So, she allowed Cameron to assume she was swayed while she made plans in her head.

The problem with trying to plan without any idea of the details was that she had no details to make a plan. This meant she had a variety of half-baked plans for different outcomes, none of which were as thorough as she might like, since she had nothing solid to work with. That was the problem with being a schemer. Overthinking everything. It could drive a person insane if they let it. Perhaps that was how Mary had become so deranged.

"Not how I want to end up," Keri said under her breath.

When all this was over, assuming she survived it, she might try and quit that particular habit. Maybe become a beach bum and plan for nothing at all, just going wherever the mood took her and doing whatever she wanted, without considering all of the possible drawbacks or consequences. However, that time was not now, she had plans to make. Lots and lots of plans with lots and lots of problems to try and iron out.

****

Dev had not been visited by his remaining colleagues at home yesterday. Alec had given him a brief summary of what had occurred at the station and told him that making an appearance there might not be possible with him already in the Super's bad books. Dev had found himself strangely disappointed he wouldn't be snuggling up on his sofa with his Angel that night. He wasn't sure at what point she'd become "his" in his mind, but she had.

He also wouldn't have minded having the sharp wits of the MCU unit helping him dig through the intricate web of deceit decorating his walls. With the mole's identity uncovered, that particular thread had been illuminated from their inspection. Finding anything with any tangible evidence to tie The Executioner to Mary McNamara had proved difficult, actually downright impossible, they had covered their tracks too well.

"She might be crazy but she is far from stupid," he mused to himself in frustration.

With that, they had instead directed their attention to their minions, seeing if they might find a loose thread there that they might give a tug, in an attempt to unravel the mess, and find something they could use to pin Mary down. They had various names now lining the wall that had previously been used to find the leak. Cameron and Conor O'Reilly topped this list. Other names included Paul Mahoney, Terry Chamberlain, Michael Ealand, obviously The Executioner, Shane Nicholson, Callum Mills, Frank Hutchins, and Jamie MacDonald, at least those were the ones they'd managed to identify.

This list had been compiled based on the information Chris had managed to collect from various contacts and been confirmed by Stephen, who added a few of his own. Though to Dev's frustration couldn't or wouldn't tell him how he was able to confirm the names or who his source was.

"Another of your informant's suggestions?" he asked with narrowed eyes.

"Does that matter?" Stephen had fired back.

They finally caught a break when Raven had been going through this list of cohorts that they had made the connection. Cameron O'Reilly lived with his girlfriend. Chris had made some calls to find out more and when he returned, Dev could tell by his face he had something good. What were the chances Cameron O'Reilly's girlfriend would share the same surname as Mary and Jack McNamara and not be related to the pair?

Raven tried to dig deeper but found no record of Mary McNamara ever giving birth. Jack's relations in Ireland were of no help either. It wasn't until Chris supplied a photograph, he'd managed to talk a friend into supplying, that they'd finally solved the mystery that was Dev's sister, Kelly Whelan. Kelly Whelan was now Keri McNamara and Dev had seen Keri McNamara before, very recently, in fact. "She's the Doctor," he exclaimed.

"Yes, I told you that," Raven said, looking at him like he was an idiot.

"Not A doctor, THE doctor. I saw her the day I came here, and you arrived," he started to explain, rifling through drawers and various pockets, looking for it.

"What are you looking for?" Stephen asked, nonplussed.

"I'm looking for her number," he snapped impatiently.

"When did you get her number? Man, that's kind of creepy. And you know she knew you were her brother. I mean, that's wrong, man," Chris shuddered.

"Not like that," Dev snarled. "She said she treated me when I was taken in, that her brother had…" he trailed off.

"Her brother had..." Raven prompted.

"She was talking about me. She knew who I was. When she mentioned her brother, she meant me," Dev realised.

"Where did you meet her?" Stephen asked, suddenly excited.

"The hospital, we need to get to the hospital!" Dev shouted, grabbing his coat, and heading for the door.

Chapter Fourteen

Superintendent Jan Wright had made her journey to London, and she'd headed to the London Met Office, and waited. She'd waited for a good fifteen minutes, before trying to call Andrew's phone, but there had been no answer. She'd rung the station, giving no name to be told he hadn't come in today. She was beginning to worry.

On the phone, he sounded like he hadn't trusted that he wasn't being watched there. Did they know about her too? Was he in trouble? Jan was getting a little bit sick of officers going missing. She had just decided she was going to head into the station and find the underlying cause of it all when her phone rang. Maybe this was Andrew now.

"Hello," she said.

"You need to leave right now," a voice told her.

"Who is this?" She asked, looking around her surroundings.

"I heard some talk on my end that The Executioner killed Andrew last night. He told me he was due to meet you today. I don't know how they got to him or what they know but you need to get out of there right now," the voice said before the line went dead.

"Shit!" she muttered, not sure she trusted the voice on the phone, but not prepared to take the risk. She remained as calm as she could before casually making her way away from the station, being as careful as she could be not to draw any attention to herself.

As she made her way for the busy London crowd, she wondered about her friend. Was it true? Was he dead? If it was true, and they had learned of her involvement, then she had just become a target. If she had somehow managed to slip their notice, then the voice on the phone had saved her from making a monumental error. As long as she was alive, she knew that there was someone in the Met working on the wrong side of the law.

Perhaps with the help of the mysterious voice on the phone, they may be able to piece it together at a later time. Whoever it was that had her number had likely taken a risk that may have exposed themselves to warn her. She believed they would be calling again, or at least she hoped so or her friend's death would have been in vain.

****

Dev and his siblings raced from the car park to get to the hospital entrance at the Queen Victoria Memorial and stopped at the reception desk. Since they couldn't be sure that she was here, they hadn't yet let the MCU team know, not wanting to warn her or scare her off by having the police turn up en masse. After Dev spoke to the lady at reception his heart sank. They had figured it out too late. According to the lady, it was meant to be her last shift today but there had been a family emergency, she had left a day before she was due to go. Keri McNamara was in the wind.

The only chance left to track her was to try and locate a home address, and they had to either get Raven to do it at home or call the team to do it officially. He wasn't sure how he felt about her being brought in by the police though. Not only would it put her life at risk if Mary found out, but she'd been helping them, even if it weren't to the extent he would have liked. He had no idea what kind of danger she may have been in, or what she had been risking helping him where she could. His own arrest still a sore spot, he wasn't keen to do the same to his long-lost sister.

"I already left her to the wolves once," Dev whispered and his family considered his words.

After discussing it, they had decided for her safety to have Raven look it up, while Dev tried to find the number she had given him. Maybe they could warn her that they knew and offer to help her if she came in of her own volition. So that was what they did. They went back to Dev's and Raven focused her skill solely on locating his real sister, collecting as much information as they could put together in such a short space of time. He had found the number she had given him, but he'd figured it might be better if they tried to see her in person first, in case she chose to go to ground. When they arrived at the house, they approached it with caution.

"Maybe we should have called it in," Chris said, having doubts at the wisdom of going without more backup.

"I don't think she would have been helping me if she intended to harm me," Dev argued.

"Yeah, maybe she wouldn't. But can you say the same of Cameron O'Reilly? What about Mary or this Executioner guy?" He countered.

"I don't know," Dev answered, suddenly unsure.

"If you're after the lady doctor and her fellow, Sonny, she has gone to take care of a sick relative.

Told me, she won't be back for at least a month," a voice called over the fence.

Turning towards it, they caught sight of an older lady looking at them.

"She definitely said that she won't be here for the next month?" Dev asked.

"That's what I said, Sonny, repeating it won't change it," she scolded.

"Oh, well, thank you," he said then as an afterthought added. "I don't suppose you have a key by chance, do you?"

"I don't," the lady replied, fixing them with a strange look, "but if I did, I wouldn't be letting random strangers in willy nilly."

"I understand, I'm with the police. I had a few questions regarding a patient who died recently. I don't suppose she left a way to contact her or a forwarding address? Any way we could get hold of her?" he pressed.

"I'm sorry, Sonny, she didn't, but she's coming back, so maybe it can keep," she replied.

"We'll see if we can find another way to chase her up. Thank you for your time," he said politely.

"You're welcome. I hope you find her," she returned.

"Me too," he agreed.

"Right, that's that then," Chris stated. "What now?"

"Now I try to call her and see if I can get any joy that way. If not, we inform the team and see if they have better luck," Dev told him.

"Let's just hope we haven't tipped off Mary by coming here. We do not need to make this any worse than it's already shaping up to be without our help," Chris said.

"Aye, that wouldn't be much help," Dev agreed. With that, they headed back so Dev could try and call his sister. Maybe they'd finally catch a break before this mess got any worse.

****

Keri had decided to leave the hospital the day before she had originally intended to. Her mother had accepted that she was working and allowed her a pass, promising to "catch her up after," whatever that meant. Instead of working, she was spying on the new location where Cameron and his father had arranged to meet with Mary. She couldn't see inside the building, but at least she would be able to see when Cam and his father left. That would finally put the bad feeling and her mind to rest. As she sat in her hiding spot, she waited for Cam and his father to arrive.

When they finally turned up, she held her breath and hoped she was wrong. Not fifteen minutes later, she saw him arrive and knew her worst fears had been realised. He stepped from his vehicle, and she watched as he entered. She had considered this outcome, and she knew Mary wouldn't want to dispose of them where there may be witnesses. She trusted the men to a degree, but never to that degree. She would also want them to suffer and that would need somewhere quiet and more remote than this current location.

For this reason, she crept towards the large vehicle The Executioner had exited from and reached underneath it. Without messing around she fixed a small tracking device in place and then retraced her steps to the spot down among the cars in the car park where she'd left her own. While she waited for the tracker to move, the burner phone in her pocket rang. Her eyes not leaving the marker, she reached for it and answered. She had only one person left unoccupied that might call it.

"Hello," she answered.

"Keri, or is it Kelly? Which would you prefer?" Dev said coolly down the line.

"Ah, you finally figured me out," she replied, still watching the marker.

"I did," he said, unnecessarily.

"Unfortunately, you weren't the only one," she said wryly.

"What does that mean?" he asked, sounding concerned.

"It means Mary found me out first," she told him.

"Where are you?" he asked, urgency in his voice.

"I am about to be in a whole heap of trouble. Don't suppose you want to help a girl out?" she asked hopefully.

"Help you with what? Where are you?" he repeated.

"I won't know until I get there," she said enigmatically.

"This is no time for games, Kelly," he said angrily.

"No games, Kier. When I get there, I will call. I'll leave it on silent. Trace me. Can I rely on you to do that? Can you send help?" she asked, silently praying for him to agree, so she would not have to deal with this alone.

"You want me to call the police?" he asked.

"I think there was another leak in the London office," she told him. "If you involve them, I'll be dead before I reach custody?"

"So, no police?" he asked.

"Preferably, no, but I'll take it if that's all that's on offer," she replied. "I have to go. Keir, darling, I will call soon."

She hung up the phone and watched as the marker moved. Taking a breath and praying she didn't die, she pulled out onto the road to follow it.

****

Dev got off the phone and immediately asked Raven if you could set up a trace on the number if it rang back. Sensing the urgency in his voice, she nodded and sprang in action to do as he had told her.

"What's going on?" Stephen asked.

"She's in trouble. Mary knows. I asked her where she was, and she said I don't know yet. It did not sound good. She asked for help, said there was another leak in London or something. I don't know if I can get the police to her in time and I don't know that if I do that, they won't find out and take her out," he fired back rapidly.

Chris pulled his phone out and called a number without taking time to explain why.

"Hey, I need some help. You remember you said you owed me a debt. I'd like to call it in. If I give you a location when I have it, how soon can you get there?" he said to the unknown person on the other end of the line.

"I don't know yet. Will that be a problem?" Chris asked them.

"Man, as soon as I know, you'll know," he finished.

"Who did you call?" Stephen asked.

"If I told you that, I'd have to kill you," Chris answered flippantly.

"Will they make it in time?" Dev asked.

"Let's hope so," Chris replied.

"I need to call Wren, tell her to keep what I'm telling her on the down low," Dev decided.

"Won't she have to tell her superior?" Raven asked as she typed.

"Possibly, but I think we can trust her. I hope we can," Dev said, his tone unconvincing even to his own ears.

"Call her," Stephen told him.

So, he did.

****

Wren had not been expecting Dev's call. As he'd rapidly explained what had happened, she raced from the canteen to the Super's office. Barging in the door, Jen Wright jumped as though she'd been electrocuted.

"DI Jones, what the devil is wrong with you? You scared the bejesus out of me," she exclaimed.

"Ma'am, we have a situation Dev called in. However, he is worried there might be another leak in London. He's concerned if they get wind of what he knows, someone or a few someones might be at risk," Wren rambled.

"Slow down, DI Jones and breathe. I need to know everything. I will not have any more damn leaks fucking this investigation up any further. Go now to the incident room and get who you think can be trusted and make it snappy. Then you can brief us all at the same time," Jan ordered.

Wren raced from the office to the incident room and nearly stumbled through the entrance in her haste. Alec and Matt looked at her in surprise.

"With me, NOW!" she ordered, and she was off again, back to the Super's office, hoping that they weren't far behind her.

When the door was finally closed and she had regained her breath, she began swiftly recounting Dev's call. Before she had finished her final sentence, the Super was moving.

"Get to your vehicles. We need to get to DI Doyle's home now," Jan Wright, commanded. And with that, they were on the move.

****

Keri had followed the marker and it had finally reached a destination. She had pulled up not far away, but she knew he would need time to unload Cameron and Connor from the vehicle and she did not want to be spotted. She rang Dev's number on her registered phone this time, the time for hiding was over.

"Hello," he answered, "Keri?"

"Kier, are you tracing the call?" she asked.

"Yes, stay on the line. Help is coming," he told her.

"I am leaving it in my car. I am going to give you the location where you will find me now. Do you have something to write this down on?" she queried.

"Stay where you are. Where are you going?" Dev asked.

"I can't do that, Keir. Are you ready to write it down?" she repeated.

"Tell me," he replied, so she did.

"Why do we need this address?" Dev asked warily.

"Because that's where The Executioner is, darling, at least he is for now," she told him, "I hope to see you soon, Keir," she finished, then left the call running and got out of the vehicle.

"Keri?" Dev called, but she was no longer responding.

"Keri?" He tried again.

The door knocked and Stephen went to answer while Dev continued to get no reply. When Stephen returned with Wren, who was quickly followed by Matt, Alec and… was that the Superintendent? Oh shit, it was.

"DI Doyle, it would seem that keeping you out of this investigation is proving to be problematic, seeing as it is determinedly dragging you back into it. I have decided it is better to join you here and get the information first hand, instead of being the last to know for a change," Jan told him.

"What's going on? Is she on the phone?" Wren asked.

"She was. She's not responding. She gave a second address, said The Executioner is there," Dev informed them.

"I'll send backup, now pass me the address," Jan commanded.

"We've sent help of our own too, just in case there was a delay," Chris added.

"What kind of help?" Jan asked, suddenly concerned.

"Nothing that will cause trouble. He is ex-military. He's on his way with some veteran friends, they are trained, and he used to be a medic," Chris assured her.

"I'll make sure the teams going in are aware that they might have company," she responded dryly.

"What should we do?" Alex asked.

"Pray," Raven answered quietly.

"Fuck that!" Dev said, "I'm going out there, they need as many hands as they can get." And he ran for the door. Wren watched him and looked to the super.

"I'll stay here and oversee this end," Jan told them. "Go and follow him. Keep him out of trouble if you can."

****

Cameron's head was swimming and more than a little foggy. His vision was out of focus. He had just gathered his wits together, when he saw his father being dragged over to what looked like an axe head on a wooden construct. He tried to speak but found he couldn't. There was also a citrusy smell in the air. Was it lemon? Why could he smell lemon? His father's limp body was placed on the wooden block at the bottom. It looked a little like a guillotine, except wrong somehow. Cameron struggled against his bonds and caught the executioner's attention.

"Ah, you're awake. I was beginning to wonder if Mary had overdosed you both by mistake," he said conversationally.

He pushed the lever and Cameron watched in horror as it fell towards his father, as The Executioner hummed a peculiar tune. As it reached the bottom, the axe blade sliced his father's head clean off before hitting the wood below with a thump. His father's head fell into a woven basket below and Cameron tried to shout in alarm, but he still couldn't seem to make his vocal cords work.

  He'd been wrong to discount Keri's feeling that something was wrong. He had been too arrogant and too sure of himself to believe he was really in danger. Keri. She would feel guilty about his death, even though she had tried to warn him. His death. He was going to die now.

  "Fucking Bastard!" Cameron choked out, swallowing down his emotions, he wasn't going to give this man the satisfaction of seeing him cry over his father's murder.

  The Executioner didn't reply, clearing away his father's carcass and sharpening the axe-like blade, preparing for a second show. He had displayed his father's head among something within the basket. What was that? Were they oranges? That was when he recognised the tune. Oranges and Lemons. That explained the lemon he could smell. Was his own decapitated head to be rested amongst the lemons? And why did he get lemons? He wished he had been oranges.

  The Executioner approached to take him to his death. He fought it, he wasn't going to go easily. In the end, The Executioner took his blade out and stuck it in his chest. Pain overwhelmed him and he forgot to fight, instead consumed by the pain. He felt his weight being lifted and placed at the foot of the strange contraption as the pain in his chest throbbed.

"Cameron, let me introduce you to my version of a Halifax Gibbet," he taunted, "You are about to become very intimate with each other."

It was then that he saw her, his Keri-blossom. She emerged from the shadows like a hellcat, green eyes flashing, blonde hair wild as she launched herself at him. Watching as she clung to him. He smiled an affectionate smile as his vision began to fade, happy to see his fierce Keri-blossom one final time.

Chapter Fifteen

Keri launched herself onto The Executioner, a thin wire she had picked up without really thinking about it in her hand. She wrapped it around his throat, pulling it for all she was worth. The wire dug into the flesh of his neck and pulled across the palms of her hands, tearing at her flesh there. If she'd had time, she might have chosen a better weapon, but she nearly hadn't made it in time as it was. When she had seen Cameron laying at the foot of a makeshift axe structure she had leapt into action.

"Just die already, you fucking prick!" she spat breathlessly, fighting to keep her hold.

The Executioner pulled on the wire with two hands and threw his weight forward, and she flew over him in surprise. She quickly pushed herself up and moved just as he made a grab for her, barely skipping out of the way. He made another lunge and she tried to move from his reach but this time she fell short and he caught hold of her wrist, clamping it tightly in his hand. She sank her teeth into his flesh and pulled back hard, smiling when he yelped in surprise, as she ripped the flesh away from it and spat it out in an unladylike manner. Before stomping her foot down hard on his and spinning away, facing him. Bellowing with rage, he grabbed her by the throat.

"Fucking treacherous bitch!" he seethed.

Unable to wrest his hands away from it, she dropped herself down, allowing her body to become a dead weight. He lost his footing as her weight's sudden drop pulled him off balance and he fell forward, taking one hand away to catch himself on a nearby wall. She spied his "tool bag" a short distance away, and used the time she had gained when he stumbled. She grabbed his thumb and wrenched it backwards off her neck, grinning maniacally as she heard the snap as it broke. He growled in anger, and she crawled quickly for the bag, reaching inside, her hand closed around a small handle. Trying to pry it loose, she snagged a finger on the edge before clutching it in her grip, just as he dragged her backwards by her ankles. Looking down at the tool she'd managed to commandeer, she chuckled at the irony.

When he'd finally managed to drag her back far enough, he reached down for her, but she twisted to her back, losing the shoe he had held to pull her. Jack-knifing forwards, Keri latched her arms around his ankle and reaching high with the scalpel, she used it to cut deep, aiming at his femoral artery. Her strike landed, and blood poured from the open wound as his weight gave out. With one last crazed lunge, he wrapped both hands around her throat and squeezed.

Feeling her airway constricted, she wondered which one of them would die first. It was quite literally a race to the death. That was when the door burst wide. A tall, well-built man entered and wasted no time getting to her. He pulled The Executioner off of her as she suddenly found air, it overwhelmed her lungs. Taking a long, deep inhale, she watched as men entered behind him.

The two men took The Executioner, examined him, and tried to stem the blood flow from where the scalpel had left its mark. They wouldn't save him though, they would be too late, she thought as she gasped heavily, trying to get the air into her lungs.

"Ma'am, are you OK? Are you hurt?" the tall well-built man asked.

She felt laughter bubble up in her chest and explode from her mouth unable to be contained. She laughed loudly, almost hysterically, crazed cackles that could not be controlled.

"Ma'am, I need you to keep it together, you are covered in blood. I need to know if any of it is yours?" he said, trying again to calm her. However, she couldn't stop the flow of her insane hilarity. Until she caught sight of Cameron. Her laughter died a stone-cold death as she let her eyes fly over him, his body still and unmoving.

"Ma'am, what are you doing?" The man questioned, clearly stunned by her erratic behaviour as she scrambled back from him.

She stumbled to her feet and made her way towards Cameron before dropping down to her knees when she finally managed to get there, spying the blood that had begun to soak through his shirt. She turned, shouting for the man who was watching her, his eyes wide, before he jumped into action, joining her on the floor, he spoke.

"He's alive. Move over. I'll take care of him. I used to be a field medic," he told her with an authoritative tone.

"Medic, you say. Remind me, does Doctor trump Medic?" she snapped back.

"You're a doctor," he repeated slowly.

"I am," she assured him. "Now help me try and control the bleeding. Do you have a medical bag there?"

"Yes, they're using it on that guy," he told her.

"Go and get it quickly," she ordered as she went to work. She heard a siren in the distance and prayed it wouldn't be too late.

****

When Dev and the others arrived at the location. It was teeming with people. He saw his sister running with a stretcher to an ambulance and swore at the sight of her. Her small frame was plastered in an horrific amount of blood. It coated her bare arms, her clothes and seemed to be clinging to her usually neat, blonde tresses. The sight Dev likened to the scene from a Stephen King film, though he couldn't recall which one. A team of paramedics assisted her as they wheeled an injured Cameron O'Reilly, into a waiting ambulance. As she drew nearer on her way, she caught sight of Dev and gave a small smile before calling out in a croaky voice, "Took your time, slowpoke!"

Dev's eyes widened further at her words, and he wondered if his entire family suffered from mental illness. Perhaps it was hereditary.

As the team looked around at the people surrounding them, Wren winced.

"What's up?" Dev asked.

"The SOCO team are going to have a shit fit when they see all these people trampling on the crime scene," she explained, her face filled with a pained expression.

"We should probably get to work cordoning this off, to try and save what evidence we can," Matt agreed ruefully.

"I'm going to head to the hospital since I can't be of any help here," Dev told them.

"Alec, you should go with him. We don't need Miss McNamara doing her Houdini act on us, especially when she's left us with this clusterfuck to deal with," Wren suggested.

"Yes, please. I would rather not be here when the SOCO team gets here and tears strips off of everyone," he joked.

"I'll come too. I would like to make sure the crazy lady is OK," a tall beast of a guy said from behind them.

They all turned to look at him in confusion. "Who are you and why are you at my crime scene?" Wren asked in a no-nonsense tone.

"I am Phantom. Chris called me," he said simply.

"Is Phantom your first name or your last name?" Matt deadpanned.

"Military nickname," he shrugged.

"You can't leave. We're going to need a statement," Wren told him.

"Didn't see anything," he said.

"Oh, fuck off," Wren said, rolling her eyes.

"It's true, most of that happened before I came," he replied.

"Most, but not all," she argued.

"It's OK Wren, Alec can get his account from the hospital," Dev suggested, watching as the ambulance set off, a little worried his sister might disappear before they could catch them up.

"Fine, I want that statement though," she insisted.

"OK lady, but if you want to get there and stop the crazy lady from leaving, I reckon we should get a shift on," Phantom indicated the ambulance pulling away.

"Let's get a move on then," Alec agreed, and they left Wren looking at the train wreck like crime scene behind her.

"I'll call the coroner's office," Matt volunteered.

"Guess that leaves me with the fun job of updating the Super," Wren stated, frowning. She was not going to enjoy that particular call in the slightest.

Dev, Alec, and their new companion arrived at the hospital just as the ambulance unloaded the other side, near the accident and emergency entrance. Staff flew out to meet their arrival. His sister emerged to deliver her hand over. She had done all she could to keep Cameron alive, but it was in the hands of the staff at the Victoria Memorial hospital now.

They wheeled him in, and a doctor arrived as they all entered, Dev and the others a short distance behind the entourage. The doctor directed the hospital staff, and they took Cameron away, leaving Keri to watch. A nurse spoke to her, kindly offering to assist her to an area where she could get cleaned up.

It was at that moment when the adrenaline from the high charged events became spent and Keri seemed to deflate. In what felt like slow motion, she fell to the floor. Phantom reached her first, barely making it in time to catch her before she connected with the cold, solid surface of the ground.

Scooping her up, he took her in his arms as the nurse addressed him, leading him to a separate area, where a second doctor made an appearance and beckoned him to follow.

They all did as he bade them, no questions asked. He directed Phantom to a gurney and told him to lay Keri there while he assessed her. Phantom gave him a brief overview of how he had found her, and Alec made a few notes in his notebook should he need to remember those details at a later date. Dev looked at his sister with concern, looking at the bruising developing around her throat.

That was when it hit him. A memory of Keri and himself in a house, their mother reading to them from a book of nursery rhymes, his sister cuddled close to her. Marco Sanchez snatching the book from her, grabbing her by the throat and then hoisting her to the window ledge. He remembered being restrained as Marco taunted their mother and Keri had attacked Marco from out of nowhere, her little form springing out and biting into his leg. His mother falling and screaming, then nothing.

"Dev, mate, you need to snap out of it. The doctor asked you a question," Alec said to him, his concern edging his voice as he spoke.

Dev looked at him then, the doctor was frowning, and the stranger seemed to be looking at him knowingly, as though he understood what he had witnessed.

"Is he in shock?" the Doctor asked Alec. "Was he with them?"

"That's his sister," Alec explained, playing off his episode as shock of the situation, not the flashback it had actually been.

"OK, take a seat in the waiting area. We have a place for her now. Will get her looked at. She has a few lacerations that need attention, and we can clean her up. I will check for any additional injuries," he informed them kindly. "Don't worry, we'll take good care of Keri."

As they watched her being taken away, they waited for additional news. Stephen, Raven, and Chris arrived to join them. Chris followed Phantom's cue and pulled aside to speak with him. Stephen and Raven approached Dev and Alec.

"The Super told us, we came as soon as we heard," Stephen said.

"Is she here?" Alec asked.

"She's gone to the scene. Wren is currently setting it up, and she'll take over when she gets there. We locked up your house and came straight here," Stephen explained. "She's sending the DCI, Richard Head, here to take control of things on this end."

Dev nodded at his brother's account and looked in the direction his sister had been wheeled in.

"How is she?" Raven asked, speaking for the first time, noting the direction of Dev's gaze.

"From what the doctor managed to tell from his initial assessment, mostly a few lacerations, some ligature marks around her neck, I think she's mostly in shock, though we don't know yet," Dev said flatly.

"How about you? Are you OK, brother?" Stephen asked, noting his pale face.

"He had a flashback." Alec interjected. "Not for long, but I had trouble bringing him back to the present."

"I remembered her," he told them.

"Who? Keri?" Stephen asked.

Dev nodded before clarifying. "I remembered her biting Marcus and I remembered my mother falling from a window."

"I see," Stephen said, unnecessarily acknowledging his statement but unsure what else to say.

They all fell quiet. Then Chris re-joined them, but Phantom was gone. Alec looked around in alarm and scanned the area, swearing as he realised he was absent.

"Fucking hell! Wren is going to kill me," he muttered grumpily.

"He told me to give you this," Chris told him, handing him some pages that appeared to have been torn from a notebook and then offered it to Alec, who looked a little relieved, though not entirely satisfied.

"Well, it's something, I guess," he sighed.

The doctor approached them to give them an update. "She's awake and stable. We have cleaned her up. She has some nasty ligature marks on her throat. Her hands are a bit of a mess, some deep lacerations from a wire and a couple of bumps and bruises, but nothing permanent, I think. There may be some scarring on her palms but otherwise she appears relatively healthy," he told them. "I want her to rest for now. She's had quite a shock, but she wouldn't until I promised to pass this along." He handed Dev a key wrapped in paper. "She said that she had pets that would need feeding," he finished.

Dev looked at an address written on the paper and the key that had been folded within it. Looking at Chris, he said. "Don't suppose you can go and check that out for us?"

Chris nodded and accepted the offer, before turning and heading for the exit. Dev sat on a hard waiting room chair, exhaustion taking over, while the others followed his lead and took up places alongside him. It was going to be a long night.

The DCI had arrived a short time later and joined their number. Cameron had been in surgery, which he'd barely pulled through, almost dying several times throughout. He was currently under guard in post op. Keri had been in and out of consciousness, the doctor insisting she needed to rest, but had allowed Dev a short visit as her relative. When he entered the room, he took in his sister's appearance. She seemed small and fragile; now clear of the blood he had last seen adorning her hair. He noted that the discoloured purple bruise mottling her skin there, her blonde hair feathering her pale face. The sleek style she usually sported had been transformed into natural, untamed curls.

"You used to have red hair," he stated, thinking aloud.

"You remembered me," she said, a small smile curling up her lips.

"I did," he acknowledged.

"How's Cameron?" she asked. "They wouldn't tell me much. They wanted me to concentrate on my own recovery."

"He had a few near misses, but he's holding on," Dev assured her.

"Good. I wasn't sure I'd done enough," she mumbled quietly.

"You did good," he praised.

"I did, didn't I?" she crowed smugly. "The Executioner?"

"DOA," he said simply.

"Good. I hated that sick fuck," she spat with satisfaction.

"Don't suppose you want to get into how you got mixed up in all this?" he asked hopefully.

"It's a rather long story. Will you have enough time before they chase you away?" she teased.

"I'm not sure, but shall we give it a try?" he persisted.

"Sure, why not? Where do you want me to start?" She conceded.

"We start with how you ended up as Keri McNamara," he said, his curiosity obvious.

"I didn't know that I hadn't always been her. I was quite young. I don't recall all that happened before," she told him.

"When did you remember?" Dev asked.

"I wouldn't say I remembered exactly. I overheard Jack discussing it. When he went over it, I had vague flashes of memory. It was your name that brought back the parts I do recall," she explained.

"So, you've been working with them all this time?" he stated. A faint hint of accusation and judgement in his voice.

"Not exactly," she told him. "I was given a choice, become a doctor and if they need a physician to attend to their staff, I would do it off the record."

"What was the other option?" Dev asked, despite being unsure he wanted the answer.

"I'm a female, Keir darling. What do you suppose I might offer otherwise?" she countered, and she didn't need to explain further. He nodded his understanding.

"So, you worked with them, but as a medical aid only," he repeated, to be clear.

"Essentially, yes," she agreed. "However, when I heard them discussing your return and the murders began, I made plans to try and oust them and have Cameron step up to take over. They wanted you dead and I thought you were committing the crimes at the time. It wasn't until I saw you the first time at the hospital, I realised you had no memory of us."

"When I came in under your care?" Dev asked.

"No, before then you came in with Marco's mother. Geena's son was missing," she corrected.

"That was when you first saw me?" he said in surprise.

"It was after that I found myself keeping you under surveillance. I knew they were trying to find you and was a little bit curious. I wanted to get to know my long-lost brother," she admitted. "I kept telling myself it was too risky, but I found myself inexplicably drawn to you. Add in the fact that you were a danger to yourself, all that wandering about without being fully aware. I couldn't just leave you that way. If they found you, it would leave you vulnerable."

"So even though you suspected I was a murderer, you helped me?" he asked dubiously.

"I realised pretty quickly it couldn't be you. I had been there watching you when some occurred, you couldn't have done it," she said simply.

"So, if you knew that, who did you think was doing it?" he queried.

"At first, I suspected Jack. He was shaken by your appearance. I thought perhaps he was killing off loose ends. It wasn't until Mary told me Jack had got Jilly pregnant and then they were murdered that I began to suspect Mary was the person arranging the deaths. Jack planned to dispose of her so his real heir could be legitimate," she recalled. "That and I caught her fucking The Executioner."

"Wow. Right. Who is he? The Executioner? What is his real name?" he inquired.

"I don't know. I never found out; he never used it. He is known only by his moniker. If Mary knows, then she has never shared that tidbit with me," she answered.

"So, once you knew all of this, why not go to the police?" he asked.

"I knew that they had people on their payroll there. I had no clue who or how many, who would I trust?" she argued.

"I see. So, what did you do?" he pressed.

"I went to her home, looking for evidence, trying to find definite proof of her guilt, I found a collection of body parts. At first, I thought that might be enough, but since it seemed likely The Executioner had been the actual murderer at my Mother's…Mary's behest. I knew I needed something better. However, I used them to alert the police. At the very least, it would cast doubt on your guilt and leave the investigation open to scrutiny," she explained.

"Hmm..." Dev said, saying no more, allowing the information to process in his head. After considering, he continued. "What happened to Jen Cartwright? Is she dead? How did she get mixed up in all this and end up missing? Also, where is Ash Carter?"

"Steady on Keir darling. There is quite a lot to cover in those answers. The simple answer is that they are at the address I gave you. Didn't you get my message?" She looked concerned.

"They are the *"pets"* that need feeding," he realised, and let out a breath of relief, "they're alive."

"They are and ensuring that was a monumental pain in the ass, let me tell you," she grumbled.

"I can imagine," he chuckled, the relief putting him more at ease despite there being a lot left to cover.

"Your time is up now, love. She needs to rest," a nurse called in sternly.

"OK," he said, reluctant to leave before he'd heard the entire story.

"You can visit again in a while," the nurse assured him.

"I'll be back," he promised Keri as he turned to leave.

"I didn't doubt it," Keri replied.

As he began to exit, Alec flew around the corner, heading straight for him.

"Cameron has taken a turn for the worse, he's coding," he clipped, and they hastened back towards post op.

"What the hell happened?" Dev snarled at the waiting nurse.

"We don't know yet. The doctors are dealing with it now," she answered. The standard script in their repertoire for situations such as these.

"Will he make it?" Stephen asked in his usual calm way.

"I will let you know when we have an update. Until then, I am sorry, but I can't tell you more," she responded kindly. "We are doing everything that we can."

Dev growled with impatience, making the poor nurse startle at the sound, as he began pacing.

"Don't worry about him, his bark is worse than his bite," Stephen assured her.

Dev slowed at his words and found himself hoping Cameron pulled through, but there was nothing left to do now but wait.

It was another forty-five minutes later before they came back and told them that Cameron O'Reilly had passed away. The reasons for that were unclear but there were several possibilities. Dev was not looking forward to his sister finding out the news, she had worked so hard to save him, had fought with a hitman to save his life, yet in the end all of her efforts had been in vain.

Chapter Sixteen

Wren had been attending the scene, waiting for the super's arrival when the pathologist had arrived. The divisional surgeon and the photographer had already been and gone, but Doctor Jodie Malone had been delayed.

"Sorry I'm late. Aside from sending out your preliminary report, I was also asked to attend another scene on the outskirts of the London area, just outside Thames Valley Jurisdiction. They had three people burnt at the stake out there, if you can believe it, blinded, and burnt," she said, shaking her head in disbelief.

"Three people blinded… like Three Blind Mice?" Wren asked. Her alarm at the concept had her staring at the pathologist impatiently, waiting for a response.

"It's possible. I hadn't considered they may be linked," she answered. "Though why would they change the location now?"

It was then that the Superintendent, Jan Wright, arrived at the scene.

"Sorry I was delayed, we've had a few developments and I got waylaid," she stated. "What have we got?"

"Oranges and Lemons and a hell of a mess is what we have," Wren answered.

"A beheading?" Jodie asked.

"With a weird looking guillotine," Wren informed her.

"What's weird about it?" Jodie inquired.

"It's a guillotine, except it looks like an axe blade. It doesn't have the slanted blade you see in the pictures. Come and see for yourself," Wren answered.

When the three of them entered the scene, Jodie whistled at the sight of the guillotine Wren had described.

"It's Halifax Gibbet," she said in a voice that sounded like fascination.

"A what?" Wren asked, disbelieving of the pathologist's almost admiring look.

"It's similar to a guillotine, but they used these in the 16th century for public beheadings, also known as the maiden, and looking at it, it may also be a match for Officer Carter's decapitation," she mused.

"I haven't seen Reece Carter's preliminary yet," Wren said.

"I only sent it over this morning. I gave you an overview at the time of the key points to hurry things along since he was a colleague of yours, however I obviously hadn't completed the autopsy then," she told them. "I was also pretty stumped by the thumb dislocations and the genital mutilations. It had a ring of mediaeval torture about it. If I didn't know any better, I would say thumbscrews and possibly the pear of anguish," she said.

"The pear of anguish?" Jan asked dubiously.

"Or something similar, yes. It has four claws and a screw and used to be used to insert into the mouth, anus and the vagina or attached to the male genitals, I think," Jodie replied.

"I think I would like to see this report. I want to know if I am to expect many more mediaeval torture device deaths in my district. In the meantime, shall we focus on the one we have here?" Jan prompted

"Oh, sorry, I forgot myself," Jodie said apologetically.

It was an hour later when Wren got a call from an unfamiliar number.

"Hello?" she answered.

"Hey, it's Chris. Dev gave me your number in case I couldn't get hold of him. He's at the hospital, so his phone is switched off. I ran into a problem and need you to verify my identity to a stowaway."

"Stowaway?" Wren frowned.

"I'll explain when you get here," he told her, then rattled off the address.

****

Jen and Ash had been shut in the metal box-like rooms for a while now. This was the first time since Jen had been incarcerated that she'd actually felt like a prisoner. Before they'd been relocated, she'd been locked in a basement, but Keri or Cameron had frequently made appearances bringing tea, coffee, snacks and meals, discussing various updates on the case and how they might prove Mary's guilt.

While she would have been more useful with access to the computer herself, they had allowed her to verbally guide them through it so they might dig around themselves. However, since they'd been moved and Ash's arrival, Cameron had been concerned that together the two of them might be a little less accommodating and make plans for an escape that may end in their death and would ruin Keri's relationship with her brother before it began, so they'd been more vigilant and careful to keep them safe and separated. It had been some time since they'd been by though, the longest they had been gone, and Jen was beginning to worry.

"It has been a while since they've been here. Do you think something happened?" she asked Ash through the wall.

"I hope not. I would rather not starve to death. It's a much slower death than decapitation," Ash complained.

"Do you think Mary got to them?" Jen said, voicing her worry. "Is she going to arrive here with the executioner and take us out after all?"

"Maybe we should look for weapons or something, just in case," Ash suggested, Jen's worry rubbing off on him.

They scouted around, looking for anything they might use should they need to defend themselves. Unfortunately, the pickings were slim.

"I'm not sure how much damage I can do with my paper cup and plate," Jen told Ash.

"The best I've got is some torn off sheet to use as a noose of some kind," Ash admitted.

"Well, that tops the paper shit I've been looking at. I mean, paper cuts hurt, but I doubt it will send them running for the hills," she chuckled wryly.

That was when they heard the door open. There were voices, but Jen couldn't hear Keri's slight Irish twang or Cameron's Irish brogue. These were deeper, and held an edge of harshness that set Jen's teeth on edge.

"Well, I don't see any pets," a voice said, seeming confused.

"Maybe they are behind those locked doors," the other voice suggested.

"She only gave me one key," the first replied.
"Maybe the keys that open them are here somewhere," the second mused.

Jen didn't dare speak, couldn't breathe. She also heard no sound coming from Ash's cell-like room either.

"I think I have them," the second voice said.

Fear shot through Jen, and she prayed they hadn't. She wasn't ready to die, and she wasn't sure she could fight two men alone, specifically because they were most likely armed, and she had a goddamn paper plate. The key clanged in the lock, and she moved to press herself into the farthest corner away from it. However, she realised it seemed further away than it had been before. It was Ash's room they were opening.

Suddenly fear for her own life fell away and was replaced by concern for Ash. She wasn't sure she could listen as they murdered him. They had grown close since they'd been here, despite the wall between them. It had been a comfort to know he was only a few feet away and she was not going to be alone. She heard the door open and waited, praying he had a better chance than she would have had.

"I can't see any—" the words were cut off as his sentence was cut short and a strangled sound came from the cell for a moment before there was a thud and a cry of pain.

"What the fuck?" the voice said. "Mate, there's a person in here and he tried to strangle me with… Is that a strip of the bed sheet?" it said, confused.

"You. Who are you?" the second voice said.

There was no reply. Jen hoped Ash had just chosen not to reply and wasn't injured or dead.

"Oi, I'm talking to you. Who the fuck are you?" the voice snarled again.

"Who wants to know?" Ash replied finally and Jen breathed again. He was still alive.

"I'm Chris. This is Phantom. Keri gave Dev the key and told us we would need to feed her pets. Yet here you are, and I see no poodles," he replied.

"How do I know that you are who you say you are?" Ash asked.

"You don't? Is it just you?" Chris queried.

Ash paused for a brief second, before he answered. "Yes."

"Then let's go. I'll get you out of here," Chris assured him.

"I'm not going anywhere until I know who you are from someone, I trust to vouch for you. Not to be rude, but my own brother tried to have me murdered. I've developed some trust issues," Ash insisted.

"Fine, wait here." Chris left and Jen listened but couldn't catch what he said as he spoke to an unknown person on the phone.

"OK bro, you have what you asked for. Verification is coming," Chris informed Ash, "Do you want a protein bar or something? You look hungry."

"If it's all the same to you I'll wait, I was drugged not too long ago. Just file that under those trust issues I mentioned before," Ash answered sarcastically.

"Suit yourself, man. If you get hungry, you could always give your arm a nibble I suppose," Chris chuckled.

"The rest of the place is clear," the other voice said, joining Chris.

"Thanks Phantom, you can head out now. Get out before Dev's friend gives you a piece of her mind," Chris teased.

"If you are sure there won't be any trouble," Phantom replied.

"I'm a big boy, she should be here soon," Chris had assured him.

It went quiet as the three of them waited. Jen wanted to ask Ash if he were OK, but he'd protected her by telling them he was alone and if this Chris guy really wasn't on their side, someone would have to let them know who had taken Ash, if they took him. So, she stayed silent wishing whoever it was would hurry the hell up and get here.

****

Wren pulled up to the address and looked around. She couldn't see any sign of Chris, so she rang his phone.

"Hello," he answered.

"I'm here. Where are you?" she asked.

"I'm inside, come on in," Chris told her.

She walked quickly to the doorway and entered, looking around. Chris was gigantic, so he shouldn't be that hard to find. Spotting his bulky frame in a doorway, she strolled up to him and he nodded to indicate the room behind him. He moved aside and said, "He one of yours?" She looked around him and her face lit up. A huge smile spread on her face.

"Ash!" she exclaimed.

"Wren?" he asked, as though he wasn't sure or didn't dare to hope.

"Yeah, who else do you know with hair like a lighthouse beacon?" she teased.

"WREN!" A screech of joy came from out of nowhere and startled them, Chris swore profusely. Ash jumped forward and leaned by the wall.

"Jen! Wren's here," he called through excitedly.

A sob came from the cell next to them and Wren's heart skipped with joy. Jen was alive too.

"Jen, we are going to get you out," she shouted to her friend.

"I missed you, Wrenny," she called back through the tears.

"Can you get the door?" Wren asked Chris.

"If there is a key on here for it then yes," Chris answered.

Wren watched like a hawk as Chris played with the lock, trying to find the key to fit it and eventually it fell away, and the door opened wide.

"Jesus, who's your father? The jolly Green Giant?" her friend exclaimed.

Chris laughed and moved out of her path. Jen moved with a speed Wren had only seen from her when her fingers were on a keyboard, barely giving her time to brace, before Jen's weight landed upon her and she was caught up in a hug so tight she could be wrapped inside the coils of a boa constrictor.

"I've never been so pleased to see anyone in all of my life," she said happily through tears of joy.

"Charming," Ash teased from behind them. Upon hearing his voice, her friend dropped her arms, her face suddenly full of concern.

"Ash, are you hurt? I heard the thump. Did you hit your head?" she began, fussing over him like a mother hen, feeling his head for lumps, reaching up on tiptoes to check it. Ash blushed furiously at the unexpected attention and mumbled that he was fine.

Jen completely ignored his assurance, deciding to make a thorough examination for herself. Wren smiled at the ridiculous sight of the tall, lean detective being pulled about by the half-pint dynamo that was Jen.

"Jen, I don't want to rush you, but perhaps we could get out of here and somewhere a little less creepy," Wren intervened.

"I couldn't agree with you more," Ash chipped in, taking Jen's arm, and pulling her along behind him, ignoring her protests as they went.

"I can't tell you how good it is to see you guys," Wren said, affectionately.

"Girl, you don't have to tell me. I have so much gossip to tell you. I've been stuck, locked up with Ash. He isn't exactly a Chatty Cathy you know," Jen moaned.

"You know, I thought that we were getting along pretty well, but the way you're talking, it sounds like you drew the short straw," Ash grumbled.

"Oh, quit your grumbling. You know I love you really," she returned, then she froze and seemed to become unnaturally flustered, giving him a weird punch on the arm, her mouth opened and, "old buddy, old friend, old pal o'mine," she finished, sounding a little like the tiger character from the children's books Wren's mother used to read to her when she was younger.

"Yeah, I'm rather fond of you too, "Jenny from the block"," Ash teased back smirking.

"What?" Jen asked, frowning.

"Like the song? Except we were stuck in a cell block. You know what...never mind," Ash rambled.

"You see what I've had to put up with?" Jen whispered to Wren who giggled at the two of them acting like some comedic duo.

"I heard that!" Ash said, petulantly.

"Maybe we should put them back," Chris joked.

"You're Dev's brother? I don't mean to point out the obvious, but you don't really look alike," Jen hedged.

"Foster brother," Chris corrected. Jen nodded and they left the building.

****

When Mary received the next call from London, she was beyond furious. She was enraged. She took it out on the room she was standing in, throwing things in her temper tantrum, barely registering them as various objects, until they smashed, and thudded as they scattered around her. This was treason. Her own daughter, her own flesh and blood, had tried to dethrone her. It was beyond treason. It was high treason.

Alistair had agreed to help her one last time as reward for taking care of their shared problem in London. However, he'd also told her he could have no more to do with the affair. She was to put an end to the entire operation once and for all. Shut the branch down and retire it. It had drawn too much attention, and she was to settle any outstanding issues, then retire herself and leave. If she chose to ignore their wishes, she would be put to death.

"As if I would allow that to happen. I belong here!" she muttered in outrage.

He had only allowed her an option to remove herself and live out the rest of her life in peace, out of respect for her and her husband's many years of service.

It would seem her daughter had got her wish. She was to be dismissed, leave the country, and live out her days in exile, while the usurper cut down all they had built over the years, and she was left to sweep it all away as though it had never been. She may have agreed to these terms, needing to use his inside help to achieve the next part of her plan. However, when she was done here, she would not be sneaking off like a thief in the night. She would be casting her eyes instead to the throne he himself sat on and take it from beneath him for daring to issue her this choice.

Before that could happen, though, there was the matter of her betrayer and her annoyingly resilient sibling to address. She wondered if perhaps her hate for their father had clouded her judgement and caused her to choose the wrong sibling as her successor. If she had kept the boy, likely Jack would have long since tired of Jilly and this whole sordid affair might have turned out a little differently. Yet the past couldn't be undone and if she were to evade the pursuit of the police, she needed to get her shit together.

"Michael darling," she called out. When he entered, avoiding the mess at his feet, she gave him an appreciative once over. When they had completed the next phase of her plan, she would likely be looking for a new consort and he was rather delicious. She let her gaze linger one last time before she re-focused her attention.

"Ma'am?" he asked, then cleared his throat.

"Get Terry and come with me. We're leaving. I have acquired a secondary location and there is much to do. Perhaps when all of this is done, I shall reward you properly," she smiled salaciously and Michael remained stoic, nodded slowly giving nothing away and left to do as she ordered. Yes, she thought it would be fun cracking that particular nut. She would have time later to play with her new toy, now though, she had an execution to arrange.

Chapter Seventeen

Dev smiled as he ended the call. Wren had excitedly recounted the recovery of their colleagues and Dev finally felt as though the tides were turning in their favour. His smile fell a little as he recalled his sister receiving the news of her fiancé's tragic loss. The Executioner had succeeded in the end. She'd been saddened by Cameron's death but had admitted that while she had been fond of her partner in crime she couldn't, hand on heart, say she'd loved him.

That admission only saddened her further, and he had left her at her own behest to deal with her loss. He'd tried to offer comfort, not wanting the strange girl he shared blood with to feel she had no one to turn to now. However, she was insistent. They'd both been alone for some time, so he understood her decision. Returning to the waiting area, he found Alec, Raven and Stephen waiting. He was also surprised to note the arrival of the mysterious Phantom, who had joined their ranks.

"Chris didn't come with you?" Dev asked him.

"He left after I did. The DI was meeting him. I believe he is still in her company," he replied.

"You're waiting for him here?" Dev pressed, surprised he had decided to return of his own volition. He hadn't seemed all that keen to be involved up to this point.

"Didn't have anywhere better to be," he said simply, shrugging. "I was a soldier for some time. My instincts have rarely failed me. It's telling me that this is where I should be right now."

Dev studied him for a moment and nodded. They could use all the help they could get. If Chris trusted him, he had a reason. His brother might be arrogant and have an attitude problem, but he was a surprisingly good judge of character. Where he had come from, he'd had to be.

"I don't mean to interrupt. I'm the new Superintendent based in London. I'm here because I believe you have a person of interest in a few crimes we're investigating in the area. I'd like to take her into custody and interview her. The charges are pretty serious," a man spoke from behind them.

"I'm sorry, who are you?" Alec inquired.

"Superintendent Brentwood. I'm replacing the late Superintendent Panderman after his unfortunate passing," he replied.

"Andy Pandy is dead?" Alec asked in shock.

"Andrew has indeed left us. His death is one of the crimes we would like to discuss with Keri McNamara. His death and that of his wife, also three as yet unidentified victims who were burned to the stake," he informed them.

"I see. Well, we would like to help with that. However, our own Super has given me strict orders to detain her and see to it that she helps with our own enquiries. We have quite a few crimes to address ourselves. She would allow you time with her regarding your own investigation when ours is concluded," Alec countered, giving the Superintendent a scrutinising look.

"I'm a superintendent!" he replied pompously, "need I remind you that I outrank you."

"No need for a reminder...Sir...however I will need to make a call to Superintendent Jan Wright before I can allow that. She is *our* Super, she's well known, she knows a lot of people, she's been around a *long* time. I wouldn't want to get in her bad books if you know what I'm saying," Alec stated, his implication clear.

"I understand. I can wait. Will she be returning with you to the station?" he asked, his anger making his face red.

"Yes, you can go there now and as soon as she's released, we will let you know," Alec answered firmly.

The Superintendent nodded stiffly and turned to leave, taking the officer he'd arrived with along with him. As soon as he'd gone Dev approached Alec and said, "I don't like him. The whole way he approached that, trying to go around The Don and steal our "witness" out from under her nose? That was more than a little sneaky."

Alec nodded in agreement, watching as they stepped into the elevator. Phantom surveyed the scene playing out silently but made no comment, just watched with his hawk-like gaze, eyes narrowing as he watched the man depart.

****

Jan Wright had received many calls today. She'd received a call from DCI Head to inform her of Cameron O'Reilly's passing in the hospital. She'd received another from DI Jones to inform her that her two detectives that had been in the wind had been found unharmed. Then she had received a third phone call from DS Morgan that had made her blood boil. Allowing herself to be relieved from the scene when CID came to take over, she abruptly ordered Matt Ainsworth to accompany her back to the station.

"What's going on, Ma'am?" Matt asked curiously.

"Matthew Dear, have you ever heard the phrase silence is golden?" she asked him, and he chuckled quietly.

They got into the vehicle and left the scene and not twenty minutes later, pulled up to the station where she exited without waiting on Matthew to join her. She strode with purposeful steps into the station. On arriving, she found what she was looking for in the incident room as she entered.

"Superintendent Brentwood I presume," she stated coldly.

"Wright, I presume?" he returned disrespectfully, leaving her earned position title off his acknowledgement, as though his new promotion gave him a right to do so.

"Superintendent Jan Wright," she corrected, enunciating each word in a clipped, icy tone.

"Yes, that's what I said," he fired back boldly.

"No actually it wasn't. That is, however, my full title. I would imagine with your new appointment it must have slipped your mind, along with your understanding of how district procedures work. Am I correct?" she bit out in an unmerciful tongue lashing.

"I came from London Met in regards to—" he started to explain, Jan took no time in cutting him off and reminding him of his place.

"That's right, London. Remind me *Brentwood,* does Welwyn fall under your authority?" she spat her ire, a remarkable sight to the staff surrounding them.

"Well, no but—" he began again.

"There is no *"but"* about it, *Brentwood*. Just a simple no will suffice. And you are correct, it's not. And yet it has come to my attention that you took it upon yourself to enter the hospital, throw your new rank around at *my* staff, and demand to take *my* witness into custody in *my* district without so much as a nod in my direction. Is that right? Tell me, *Brentwood*, is that how London is to be run now? Did they perhaps consider offering you a workshop on how it works as a Superintendent? Or did you presume in your arrogance to think you know everything you need to know already and decided that you in some way outrank me because you deem it so? Do I need to speak to your superiors regarding how you conduct yourself in areas that *aren't* your own?" she said, levelling him with a frosty glare.

"I do apologise, I was informed you were currently on scene," he tried in earnest to back track.

"Did it not occur to you to call ahead?" she queried, giving him no quarter.

"I... I didn't think," he stuttered.

"No *Brentwood*. You didn't think, so I suggest you leave this station and consider how you wish to approach this from here on out. Perhaps have a do over, and try following the proper channels," she concluded, eviscerating the stunned man, and making him shrink under the weight of her glacial gaze.

"I can't apologise enough," he answered, cowed by her intimidating stance. "I'll arrange to discuss this at a more suitable time, tomorrow perhaps?"

"Perhaps," she threw out dismissively. "Have a good day, Superintendent." She watched him make a hasty exit, her wintery blue eyes following his retreat, as he made good his escape from the station with hurried steps and her posture eased.

"Ma'am?" Matt asked, his voice full of admiration.

"Yes, Matthew?" she responded, humouring him.

"I think when I grow up, I want to be just like you," he teased.

"Oh, do be quiet Matthew, you old fool," she scolded, the hint of a smile playing at the edge of her lips the only indication she was amused at his words. "Now come along, there's work to be done."

****

When Wren had arrived back at the incident room with the two misplaced detectives in tow. Matt had ambushed them. There was now a myriad of conversations taking place, an incoherent jumble of words as each person excitedly tried to relay their tales, not listening to the other parties' own words.

"Hello?" Jan called the room to attention. "It is unlikely we will be able to appreciate all that needs to be discussed if we continue to drown each other out by talking over them. Now how about we do this in a more methodical way? One at a time should work."

Everyone immediately settled down as Jan conducted the cacophony, adding relevant details to the big board as they reprised their accounts in a more orderly fashion. Once they were done, Jan assessed all they had learned and came to a conclusion.

"It's time we spoke with Miss McNamara. Wren, could you go to the hospital and see to it that yourself and Alec escort her in as soon as she is discharged? We really could use her testimony. I believe it might help us muddle through this tangle and give us a solid case against Mary McNamara when we locate her and bring her in. Ash, you should go and get that bump on your head checked, then go home and rest. If you're both to join us back at work in the morning, I want to ensure you are in tip top shape. No arguments," she said firmly as Ash made a protest. Jen nodded, seeming to agree that Ash should be checked over.

"What about me, Ma'am?" Matt asked.

"You should also go and rest. It'll be a long day tomorrow," she answered.

"It's been a long couple of weeks, if you were to be accurate," Matt said quietly under his breath, but her hearing was as sharp as ever.

"That's quite enough out of you, Matthew," she admonished.

"I'm sorry ma'am, but—" he said.

"You know, I would quite like to ban the use of the word "but" from the English language. It is inevitably followed by an excuse of some kind," she mused conversationally. "Can't say as I have a lot of patience for excuses."

With that, they all dispersed to do as they'd been directed. Wren herself was more than a little excited to catch up with Dev. She'd had little time with him since she had seen him a few days ago in his home and she found that she missed his company. He hadn't told her with words that he had forgiven her for her actions, but he had been decidedly warm towards her despite it, so she hoped that all was forgiven.

Although she wasn't entirely sure he could hold her doing her job against her indefinitely. Her ex-husband would certainly have done so. She glowered at that thought and pushed him from her mind. The less time he spent in there, the better.

"Some things are best left in the past," she mumbled.

Since Wren and Ash were both heading in the direction of the hospital, the other two, seemingly reluctant to be left out of the group, accompanied them. Matt because he was still a little put out at being left out of the loop the last time, when they had been looking into the leak situation. Jen, Wren suspected, would not finally be at peace until she was sure that Ash was as uninjured as he claimed to be, though she hadn't admitted as much.

When the team finally descended on the hospital, it was a chaotic display. Jen had launched herself on Dev, happy to see him out of custody and in their midst. Ash had frowned at the sight, looking more than a little put out at her antics, though she didn't seem aware of this, too caught up in the moment to notice.

Dev introduced everyone, beginning with Alec since Jen had been missing upon his arrival to the team. Followed by his foster family and, when he finally went to introduce the mysterious Phantom, Jen stiffly replied that they had met. Clearly still more than a little pissed that he had hurt Ash, even though it had been to stop the breath being strangled out of himself.

"How's Keri doing?" Jen asked. "I heard about Cameron. I know he wasn't exactly a good man, but he did treat me well and he adored her."

"Hard to say really. She has taken it better than I assumed she would, but she's quiet and pretty shut down. She seemed a bit more of a live wire before he died. We aren't exactly well acquainted," Dev surmised.

"If it isn't too much trouble, I would quite like to see her," Jen said cagily.

"I'll come along," Phantom said, surprising everyone.

"I don't think you will, you big oaf," Jen snapped, poking him in his large chest, "don't think I've forgotten you attacking Ash and giving him that great lump on his head."

"I think you are confusing the order of those events. He was strangling me with a bed sheet," Phantom corrected.

"He isn't actually wrong," Ash agreed, trying to smooth things over.

"You can wind your neck in too," Jen shot him a look, silencing him. "Don't you have a lump to get checked?" she asked, shooting another pointed look at Phantom, who held his hands up in surrender, shooting Ash a commiseratory look.

"What was that look?" Jen asked, accusation clear in her tone.

"No look," Phantom bald faced lied, before smiling and giving a chuckle. He looked back at Ash and said,

"You're going to have your hands full with that one."

Ash reddened and Jen, thrown by his words, spluttered and went quiet with her mouth agape. Phantom began heading in the direction of Keri's room and Jen, finally over her momentary loss for words, followed behind taking snippy pot-shots at him as they went. As the two departed, Ash, still a little red in the face, mumbled something about seeing the doctor and left too.

Raven and Alec appeared to be having a conversation off to the side, though they weren't close enough for Wren to hear its contents. Stephen and Matt made a vague reference to drinks and Dev nodded his agreement and they wandered off in search of coffee. That left the two of them standing in silence.

"Hey," she said awkwardly, shifting uncomfortably from one foot to another.

"Hello Angel," Dev replied, his mischievous eyes twinkling in amusement.

"Are you doing OK?" She asked.

"Better now you're here," he told her softly.

"Oh," she said, falling quiet. He chuckled and moved closer with slow, predatory movements, stopping just a hair's breadth away. Reaching out with his fingers, he snagged a random snowy lock of hair that had come loose from its bonds and tucked it behind her ear. She shivered at the slight brush of his fingers on her earlobe and the moment was disrupted by Alec's teasing voice calling across to them.

"In a hospital, people, we're in a hospital."

"Aye, you eejit. It would be hard to forget," Dev shot back, his irritation at the interruption not exactly subtle.

It was then that the doctor approached Dev.

"Good evening. I'm just coming out to let you know we're happy to discharge your sister now. We are, of course, sorry for her loss. There is no reason why she should remain here any further," he informed them. With his update complete, Wren looked at Dev and told him. "We're going to have to take her in."

"I know. Let me speak with her first and I'll see if Stephen is happy to tag along," he agreed.

"OK," she said simply. Dev reluctantly released her and stepped away, heading in the direction Jen and Phantom had gone not moments before

Chapter Eighteen

August 19th, 2014

It had been the early hours of the morning when they'd all left the hospital. Keri had reluctantly agreed to being taken to the station, though Phantom protested that she was not exactly in a fit state. Dev had been surprised by his strange intervention, but he had been shut down by Keri, who had been aggravated by his overbearing nature and insisted that it was time to get it all over with. It would appear she had accepted the truth that going it alone, while brave, had perhaps not been the wisest decision.

Though Dev wouldn't be the one to say it. With all that she'd lost, she had still come to his aid regardless of the misguided way she had chosen to do it. With nothing further to do, he had headed home. He was still not allowed to be at the station, and he had no other place to go besides home. Raven and Chris had accompanied him. Stephen had set off leaving Wren and Alec to sit in with Keri, who was being taken into custody.

Ash, Jen, and Matt had also said their goodbyes, while Phantom did what phantoms do and had vanished into the night. No farewell or fanfare, just gone. They had arrived back and also said their good nights and headed home to catch some sleep. It had felt like such a long time since he'd had more than a few hours to do so. It was, however, no more than five hours later when a strange sound caught his attention and he stirred, drowsy. He crept stealthily to his bedroom door, closing it quietly behind him as he left so as not to disturb Raven and Chris. Heading to the front door he considered that it might be Stephen, finally returning from the station.

"Stephen?" he called with a whisper, not wanting to wake the neighbours. When no reply came he frowned and opened it. When he found the new Superintendent standing in front of him his frown deepened.

Before he had a chance to ask any questions, the Superintendent's hand shot out and stabbed him in the neck. Fluid flooded into his system as he decompressed the cylinder containing it and injected him with the contents. Dev pushed him back with all his might stumbling forward toward him. The man grabbed at him, attempting to pull him towards a vehicle.

Dev dropped down and the man straightened and looked at him in frustration, turning to look behind him. He shrank back in fear as a large, threatening form towered over him. Chris grasped him by the throat, lifting him clear off of his feet, his anger radiating in pulsing waves as his muscles rippled, straining against the dark T-shirt.

"Where the fuck do you think you are taking my brother?" he growled with menace.

Superintendent Brentwood spluttered, unable to reply with his airway constricted under Chris' large paw of a hand. A shot rang out. Dev barely registered the sound as the world swam before him. He saw a haze of red spurting from Chris. Brentwood was skewered along with him. He suspected that a bullet had pierced them both. They fell seemingly in slow motion and the last thing Dev saw was the vague outline of Terry Chamberlain looming above him as he finally fell victim to the drug he'd been given.

****

   Raven had woken to the sound of a loud bang and the screech of a car, pulling quickly away, as she tried to account for the sound. Had the car backfired? Wiping the sleep from her eyes, she listened but heard no further sound. Deciding to grab herself a drink, suddenly parched, she headed down the stairs, and caught sight of the front door ajar. Frowning, she pulled her long night-shirt lower and approached it warily.

"Dev?" she called, nearing the opening. "Chris?"

"Raven..." she heard faintly from the other side of the opening. Moving less cautiously now, she opened the door wide and gasped at the scene before her. The sight of the Superintendent from London Met stared up at her. His eyes were wide and looking to the side, his mouth twisted in pain, his body unmoving. She became frozen, unable to take her eyes from the creepy picture it made.

   She stared at him in silent horror as his gaze stared back at her, unblinking and more than a little unnerving. She waited him out, unsure if he still lived. His chest seemed like it might still be moving, but as he remained unblinking for a time, far past what a living person might, she decided he must be dead.

   "Raven," Chris called again. He hadn't called her in a while, though she may not have registered it if he had. The shock of seeing the creepy, glassy eyes of the staring Super had temporarily held her transfixed.

   "Chris?" she finally replied.

"Call for help," he instructed, his words broken with gasps of air.

"Call who?" she answered, her current state of shock making her slow to follow his instructions.

"Alec. Wren. The police, Anyone. Raven, call any of them dammit," he sputtered breathlessly.

Raven ran to get her phone and the screen was hazy, she wasn't sure why. It was then she realised that tears were trailing from her eyes, blurring her vision. Wiping them away, she dialled the first number on her contact list. Alec Morgan. He'd know what to do.

****

Alec was dead on his feet. The Superintendent and Wren had begun to interview Keri as soon as they had arrived. Stephen had also been there representing Keri as her defence attorney at Dev's insistence. He'd been taking a short nap, unintentionally. His shift had lasted long past the time when he would have finished and he had found himself drifting off, his tiredness consuming him.

The ringing of his mobile phone had pulled him from his slumber, and he checked the time. It would appear he'd lost an hour and a half. He reached for his phone, answering the call, what he heard had him up, awake and moving faster than green grass through a goose's ass. He made a mad dash for the interview room and knocked on the door frantically. Wren appeared and asked him what the rush was, they were nearly done for the night.

"Raven called. Chris has been shot, there's a dead superintendent on Dev's doorstep and Dev is missing," he recounted. Wren called for the Superintendent, and she stepped into the hallway as they relayed the message one more time. With that they left some fellow officers to escort Keri back to a holding cell while they raced to Dev's home to attend the scene, Stephen not far behind them.

****

Raven had rushed Chris' aide, trying to stem the bleeding as soon as she had hung up the phone. He'd been considerably luckier than the Superintendent, who had bled out a lot quicker when he'd been shot through his throat, hitting an artery. The ambulance had pulled up seconds before the police vehicle that had peeled into the street behind them. Wren and the Super had begun coordinating the scene while the paramedics took care of Chris.

Alec had got Raven some trousers to put on so would be able to go with Chris to the hospital, promising to follow in a vehicle behind with Stephen. As she jumped in with him, the paramedics worked hard on the journey to get him stable. They finally arrived and they were met by the entrance to unload the gurney and wheel Chris in. He had been unconscious for a while and Raven worried that she'd acted too slow in her shock.

They took him straight through to surgery and she was shown to the waiting room alone. She huddled into a ball. It was something she'd done since she was young to block out the world. She'd been sitting there for what felt like an age when she felt somebody pick her up and put her down on their lap and wrap her up tight.

"Don't cry, Raven," Alec whispered, "I'm sure he'll be fine. He's in the best place now. Stephen is just finding out what's going on and he'll be right behind me."

Raven hadn't even realised she'd been crying, but with his words a sob escaped her.

"What if it's my fault he dies? I hesitated. I froze. If I could have gotten him help sooner. What if he dies because I wasn't quick enough," she said between tears.

"Chris is a fighter. He won't give up without a battle to the end," Alec tried to comfort her.

"ItsyBit?" Stephen said gently. "It's not your fault. None of this is your fault. It's mine. I called you here. I got you mixed up in all of this. You wouldn't be here if it weren't for me."

"Can we stop playing the blame game? Chris chose to be here, the same as all of you. The only person to blame here is the bastard that shot him," Alec cut in.

Raven tried to curl up on Alec's lap, huddling in tight, blocking it all out but Alec pulled her closer. "Don't block us out. We're all in this together. You aren't alone anymore," he said, as though reading her mind.

Sitting in the waiting room, they all awaited the verdict. Stephen offered to get coffee and Raven lifted her head, glancing at Alec, as if needing someone to tell her it would all be OK.

"He'll make it won't he? Tell me he's going to pull through this," she pleaded.

Alec looked at her, his expression pained, and he shook his head. "I can't do that, Raven. I can't make you that promise. What I can promise is I'll be here with you every step of the way."

She nodded, even though his answer wasn't what she wanted to hear, but she respected his honesty. She had been unfair to ask it of him. He could no more promise Chris'd live, than she could promise that Dev wouldn't be joining him. It was then that she realised that Dev was still in trouble, taken by the murderer. She might lose him too, and the tears began to fall once more.

****

Wren was more than a little afraid for Dev. He'd been taken by Mary. She wasn't known for being merciful. If they didn't find him soon, then the last time she'd see him would be at a grotesque crime scene. She wasn't sure if she could take that.

"You have to keep it together," Jan said suddenly. "If you fall apart, we might not get to him in time. Now is not the time to think the worst. Now is the time to be your absolute best."

Wren took in these words and knew that the Super was right. If she behaved like all was lost, then it could very well end that way. For now, he was alive. She just hoped he would stay that way. Matt and Ash arrived at the scene, joining them.

"What do we know?" Matt asked.

"Not much from what we've managed to establish. Superintendent Brentwood was playing for the other side. He drugged Dev on the doorstep, tried to take him. Chris intervened. Terry Chamberlain shot at him. The bullet got both men. Brentwood died on scene, the bullet caught him in the throat, hitting his carotid artery. He bled out quickly. Chris sustained a similar injury; however, it nicked the artery instead of hitting it directly. We think Terry had been aiming for a headshot but missed, killing Brentwood, and leaving Chris Doyle in critical condition," Wren surmised.

"And Dev?" Ash asked.

"Terry Chamberlain took him. Raven heard the shot and a vehicle leaving in a rush. She thought the car had backfired but found the door open. She called it in and tried to help Chris. They're on the way to the hospital with Alec and Stephen," Wren told them.

"Will he make it?" Matt inquired quietly.

"We don't know. He lost consciousness as they were attending to him and put him in the ambulance," Wren replied.

"So, what do we do now? Do we have any way of trying to find Dev?" Matt wondered aloud.

"Not that we've found yet, we just have to hope that we find something before Mary has a chance to do something that can't be undone."

****

Dev began to rouse from his drugged stupor, He tried to look around, but didn't quite have all his faculties. He'd managed to open his eyes but had yet to have control of anything more.

"Hello there, Sleeping Beauty," he heard Mary say. He would recognise her cold, calculating voice anywhere. It was ingrained in his memory since their last encounter. He said nothing, hoping if he seemed like he was still only semi-conscious, it might stall the proceedings.

"Now, now, no use trying to pretend I already saw your eyes open, silly boy. You don't have to worry just yet. You will be with the living a little while longer. We still have another guest to join us for the party," she told him.

"Party?" Dev asked.

"Yes, I decided it was only fitting that since the pair of you began this journey together, that I let you have a farewell party together too," Mary explained, though Dev still wasn't sure what she meant.

"You know it wasn't meant to be this way. I talked Jack into sparing you all those years ago. He did change his mind, however, but me and Cain arranged it so you could be free from it all," Mary continued.

"Cain?" Dev inquired, his still addled brain, not understanding where this Cain fit into the story.

"Oh, that's right. You knew him by his moniker. Cain was The Executioner; he was the one who took care of your imbecile of a father. I rescued you, allowed you to live and even planned to have you join the family business when you finally got out of jail. Unfortunately, your sister ruined that for you. You might have lived, if not for her, you know," she informed him. "Your sister ruined it all. If she had just been patient and waited for you to serve your sentence, you could have had that reunion she couldn't seem to wait for."

"You set me up," Dev accused.

"I did. I felt bad about that, but you see, you were the perfect full guy. I went to a lot of trouble to get you here just for that purpose. You see, Jack had got his mistress pregnant, and I knew I would be surplus to requirements. I needed them to die so I might live, you see. You were up in London, though, so I needed to arrange for your little mishap. Only once I could give my little friend an excuse to make you more available, could I finally get you where I needed you," she rationalised, "I got to take care of my minor problem and avenge our family all in one neat, tidy package. I took out all of the trash. You should be thanking me, really."

"Thanking you?" Dev scoffed, "You plan to kill me? Why would I thank you?"

"Well, that's gratitude for you. If not for me, you wouldn't have lived to see your ninth birthday," she huffed.

"If you allowed me to live this long, why kill me now?" he asked, wondering if he might be able to dissuade her from this path.

"Unfortunately, you are to be your sister's punishment. She betrayed me. ME, in favour of trying to free you, that can't go unpunished. I'm afraid high treason must be dealt with unmercifully," she declared.

"High treason," Dev repeated, looking at her crazed expression with a sinking feeling, "So Keri will be the other guest at these…festivities?"

"She is," Mary confirmed, barely able to contain her glee.

"How? She's in custody," Dev pressed, curiosity getting the better of him.

"Don't worry, darling, it's all in hand. I have someone arranging for her attendance as we speak," Mary assured him.

"Anyone I know?" Dev asked.

"Look at you! A detective to the very end. Unfortunately, you won't be alive to solve that mystery," she taunted, "Now I'm sorry to love you and leave you, but I really do have arrangements to make. Party planning is such tedious work. Rest well, Keir," she said, before leaving him alone with only his thoughts to keep him company.

****

Keri was being led back to the holding cell when a new face stopped the officers. She wasn't sure what was being said between them, however she was now being led towards the door.

"Where am I going?" She asked.

"You're being taken by officers at the London Met Office in connection with some cases they have reason to believe you have information on. Since we have your statement here, they requested that you be transferred to them," the stranger replied.

Keri said nothing. She was trying to place where she'd seen this man but couldn't seem to. He either wasn't important enough to register or hadn't been relevant enough to put a name to the face. She was more concerned that it was the London Met Office that requested her presence.

"I'd like to speak with the Superintendent," she stated.

"No can do, I'm afraid. She is currently on a scene at the moment," he replied, dismissing her as they left the building.

Keri decided she wasn't particularly fond of that answer. She was restrained, so she couldn't really bite him. However, perhaps she might be able to outrun him. Dropping her weight forward, she managed to get out of his grasp. Abruptly she thrust back with speed and using the back of her head, landed a well-placed blow onto his nose. He swore loudly and despite the throb of pain to her crown, she took the opportunity to run. However, she didn't make it as far as she'd hoped. He was surprisingly quicker than she had first thought, grabbing her quickly and putting a firearm to her head.

"That will do, one more false move and I will shoot you. Now be a good girl and get into the car," he snarled.

With no other choice, she did as he ordered, shutting the door to the vehicle behind her. He wiped the blood dripping from his nose and muttered under his breath. Key in the ignition, he started the engine and drove the vehicle away from the station. When he began taking a route that did not go to the London Met, she asked him the question on her mind.

"Why?" She didn't need to explain the question. He knew what she was asking.

"She took my wife and kids, said it was either you or them. You're involved in this; my family are innocent. I made the choice I had to make," he replied.

"She will probably kill all of us. You know that, right?" She informed him.

"Why do you think we're going in the police vehicle? I needed to get to them but I'm not an idiot. Hopefully once they realise you're gone, they'll find us and maybe we'll all live," he told her.

Keri shook her head at that. "Maybe," she said, though her tone said she thought differently.

****

Superintendent Jan Wright got the call and couldn't believe what she was hearing. "The DCI did what?" she asked, still too stunned by what she had just been told to comprehend what they were telling her now. She asked them to repeat it as Matt watched, looking at her in question.

"What's going on?" Matt asked.

"DCI Head took Keri from the officers that were taking her to the holding cell," she said in disbelief.

"Why?" Wren inquired, confused.

"He told him that she was being transferred to London Met for questioning," she recounted.

"If that were true, why are they informing you now?" Matt queried.

"Jen found out through the grapevine, wasn't convinced it was on the up and up, she is tracking him in a police vehicle. She says he isn't going to London," she repeated the news, still trying to make sense of the situation.

"So do we think he's taking her to Mary?" Wren asked, jumping to the most likely conclusion.

"It would appear that might be the case," Jan agreed.

"So has he been in on this the whole time?" Matt wondered.

"I have no answers to that, it's possible but I can't be certain," Jan answered.

"Jen is tracking him, so we still have time to find them?" Matt asked.

"Then we should go," Wren said.

"Let's roll," Jan confirmed.

Once they got to their vehicles, Matt called Jen for the location that they were setting out for, the police vehicle's last known GPS coordinates. When they arrived at the location where the vehicle had stopped. They raced towards it. As they approached, it became clear that things were not going to be as straightforward as they had hoped. The vehicle had been left stranded, the door to the back open wide. Keri and the DCI were not there.

They found a building nearby, and the officers in attendance cleared the surrounding area and began cautiously surrounding the building, covering any exits. Wren and Matt entered first. They proceeded slowly, careful to survey the scene around them. Looking for any danger that may be lurking. By the time they found DCI Head, he was already dead, a clean shot between his eyes. Whoever had been here with him was gone, and Keri was gone with them.

"Did we find anything?" Jan said, slowing as she saw the DCI in a pool of his own blood.

"Ma'am, we have something, we've found a woman and two kids," an officer called from the back.

"Who are they?" She demanded.

"The DCI's family ma'am. They said they were taken by some men. One had credentials; it was Superintendent Brentwood. She was told her husband had been mixed up in something on a case and they were being moved for their safety," he replied.

"That sounds like a familiar reason to move someone," Jan observed, recalling that had been the very same reason for DI Doyle's arrival. Matt swore and Wren hung her head. The DCI had made the wrong call. He was lucky his family hadn't died along with him. It meant that they hadn't had enough time to spare to finish the job. It also meant that Mary now had both Keri and Dev. They'd got here too late.

Chapter Nineteen

August 20th, 2014

Keri had been taken from the police vehicle and drugged. She was finally coming around when she heard him.

"Keri? Keri, are you awake?" Dev called.

"What? Where are we?" She queried, still disorientated.

"I'm not sure. It looks familiar though, like I've been here before, but I don't know when," he told her.

"I can't see you. Where are you?" Keri asked.

"I'm behind you," he said.

"Oh no you're not," Keri teased.

"Yes, I am," Dev said, not getting the joke.

"You didn't see many pantomimes when you grew up, did you," Keri said.

"I was a foster kid. What do you think?" Dev answered.

She tried to move her head so she could see behind her, but her head spun. Closing her eyes, she waited for the room to stop spiralling around her.

"Are we going to die now?" She thought the question aloud.

"It doesn't look good, that's for sure," Dev admitted.

"So we are," Keri said, interpreting his words and translating them into what she thought he'd meant.

"We aren't dead yet," he corrected, "That means there is still time for the odds to change."

"I wouldn't say the odds are looking to be in our favour right now, would you?" She pointed out.

"No, I don't suppose they are. It doesn't exactly seem like the time for optimism, but they know who they are looking for, so it seems unlikely she will get away with it. They just have to find us," he tried.

"She might not get away with it, but she will succeed in doing it," Keri concluded, before adding, "Not exactly a comfort, but better than nothing I guess."

"I don't imagine for a moment that this will be the case, but can you move at all?" Dev asked.

"If you mean, am I wrapped up like a Christmas parcel, then the answer is yes," she told him.

"And I suppose there isn't much chance that you can get loose either," he stated.

"Outlook not so good," she replied flippantly.

"Did you just quote a Magic eight ball?" He chuckled.

"Did you just admit you know the answers on a Magic eight ball?" She responded, teasing him.

"Touché," he relented.

"So did she give you any hints as to what we might expect now?" Keri wondered, "Are we going to be decapitated? She is favouring that method recently."

"At least that would be quick," Dev surmised.

"Not if she tortures you first. Reece got the full *"Mary, Mary Quite contrary"* treatment," Keri contradicted.

"What is the *"Mary, Mary"* treatment?" Dev asked, puzzled.

"You didn't figure it out. That's hilarious. She was so proud of that one. The rhyme *"Mary, Mary"* was said to be about the torture Bloody Mary treated her subjects to, silver bells are a reference to thumbscrews, cockle shells were devices for genital

251

torture, and the pretty maids all in a row, was Protestants being lined up for *"the maiden"* to be decapitated. Or it was a reference to the rows of graves from the victims beheaded. I forget," she rambled.

"So, we aren't rooting for decapitation then, either" Dev joked.

"I'm personally hoping to be shot. Not much torture involved with a bullet to the head," she considered.

"Tell that to Vincent Walker," Dev countered.

"Oh yes, I'd forgotten about him," she replied, "can't say that skinning would be my favourite choice. Better than burning though."

"Burning? Like at the rose and crown?" Dev asked quietly.

"She's quite fond of those too. Whether it's tied to a stake or not, burning would be a bad way to go," Keri mused, "sounded bad when I heard it anyway."

"You heard people burning?" Dev queried, horrified.

"It's in my statement," Keri supplied, "not that you would know since you're on suspension."

"So, we don't want to burn, decapitation, or skinning. What option does that leave?" Dev asked nervously.

"I have a feeling it would be better not to find out the answer to that," Keri answered quietly.

The door opened and Mary stood in its frame. "Ah, did we enjoy our little reunion?" She inquired.

"We haven't quite caught up yet. You know, we have years to talk about. Perhaps you could come back a little later, say next year sometime, maybe the one after, just to be sure we are thoroughly reacquainted," Keri quipped.

"Always with the smart mouth, Keri, darling, I always suspected that your mouth would get you in trouble one day and here we are," she replied. Putting her arms out indicating the surroundings, before continuing, "Do you like the party venue? It's a particular favourite of mine. It was where your father died, so I'm rather partial to it. I'm surprised you don't recall it, Kier. You have, after all, been here before."

Dev's memory clicked into place as he recalled his flashback, so that explained the familiarity.

"Unfortunately, it's become somewhat derelict since you last visited. Being a crime scene for a murder will do that to a place," she taunted,

"Maybe it's haunted, should we expect a visit from dear old dad."

"So, what entertainment do you have planned for the evening," Keri said in a blasé manner, that was out of place in their current situation.

"Oh, don't worry, darling, it will be spectacular. Not the work of art Cain would have delivered had you not killed him, but still quite the spectacle," Mary assured her.

"Oh, and I forgot my party dress," Keri replied sarcastically.

"You won't be needing one, darling. It would only get in the way. So hard to be hung, drawn, and quartered in a gown, I imagine," she stated coldly.

"Pardon?" Keri said, suddenly less amused.

"That is the sentence for high treason after all," Mary said, smirking as she delivered the news.

"Erm, didn't they use horses for that?" Keri questioned, not entirely sure what else to say to that.

"I know," Mary admitted, seeming saddened by the lack of equestrian assistance, "I have had to take some creative licence with that I'm afraid. Of course, we are skipping ahead. That will be the finale. First, you will get to watch your brother as he is punished for your crimes." Keri remained silent at that. "Don't you want to know how he will be punished?" She asked, smiling maliciously, knowing she had finally hit a sore spot, digging deep to assuage her rage at Keri's perceived betrayal.

"How will I enjoy the surprise if you ruin it?" Keri responded, faking nonchalance. Dev winced at the statement.

"Very well, darling, have it your way," Mary conceded. "Now enjoy your remaining time together. The party is going to start soon," she crowed, leaving the room once more.

"Well, isn't she a Peach?" Dev muttered sarcastically.

"Try living with her," Keri replied.

"I think I'd rather be tortured," Dev shot back, and the two of them paused at his inappropriate joke, before equally inappropriate laughter burst out of them. When the hysterics waned and they sobered, Keri asked, "Is it too much to ask that your friends get here before we receive our punishments?"

"I don't think so, I've been wishing for that since I got here," Dev assured her, and they finally fell silent, both praying for help to arrive.

About twenty minutes later when Terry came in, grumbling under his breath about Michael moving his ass and getting here to give him a hand. Dev felt the puncture to his neck and realised he was being drugged again.

Likely because moving his weight would be difficult enough without him struggling and making it harder. As the world began to fade out, he wondered what he would find once he re-awakened.

"I'm glad we finally got some time together, Kier, I just wish we'd had more of it," Keri said sadly, before he lost consciousness and heard nothing more.

****

Stephen was still in the waiting room with Alec and Raven. Chris had finally come out of surgery and though he was currently stable, he had died during surgery, but the team had managed to revive him. However, they had informed them, they couldn't be certain if he would pull through.

He decided he could no longer be in this place for the time being, the waiting too much for him, particularly knowing that Dev was somewhere out there, alone and in peril. Stepping outside for some air, thinking he may get an update on any progress finding him. After a few minutes, his phone rang, and he listened as the voice on the other end relayed his message. When the call concluded, Stephen rushed back to reach Alec.

"We have to go," he said to Alec.

"But Chris," Raven began.

"We can't do anything more for him now but wait, I have a location I need to check out," Stephen told her.

"If you have something and it pans out, it might be dangerous. You stay here with Raven, I'll go, I can ring the others on route, and they can head out to meet me," Alec said firmly.

"Fine, but I'll contact Phantom, I think Chris said he was based near there. He can meet you and cover you until the others catch up," Stephen insisted. Alec nodded his agreement.

****

Keri watched in disgust as Terry had arrived at the entrance of the room. He was wearing a stupid horse mask, one of those ridiculous joke ones originally sold by a novelty purveyor as a Halloween costume.
 "Oh, you have got to be kidding me!" Keri exclaimed as he wheeled in a sack barrow.
Terry strapped her onto it and proceeded to wheel her from the room and she realised their time was about to run out. As Terry dragged her along on the sack barrow, she noted the strange decor adorning the walls, the royal standard for Mary I was displayed many times, each one a combination of the Tudor arms, the lions of England and a blue quarter to represent France. A golden harp on it, with wings protruding from its back end, while a lady posed at the front end like a figurehead on a ship.

There was also bunting hanging from the warehouse ceiling and banners, as though there was some kind of celebration, and she was the lead procession. Or more accurately, Terry the horse led it. If she was going to die, was it too much to ask to not be led there by a Halloween horse-headed henchman?

"She does know she isn't really the Queen, right. Because we have one of those already," Keri stated dryly but Terry said nothing.

She entered the main hall of the storage facility, and saw her mother in the centre at the far end. She sat on a white throne-like chair, the fleur-de-lys etched into it, draped with rich fabrics. Dressed in costume as the Bloody Queen, no less. She really was a couple of sandwiches short of a picnic. She took a look at her surroundings further, noticing an array of torture devices, none of which particularly comforted her.

On one side of the room, she saw the pear of anguish, several thumbscrews and what appeared to be a breast ripper hanging on hooks along the wall. A rack, consisting of a rectangular wooden frame, slightly raised from the ground, a roller at both ends, lay in one area, however Dev didn't appear to be restrained there. She wondered if that was how Mary planned to "quarter" her but chose not to linger on that thought and continued her perusal.

"Wow. The décor really leaves something to be desired," Keri quipped. Again Terry remained silent.

Her eyes rested on an A-frame shaped metal rack, she had read about this when she'd taken history in college, it was a scavenger's daughter. As opposed to the first rack, the scavenger's daughter had a person attached and was compressed from both sides, pushing the knees into a sitting position and the head in the opposite direction. Essentially compressing the body into itself, often leaving victim's bleeding from the nose and ears.

She let her gaze fall then upon a pillory. It was set with two parallel wooden boards clubbed together with holes for necks and wrists. The victim placed their head onto the board and the pillory was closed and they couldn't escape. You didn't really come to any harm from the pillory itself, however, that would put you at the mercy of somebody else, leaving you open to all manners of torture.

"Where did she even get this shit? Did you rob a museum?" Keri wondered aloud.

"It was here when I arrived," Terry said blankly and she looked at him in surprise.

"He speaks," she teased, "I thought for a moment she'd cut out your tongue."

"No, that was Paul," he replied quietly. "Needless to say I tend to keep my mouth shut these days."

Keri looked horrified, falling silent at his words, speechless. Not for long though.

"Speaking of cutting out tongues," she uttered, her eyes falling on a hollow brass statue resembling a bull.

She recalled a time when Mary had boasted that she owned one. Victims were placed inside after having their tongues cut out. It was sealed shut and then they would light a fire around it. This would cause the victims to scream in agony. However, with their tongues cut out, it made a sound that resembled a bull's call, much to the amusement of all who came for the spectacle.

Next in the little warehouse of woe, she noticed the Iron Maiden. The Iron Maiden was an upright sarcophagus with spikes on both sides of the shell, strategically placed so it would pierce several of the vital organs upon its closure. Not a quick death, but one that would leave the victim bleeding over several hours. She had always been led to believe it was a myth, a story that had been passed around to put the fear of God into people back in the day.

"Holy Mary, mother of God," she mumbled.

Her ride finally drew to a stop, Terry, stood the sack barrow to a halt and lifted her back to a standing position, though still attached. He held onto it firmly so her weight didn't pull the barrow forwards, which would mean her face planting onto the cold stone floor beneath. He drew in several breaths the strain of wheeling her in, the probable cause of his overexertion.

It was then that she noticed Dev's unconscious form lying on a wheel like structure, what the fuck was it? Was he naked? That couldn't be a good sign and also not an image she wanted in her head of her brother. Turning her head away from the sight, she noticed one final structure. Oh, fun. It had a noose. Lovely. From what she could recall, during a quartering they weren't killed by the hanging, they just hung them up until they were close to death before the disembowelment part. Then they were either ripped apart by their arms and legs, possibly by the rack in the corner, or being beheaded and cut into four pieces. She was hoping for the beheading, slightly less pain but not by much.

"I won't hold my breath though," she mused aloud. She didn't really talk to herself often, but it filled the eery silence.

Terry unstrapped her and carried her upwards. The noose was placed around her neck and tightened, and she realised it was really over. Dev was about to die while she stood here wearing the rope and then her turn would come.

"Nearly ready for the show to begin, Darling. We just have to wait for your brother to wake up, do you like it? These were all gifts from my darling Cain. Some of them he handcrafted himself, he was such an extraordinary artist, always keen on the details, a torture chamber fit for a queen, he'd say," Mary called out cheerfully, delight lighting up her face.

"Oh, it's something, alright," Keri replied.

"Yes, you know the Iron maiden over there is something of a myth. Although it is said to have been used during mediaeval times, although, there is no recorded incident of one being used. After I finish with your brother on the breaking wheel, we can give it a trial run," she mused.

Keri hoped they had given Dev an extra-large dose.

****

They were still finishing the crime scene at the last location, when Wren received Alec's call, and she wasn't sure how quickly she would be able to get to the location. Rushing to speak with Jan, she hurriedly told her of Alec's message. The Don assured her that she would call it in and gave her permission to leave the current crime scene.

Wren raced to her car; the location she'd been given was quite a trek out in the other direction. It was going to take some time to get there. Hopefully, it wouldn't take the backup long to arrive either.
She pulled on her seatbelt and peeled away from the curb, pushing the speed as much as she could without causing an accident, Dev and Keri had been gone a while now, if she had any hope of saving them time would be of the essence. She just hoped they had held out and she wasn't going to arrive to find their mutilated corpses. She could go a bit faster.

Chapter Twenty

Mary had come down from her throne and was pacing impatiently for Dev to regain consciousness.

"How much did you give him?" she screeched at Terry.

"I don't know, I haven't drugged anyone before," he replied.

It was then that she saw it, a flickering of his eyes. Had he been faking it? She smiled widely and stepped toward the wheel.

"The jig is up, darling. I saw your eyes move," she chuckled with malicious intent, "that means it's time to begin. I wonder Keir, have you ever heard of the Breaking Wheel? Known to some as the Catherine Wheel. If not, let me give you a breakdown. Get it?" Mary paused as though waiting for his response, before continuing, "That was a joke. I take this club and beat you with it, repeatedly breaking as many bones as possible. Did you hear that, Keri, darling? I do hope that you can. I wouldn't want you to miss anything. It is your punishment, after all, to watch as I break your brother into pieces and let him die as his body is crushed beyond repair."

It was then that the sound of Terry and a man she couldn't place interrupted her, fighting on the platform where Keri was tied into the noose. As Mary watched it unfold with disbelief, she was incensed by the sight that was playing out before her.

"No, no, no, no! How dare you disrupt my court?" she fumed.

****

Mary marched back towards the wheel, and in a fit of temper swung the bat, connecting it with Dev's arm. He let out a bellow of pain as it slammed into him, bone crunching beneath its weight. The two men still battled it out above, while Mary stomped back towards the platform. She threw the bat in a temper. Quite why she thought it would reach them, Dev couldn't be sure; the platform was raised and still out of her range. He was only glad that the bat was no longer in his vicinity.

As Phantom seemed to be getting the upper hand, Terry fell back, barging the restrained Keri forward and knocking her from her perch, as the rope pulled tightly around her throat. She grasped it, desperately clawing to get air as she swung.

Phantom, distracted by the sight of her hanging by the rope, took his eyes off of Terry, who launched himself at him. As Keri hung, her body beginning to lose the fight for life, Phantom strained to gain ground; seeing her struggle he gave a push in desperation. He finally managed to wrap his hands on either side of Terry's head and twisted for all that he was worth.

There was a sickening crack, like the one Dev's arm had made not more than a moment ago. Phantom pushed at the lifeless body of Terry, throwing it off him and lunging forward to snatch up Keri's body pulling it up and taking the weight of the noose from around her neck, loosening the tight grip it had on her throat.

"It's okay. Breathe," Phantom told her and she sucked in air.

Mary rushed closer to the platform, her screams of rage echoing off the walls as Phantom rushed to get Keri away from the rope and breathing. He finally managed to balance her weight on one shoulder and pry the noose from around her neck. Realising her plans had been ruined, Mary turned, picking up an iron skewer and then brought her attention back to Dev. Keri might be temporarily out of harm's way but Dev was a sitting duck. Or considering the hungry look of vengeance on her face, a meal on a wheel.

After moving closer to the platform, distracted by the unplanned breach above her and her subsequent hissy fit following it, she found herself a fair distance away from where Dev lay open and vulnerable. Now, though, she focused all her fury on him and ran, covering some of the distance, intending to stab the torture skewer into him.

She was so busy focusing on Dev, that she didn't see Alec throw himself at her from the side. As he shoved his weight into hers, she lost her balance. Twisting to see who had side swiped her, she lost control of the small spear and the skewer pierced Alec. He let out a yelp and fell, and his blood spilled.

Mary regained her footing, pausing to pull the skewer from Alec, making blood spurt from the wound as it pulled free. She realigned and made a second attempt for Dev. That's when he heard Wren's voice shouting from the doorway.

"Stop! Put down your weapon and get on the ground!"

Mary, too crazed or no longer caring, didn't stop as Wren had ordered and continued to run. Just before she connected, a shot rang out and she fell. Wren ran from her position, racing over to Mary, checking she was down, as Alec groaned beyond. As she lowered herself to roll her over, Mary reached up and grabbed at her. Wren squeaked in alarm, the deranged woman throwing herself at her, and they wrestled on the ground for purchase, each fighting to be the one left standing.

Mary grabbed at Wren's hair, pulling her by it while simultaneously pushing her body up and over, managing to roll herself on top and Dev's heart stopped as he howled out his rage. Fighting desperately at his bonds, the rope scraped along his skin, making raw and bloody abrasions.

Mary smacked Wren's head onto the concrete and Dev fought harder, the pain in his body didn't register compared to the weight of the pain in his chest, watching helplessly as Wren's head connected, blood seeping through her white hair.

"NO!!" he shouted, fear clutching at his heart while the cry strangled out of his throat.

As Mary struggled to her feet, Phantom had taken a position before Dev, prepared to tackle the unhinged creature. It was then that Michael appeared from nowhere, pointing a gun in their direction. Mary, seeing him, smiled.

"Shoot them! Shoot them all!" She ordered in a screech.

Phantom dropped lower and made for Michael, forgetting his mission to cover Dev, and assessing the new threat. Mary seized the opportunity and lunged at Dev, her hands wrapping around his throat as she loomed over him.

Two shots rang out. The first sent Mary up and spinning as it clipped her shoulder, she evaded the second, but the action had her losing her footing, sending her crashing backwards into the open sarcophagus. The spikes dug into the flesh of her back, and the sudden impact of her weight knocked it off balance. It teetered as it rocked back and Dev watched in horror as it seemed to hang, balancing on the back edge for a prolonged moment before gravity had its way and it fell backwards to the ground. The doors swung as it fell, the momentum slamming it closed, not dulling the awful sound of ear-splitting screams that came from the inside as the spikes finally found their mark.

Dev watched in nauseated fascination as blood oozed from within, all that was visible of Mary were her feet poking out from the open base. Her screams died down to a gurgling sound—not unlike the sound a bath makes when water is drained away— replacing them before that too faded.

Finally managing to drag his gaze from the terrifying sight of the human shaped coffin, he refocused on Michael in the entrance way. Phantom, noticing his shift of focus, followed his gaze, moving first his eyes and then himself as he began to stalk towards him.

"Wait, stop him, I'm an undercover cop," Michael shouted.

Phantom's intent faltered and he looked to Dev, who attempted to shrug and then remembered he was still strapped down. Out of the corner of his eye, Dev caught sight of Keri perched on the platform. Watching the sarcophagus with glazed, expressionless eyes, as though undecided about what she should feel, unconsciously rubbing at her neck and wincing in pain. Phantom watched Michael warily, unsure what to do.

"Are you just going to stand there or are you going to help the injured people? You're a trained medic, right?" Michael asked.

Phantom bristled at that, standing taller, looking even more threatening. "How do you know that?" he questioned; his mistrust of the man increased at this statement.

"Chris told me," Michael shrugged.

"How do you know Chris?" Dev cut in, going stiff, his whole-body alert.

"Don't you recognise me, brother?" the voice said, amusement clear in his voice.

Dev's mind raced as he tried to solve the puzzle then his eyes widened in shock as he figured it out.

"Gabe?" he asked.

"The one and only," the man grinned broadly.

"You know him?" Phantom asked, still not convinced.

"Aye, I know the bastard. Good to see you Guardian," Dev laughed but his laughter fell away when his eyes rested on Wren.

"Angel?" he called.

Phantom followed his gaze once more and he hastened to rush to her, seeming more at ease now the threat had been identified.

"Is she OK?" Dev asked.

"She's still alive," Phantom called back.

"Are you going to stand there and watch or untie me, you fecker?" Dev threw at Gabe.

"That depends," Gabe retorted, "are you going to put your dick away after I do?"

"Ha bloody ha. Get me the feck out of this thing," Dev ordered.

Gabe headed to him, quickly doing as Dev bade, when he was finally free he began to make his way to Wren. At that moment, a shout came from the doorway.

"Police! Everybody down on the ground. Nice and easy now."

"Feck me!" Dev groaned, still buck naked and his arm hanging limply on one side, he awkwardly lowered himself to the ground with Gabe's help. Everybody who was not already down on the floor followed the order and Gabe finally lost his battle of holding back a laugh and began to chuckle.

"What the feck is so funny?" Dev said, looking at him like he'd lost his marbles.

"Man, you're going to have to leave here with your dick swinging in the wind, while your colleagues watch. I hope it's still warm outside." He laughed aloud as he said it. Dev shot him a filthy look.

"Thanks for those kind words, you asshole," he snapped.

"You're welcome Dev, you are very fucking welcome," he spat out between laughs.

"While you laugh about that, I want you to remember the many, many hours you're going to spend in holding, then in interviews while they confirm your identity," Dev said smugly. Gabe's laughter died instantly. "Yeah, hadn't thought of that, had you?"

"No, but on the positive side, at least I'll have clothes on," Gabe fired back, and began laughing again.

The police began to cordon off the scene while they waited for the paramedics to arrive. Jan Wright entered the scene wearing protective clothing to try and preserve what they could, and Matt was not far behind her.

"DI Doyle, your arm is looking a little worse for wear and do I want to know why your clothes are missing?" She asked.

"It was not a choice," Dev replied sulkily.

"Get him a blanket or something!" Jan ordered one man and then turned back to Dev. "Give me a rundown, any dead?"

"I am not entirely certain. I would estimate at two dead and four injured, me included," Dev told her.

"We heard shots fired. Who was shot?" Jan asked.

"That was me," Gabe told her. "I was given the gun by Mary. I shot the first when she ran at Dev and two more when she attempted to kill him a second time. None were kill shots," Gabe told her. "I am an accredited firearms officer. DCI Hank Gordon insisted in case of an emergency."

"That will need to be reported. Where is Mary?" she asked.

"In that," he informed her, pointing at the device now horizontal on the concrete.

"What is it?" Jan queried in surprise.

"It's a bit like one of those Egyptian things except with sharp protruding nails or spikes or something," Dev tried to describe to her.

"So, we can't open it to confirm if she's dead?" Jan pressed.

"I wouldn't recommend it Ma'am, if she has somehow managed to survive in there after being shot, opening the door will pull the spikes free and she will bleed out," Dev confirmed.

"So, we're going to need to bring in the fire brigade," she surmised.

"It's Schrodinger's Cat," Matt said glibly.

"What?" Gabe asked, looking confused.

"You know the theory that if you put a cat in a box with no food or water, then it will die. It was alive when it went in, and you cannot tell if it's dead until you open the box, so it is both alive and dead. Or something like that," he explained haphazardly.

Ignoring Matt, Jan approached the sarcophagus and evaluated it. "I'll call in the fire brigade," she said. Matt appraised the coffin-like box next to her, looking at her feet protruding from the base, he joked, "we aren't in Kansas anymore Dorothy."

At his reference to the wicked witch under the house, Jan scowled, "DS Ainsworth, why don't you do something useful. Go and check on Alec. You down there, Phantom, is it? That is a ridiculous name, how is DI Jones doing?"

"She's coming around, it's a nasty blow though," Phantom called from the ground.

That was when the paramedics arrived. They began by attending to Alec and Wren, Phantom had been given leave to move and went to check on Keri further, seeing how she was faring after her hanging. Dev was having his arm secured as they began to load Alec and Wren into the ambulances.

The fire brigade had finally arrived and with assistance attended to Mary. They were assessing the best way to detach the top, they would have to be careful not to disturb the protruding spikes and cause her to bleed out. From there they could check her vitals and if she were still alive, inject her with tranexamic acid and mefenamic acid to slow her heart rate and keep the bleeding to a minimum, before they could insert several IV's and take her to the hospital in the chamber where they could attempt to save her life.

"It's going to be touch and go. I would be surprised if she makes it to the hospital," a man told Jan and she nodded while Dev watched on, waiting to be given direction.

In the meantime, the divisional surgeon had pronounced Terry Chamberlain as dead, and the pathologist was now dealing with his body. A paramedic finally approached Dev after the others had been loaded up, he had been the last one left to transport, and he'd had to wait on a later one. They asked him questions as they got him inside with the blanket he'd been given when the initial responders had arrived, wrapped tightly around him, allowing him to maintain his dignity. Gabe had joined them, and his last glimpse of the scene were the sparks from the rotary saw as they began cutting the head off the torture device. Secretly, Dev hoped with everything he had in him, that Mary would be dead. Despite the fact she had earned her karma he would not wish that much pain on anyone, not even her.

****

Stephen was at the hospital when the injured were brought in. Wren had been cleaned up and, since she'd regained consciousness, the cut on her head had been cleaned and stitched. She was being held overnight with a suspected concussion, much to her disgust. Alec was in surgery, though he'd been fortunate, and the skewer had missed all major organs, so if the surgery had no issues and he showed no sign of infection, he would be up and about before too long.

Dev was also having surgery on his arm to stabilise the fracture. He was looking at a good twelve weeks of recovery, which would give him a chance to attend regular visits with Doctor Jean Winters. He would also be able to resume his role at the station once he had fully recovered, now that the case had been solved and his suspension would be lifted.

"All of this because of one crazy woman," Raven had observed, shaking her head in disbelief.

Keri had been a little groggy but was alert on arrival. During her physical exam, the doctor had noted the ligature marks on her neck. However, her breathing was normal, and her voice remained normal. The doctor considered getting her in for a CT angiogram, to be sure. He had further cause to worry, since she had not long-ago sustained damage to her throat at the hands of The Executioner, so had suffered from previous trauma in that area.

He decided to proceed with it, in order to characterise and determine the frequency of the dissections in the super-aortic arteries, or in layman's terms, looking for any tears that may have occurred in the inner layer of Keri's main artery and also to check for injuries that may have been sustained to the spine or the cartilages in her throat. This would confirm any signs of damage that may cause her further health issues from her incomplete hanging.

"Damn lucky Phantom got to her in time," Stephen mused aloud.

That left Mary. Now, her case was not so clear cut. Stephen had been surprised to see her wheeled in with the lower half of a human shaped metal shell attached beneath her; she had large spikes protruding from her body in several places, the top of the contraption had been removed and there were a team of doctors waiting for her arrival, rushing her through with more than a few medical attachments in place.

Looking at her, Stephen considered it a minor miracle she had remained alive up to this point. It would have been a kinder death if she had died instantly, he did not want to imagine the pain she would have been in before they had arrived at the scene. Still with the time it had taken for them to arrive, long after the others, it would take a miracle for her to survive.

"How is she still alive?" Raven asked with a horrified look on her face.

"She made a deal with the devil and it's not time for her to die yet else the bargain isn't complete," Stephen quipped lightly and she poked his arm, making him wince.

The doctor who had been monitoring Chris had come to give them an update on his condition and it would appear he would make it, which had been good news to Raven who had still been harbouring guilt at her slow response in getting him help. When they had been allowed in to speak to him, he hadn't seemed quite as boisterous and arrogant as he usually preferred to portray himself. Instead, he'd seemed quiet and subdued. He had been more than a little concerned with Dev's well-being, nobody had yet updated him on Dev's recovery from the scene and he had assumed he was still missing.

He'd been considering his own share of culpability for Dev's capture, blaming himself for not checking for more than one abductor, instead intervening without thought and getting shot for his lack of foresight. He brightened a little upon learning he had been found but went quiet as they recounted what they knew of the scene he had been found at.

"Gabe was here?" Chris asked in surprise, a mixture of anger and something else in his tone. Stephen confirmed the answer with a curt nod.

"Gabe was here at the hospital for a brief time but has been detained at Superintendent Jan Wright's request." Stephen explained, "though it's off the record as he's working a case."

As the only person not injured in some way in attendance, Jan had taken him first for his statement. Wanting to begin unravelling the case and compiling evidence, should Mary survive, though it was doubtful.

"What kind of case?" Chris asked.

"The kind we aren't allowed details of," Stephen said simply.

Phantom had mysteriously vanished when the Superintendent had arrived, though he had reappeared sometime later and was waiting outside Keri's consultation room. He'd also stopped in on Chris when he had been allowed. Stephen was not entirely sure what his deal was. He was ex-military, had no criminal record and no reason to want to evade the police.

When he'd asked Chris about it, Chris had told him that he had history with a corrupt superior in his military days. That particular situation had ended with severe consequences and had left Phantom with more than a little bitterness as far as the authorities were concerned.

Overall, despite the body count of victims being high in this particular case, Stephen was pleased it had finally come to an end; that Mary had finally been apprehended, whether dead or alive, remained to be seen. Between the statement given by Keri and the account given by Gabe, concerning his time spent as Michael Ealand, they had more than enough evidence of criminal activity in Mary's case. Add in the evidence taken on scene, the various torture implements and structures currently being assessed for physical evidence connecting them to several of the murders, plus the statements due to be given by Wren, Alec, Dev and hopefully Phantom, they would have enough evidence to sink Mary. Should she somehow manage to pull through she would be locked up for a considerable length of time for her crimes.

"So, is it over?" Chris asked.

"It's over for Mary," Stephen replied, not sure how long it might take to wrap the case up entirely.

Keri's testimony concerning Mary, had also tied up several puzzles, one such being the removal of Jilly's womb. She had been informed she'd been pregnant, unaware of her ectopic pregnancy and had only realised after she had already started her mission of destruction, that she had in fact been lying. One woman's lie had been the catalyst that had started the ball rolling on this deadly crusade. Liam Whelan's case had also been closed. It had also resolved several murders committed within the London Met authority and the three burn victims had finally been identified.

They had also been able to resolve the murder of Andrew Panderman and his wife.

He had been looking into a leak in the London Met; they had found evidence that directed them to none other than his successor John Brentwood, he had also been the one to insist that Devlin was under threat and could put other officers at risk should he remain there before the threat had been resolved. This had resulted in his transfer as the board had taken his statement under advisement and done as he'd suggested. Since he was dead that particular line of inquiry ended there.

"What happened to the DCI's family?" Chris asked, cutting into his thoughts once more.

"They've been taken in for questioning," Stephen answered patiently. His brother didn't like being in hospital and not in the thick of it all.

It was discovered through hospital CCTV that the DCI, Richard Head had been inside Cameron O'Reilly's room not long before he had flatlined. They believe that he may have been responsible for Cameron's premature death, under threat of punishment, while his family had been held hostage. There would be an investigation into that, which would be confirmed and concluded later.

Jen had submitted evidence she'd uncovered linking Mary to The Executioner before Keri took her, and she had also taken the evidence that Raven had found linking to Reece Carter and his part in the whole mess. She had followed the same trail, using official channels to add it to the list of evidence for submission, should a trial need to take place.

"Am I going to be stuck in here much longer?" Chris asked sulkily and Stephen sighed. He wondered how much of a pain in the ass Chris was planning on being for the time he would spend here. He really was a terrible patient.

"I'm sure you will be out in no time," Stephen assured him, "I'm going to go and check on Raven."

He observed Raven sitting huddled in her waiting room chair; together they had been here for most of the day. Raven hadn't been away from this area since they'd first arrived. Letting out a tired sigh, he approached the human cocoon that was his sister and, putting a hand on her arm, realised she'd fallen asleep.

He wasn't sure how she could sleep in that position but a combination of stress, worry and exhaustion had finally taken hold of her, and she'd given in to it. He spoke to a nurse, and she assured him that should there be any need to contact them she would call. Reaching down he lifted her up and carried her out of the hospital. With everyone stable he decided they should get some rest.

Chapter Twenty-One

Gabe sat in his holding cell considering his interview, since Dev had confirmed his real identity. It was more of a formality to keep his cover as he'd been arrested as Michael Ealand. Originally he'd been working undercover in the London area as a low-level stooge, working his way into the operation when Alistair had approached him.

He'd asked him to go and join Mary's branch in Welwyn. Since her husband's demise, they did not trust Mary and her assassin to oversee their business arrangements. Although Mary had insisted business would run as usual, they didn't like change. If something was working, why fix it? They had also heard rumours that Mary had become unstable and was drawing a lot of unwanted attention. They wanted eyes in there, watching her so they would know if she had become a liability.

He'd also known that Andrew Panderman was looking into the London Met leak and, at Stephen's request, they'd teamed up, with Andy becoming his handler. Andy was looking into it from the Met side of things, and he from within the crime syndicate. It also meant that he would be inside Mary's operation, which, should Dev become a target, he would have better odds of intervening on his behalf.

He had informed Alistair of Mary's descent into madness, and he had been issued a kill command. If she became a risk to their own interests, he was to take her out. As far as they were aware he had done so, this would mean he would be able to keep his cover. Although Mary had been dealt with, he still had work to do on the London Met side. Now that Andy had been killed in action, Jan would assume his role and he would let her know of any findings. Andy had been an old friend and her own life had been in jeopardy because she'd been keeping his confidence as he investigated. Since she was already "in the know," it made sense for her to replace him.

"It's been a pleasure finally meeting you, Guardian." Jan said with a small smile and Gabe looked at her in question. Only a few people knew the nickname he had been donned with as a child.

"Should I ask how you know that name?" he inquired with suspicion.

"You are not the only person who knows things," Jan said enigmatically.

Jan had brought him in as Michael Ealand, but the report she took will be kept under the radar until he had completed his undercover work. Until then, on paper, he had been taken in only as a worker, but had offered no statement since he only worked the legitimate side of her business. He would be released due to lack of evidence, and would return to his original operation.

Alistair had instructed him to return now that Mary had been dealt with. Although her death had yet to be confirmed, he was satisfied that she would no longer be any further hindrance so long as she kept her mouth firmly shut. Which wouldn't be much of a problem since she had yet to survive. Only time will tell, but the prognosis was not looking good for her survival rate.

Now, however, he had only to concern himself with how he was going to spin this and return to his own mission. Mary had only been one snake in the nest. It was like a hydra. You cut off one head and two more grew back in its place. He needed to cauterise it to finish the job. Only then would his work be done. He would have to leave again soon.

"I'll look forward to hearing about your progress. Take care of yourself Gabriel," Jan told him and then she saw him to the door.

"I will try," he said and, when she dismissed him, he left the station.

He wished he had more time to spend with his family. It had been so long since they'd all been together, he hadn't even realised that he had missed it. When he joined the Army, he hadn't really appreciated his foster family. They were not related by blood, after all. He had since learned, though, that blood was not always the definition of family. Sometimes family were the people you trusted to have your back when the shit hit the fan.

He had enjoyed infiltrating Mary's operation only because he had finally felt he had rejoined the family he had once taken for granted. Now he was going to have to leave them and if he was honest, he didn't want to. After all this was over, he could move down this way, leave the cloak, and dagger lifestyle behind. Settle down. First, though, he had to go Hydra hunting.

****

Dev felt drowsy, and if he was being truthful, he was tired of waking up feeling that way. He did not much like being drugged, even though on this occasion it was willingly.

"Hey, sleepyhead," he heard.

He allowed his eyes to drift open. Before him was a slightly battered but ever beautiful Angel. Her violet eyes were a little clouded with what he thought might be concern.

"Angel," he said with a croaky whisper.

"Hi, how are you feeling?" she asked.

"A little like I was tied to a wheel naked and had a bat slammed into my arm," he told her, "you?"

"Huh. I feel like I spent the longest two weeks of my life worrying. All my friends were being tortured and unable to find them, before being battered against concrete," she teased, playing along.

"Only friends?" he couldn't help but ask.

"Yes. So, there is something I might consider remedying," she pretended to consider. Dev growled low in his throat.

"Do you not think I've had enough torture in this lifetime?" he said in an exaggerated plea that made Wren giggle. When he stuck his tongue out at her, she became thoughtful.

"I was really scared, Dev," she said simply.

"Why Angel?" He asked, hoping he knew the answer but wanting to hear it anyway.

"I thought that our time together was up, and I hadn't had a chance to really enjoy it yet," she said softly.

"Is that so?" he inquired, and she nodded.

"What on earth are you doing out of your bed?" a nurse asked in shock, "you, young lady, are supposed to be getting rest and be where you are supposed to be so someone can check on you. Head injuries are no laughing matter, my girl," she scolded.

"But if I didn't check on him, I would not be able to rest. So, I snuck in to put my mind at ease. Trust me, my health depended on it," she said, laying it on thick.

"Well, as you can see, he is perfectly fine. Now wait there and I'll call someone to assist you back to your bed," the nurse said reproachfully.

"I made it here all by myself. I will just go back and—" Wren began.

"Oh no you will not, Missy. You already got here unassisted, putting yourself at risk. There will be no more misadventures for you," she told Wren firmly, interrupting her.

"Well, she should stay here, and she could move in with me. We can keep each other out of mischief, and she won't wander the halls getting into trouble," Dev suggested hopefully.

The nurse gave him a look that told him not to encourage her, then sighed, "I'll see what I can do."

"Yay!" Wren cheered and Dev chuckled, the unusually cheerful comment tickling him.

While the nurse went off to make arrangements, Wren took the moment alone to settle herself on Dev's good side and huddle into him. Resting herself with her face pressed towards his so as not to irritate her injury, as Dev wrapped his good arm around her. After a long moment, silently finding peace in each other's embrace, she slipped back off in case the nurse disapproved.

****

Keri had been in the examination room for hours and honestly, she was bored of being poked and prodded. Her throat hurt, and hospitals were dull on this side of them. She left her area and wandered down to the surgical ward. Recognising her, the nurse nodded and allowed her through and she walked in, checking the board to find what she was looking for. She walked into the observation suite and watched as they worked. It was a long surgery with so many potential problems. It was a literal death trap of pitfalls. There were a lot of doctors and attendants, each working on different issues and Keri would have been itching for a case like this one if she had been working or if a part of her didn't want the bitch dead.

"What are you doing?" A voice startled her.

"How did you get back here?" Keri spat back, answering his question with her own.

Phantom shrugged noncommittally. "You didn't answer the question," he pressed.

"Neither did you," she retorted.

"I asked first," he said stubbornly.

"I'm a doctor. The nurse let me in. I worked here. Seems not everyone got the memo that I had left," she answered, knowing that was not what he had meant.

"I know that, but why are you here? Watching them trying to save the woman who intended to hang you until you were barely alive, gut you while you were alive and rip you apart as you died? Why would you watch them as they try to save her?" He embellished the question, clarifying it so she could not pretend to misunderstand his meaning.

"Why not?" she countered.

"OK, I will rephrase. Are you here because part of you was hoping she lives or so you can be sure that she dies?" he tried again.

"She caused a lot of suffering," Keri hedged.

"She did," he agreed.

"She was going to kill Cameron. She arranged to have him die and I had worked so hard to save him," she continued.

"She did that too," he concurred.

"She tried to kill my brother and me, and she did kill my Father," she said, her voice breaking up. What was wrong with her?

"It's OK to be upset and it isn't weak to cry," he stated.

"I know that," she said, nodding.

"Look at me, Keri," Phantom commanded gently.

"No, you weirdo, I don't even know you," she said defensively.

"Now that just isn't true. I was there when you nearly had your life strangled out of you. Twice. I also know what it's like to live your life constantly looking for threats, never knowing when it might be your turn, if they would finally decide your life was up and end you. I also know what it's like to "rub some dirt on it" and become so detached from people that you no longer feel like you are human. To make it all like it's a joke. We know each other. I know you, better than anyone else, even if they have known you longer. So, I am telling you, it is not weak to cry. You have forgotten how, haven't you?" he finished. It was then, as if she finally heard him, really heard him, that she let the tears fall.

It was not the explosion of feeling like a dam exploding. It was still controlled. It was hard to completely let go of the years of conditioning. Yet she allowed that one small show of emotion. He pulled her in and shielded her with his arms, knowing she would feel weak if someone saw her. He gave her privacy and allowed her to feel just for a moment.

"It isn't weak to feel what you feel. It is a strength to remember your humanity. It's what sets you apart from Mary. What she became was inhuman, a psychopath. Not allowing yourself those feelings stops you from really being connected. You have been living a half-life for so long that you have forgotten how to embrace your emotions," Phantom began, "you've been living like Rapunzel, trapped in a tower, unable to reach the real world. It was necessary in the life that you had to live, but that's over. You can leave the tower now."

She was no longer certain if he was talking to her or himself. Though she couldn't really imagine him with the flowy, gold locks. They stayed that way for what felt like forever, and she took what he offered. A moment to let the walls come down. Then the sound of Mary crashing ended it.

As he turned her around in his arms and held her while she watched, knowing without being told that she needed to see with her own eyes, that the nightmare was over. They pushed to try and save her, a flurry of activity ensued as they shouted in quick, rushed communication to address the source of the problem. It was all in vain.

After solidly working to get the procedure back on track, Mary had finally given up the fight. She was, without doubt, gone. They all stopped. The exhaustion from hours of labour proving ineffectual. The trauma to her body was too extensive for her to be revived. They hung their heads in despondency before the lead surgeon called time of death.

That was when Keri breathed again. She was unsure whether to be relieved or if she should feel pity for the woman who had never learned how to genuinely love someone beyond herself. Then she prayed that she didn't become her.

****

Alec awoke from his surgery feeling a little worse for wear. He had spent the best part of a day with Steven and Raven while they waited for news on Chris' surgery. He had been here when Keri had been brought in, and the one thing he had noticed was nobody had been waiting for him. He had woken up with no one wondering if he would pull through. And although he knew that Dev and Wren had both been admitted alongside him, he mourned the loss of people hoping he would make it. He supposed Dev would have stayed if he weren't here himself, but it wasn't the same. What kind of person did that make him if nobody cared if he lived or died?

"I suppose nobody cares when you are just the sidekick," he said to himself wryly.

His thoughts turned to the people outside and he found himself wondering if Stephen and Raven were still here. At least he had a comfortable bed to lie in, while they'd been in those hard, cold chairs for hours. Might be a harsh reality to realise nobody would be there if he died, but it was harder still having the people you cared about lying in the hospital, and not being able to do a damn thing about it. To sit helplessly, waiting to know what their fate would be and knowing that you had no say in it. To have to put a brave face on for them and try not to let on that your heart is being ripped out from your chest because it isn't about you.

Their possible death isn't yours to suffer through, you have to continue on as though you are fine with it. Make arrangements. Sign the documents, fill out the forms. Inform all of the family that need to know that they are there. You just push it all to the back of your mind and become a robot, waiting, and repeating all of their information to each person who asks for it. Over and over. To remain steady when all you want to do is fall apart.

"Guess I should stop feeling sorry for myself. At least I'm not leaving people to worry about me if I die," he muttered.

He hoped that they had gone home for some sleep and that they had thought to eat, Raven was only a slip of a thing as it was. With not one but two brothers here, the stress of worrying for their lives had certainly put them through the wringer. He imagined that Stephen would ensure that they'd both eat, he seemed like the dependable sort. As he tried to rest some more, he found he couldn't quite seem to stop his mind from ticking over. He called for a passing nurse and when she came to him asked the question burning in his mind.

"Are Raven and Stephen Doyle still here? They were with Chris Doyle, he was shot. Their other brother is here too, Devlin Doyle," he asked.

"Do you mean the lawyer? He left a little while ago carrying his sleeping sister to the car. He's such a sweetie," she replied, looking wistful and sighing.

He rolled his eyes a little, before asking if she could keep him informed. She told him he should stop worrying about everyone else and get some sleep.

Unphased by her disapproving look, he inquired about getting an update on the others, but she sighed and went to check. Alec waited for her to return. When he finally got the update that everyone was hanging in there, he was able to relax and sleep.

****

Stephen was exhausted from the combination of working his day job, taking care of his sister, watching over his two brothers, and trying to keep the others' confidence while he dived into the depths of the criminal cesspool. The aftermath of the case had been hectic, with casualties and deaths being addressed and dealt with. He'd worked tirelessly, compiling all that they had found to ensure Dev would be completely cleared of all suspicion. Raven was still sleeping, and he was pottering around Dev's home slowly, willing himself to find motivation to get himself moving and head back to the hospital.

A knock came from the door, and he became immediately alert. A mixture of hyper-awareness and paranoia took over him as he approached the door warily. He checked the spyhole and found Doctor Jean Winters on the other side. Putting a finger to his lips as he opened the door silently, he indicated for her to remain quiet, so as not to wake Raven. He led her through to the living room and closed the door behind them.

"Dev didn't turn up for a session. I was worried," Jean began.

"He's in the hospital, things took a bad turn, but everything is over. Mostly over," he corrected, recalling Gabe's message. Not what he would have liked, as farewells go, but he understood.

"I'm so sorry. Is he OK?" she inquired.

"Yes. And no," Stephen answered honestly.

"I see. And you? Are you OK?" she asked gently.

"I have been better," he admitted.

She took a seat and gave a small smile, patting the couch in a teasing way, poking fun at the trope reference to her profession. He made no move to sit down, instead choosing to remain standing deliberating in his head.

"Do you want to tell me about it?" She pressed, seeing his indecision, pushing for him to unburden himself of the weight of his own thoughts.

"I–" He hesitated and tried again. "I'm the one that holds things together. But I am struggling," he said, trying to put what he was feeling into words that made sense when he wasn't entirely sure he comprehended them himself.

"What are you struggling with?" Jean prompted.

"I feel…overwhelmed. It's too much I need…I don't know what I need," he replied.

"You perhaps need a release to vent some of the feelings you've been suppressing," she ventured tentatively.

"Yes–No. I don't know. I need…I need..." he lurched forward and slammed his mouth down on hers. Her surprise caused her mouth part, and he used the motion to his advantage, sweeping his tongue inside and lapping at her own. Their tongues duelling in the fire of their combined passion. It was so uncharacteristic of him.

He was usually so controlled and concise but now, in the moment, he was untamed and almost savage in his need for her. She got swept up in his urgency and matched it, plucking her from the seat and with one fluid motion he laid them both onto the plush sofa. Allowing their bodies to collide in a maelstrom of the senses.

As the storm inside him subsided, his frenzy eased enough that he managed to regain some measure of his composure, the kiss becoming less feral and tempestuous, morphing into something more exploratory and sensual; transforming from lustful and necessary, to a kiss of reverence and wonder.

When they finally broke apart, their breathing falling in rapid pants, he eased away, putting a little distance between them. While fighting back the urge to lose himself in her and find solace away from the cacophony of chaos raging inside him.

"I'm sorry, I shouldn't have done that," he offered an apology, caught off guard by his lack of propriety.

Jean's face became thunderous for a fraction of a second before her carefully constructed mask fell back into place.

"I have to go," she replied, pushing his weight off of her, and he watched in confusion as she made her way to the door with an unsteady gait.

Raven, who had appeared in the doorway, moved aside to allow her to pass as she muttered her thanks and left quickly down the hallway to the front door. Stephen watched frozen, unsure what to do, still too stunned by the unexpected encounter to stop her. As the sound of the door being abruptly opened and closed filtered through, he finally registered Raven's look of disapproval. She reached up and gave him a slow clap.

"Oh, nicely done, Stephen. You handled that beautifully," she congratulated him, sarcastically.

"I–" he started, but for once, had no words to impart, as he dragged a hand through his unkempt hair, frustrated with himself.

"I shouldn't have done that," Raven parroted in a snarky voice, "that's not what a girl wants to hear after a kiss like that."

"What was I supposed to say? I damn near mauled her!" Stephen bit out.

Raven chuckled derisively. "You don't say that Baby Shark, anything else, but never that."

Stephen bristled at the use of the nickname. He hated the use of it, only adding salt to the wound she had delivered with her observation. Looking at the doorway Jean had left through, feeling like a complete asshole. He had royally messed that up.

"I'm not sure how you intend to fix that, but I would try using that brilliant mind of yours to figure it out. Quickly," Raven advised before sashaying out of the room.

"Well, Fuck," Stephen said to the air before sitting down, empty and depleted. After replaying the scene over in his head a few times trying to figure out what he could do to mend fences, he shook it off, sighing. He decided it was a problem to ponder at another time. They needed to get back to the hospital.

Chapter Twenty-Two

Dev woke up in hospital to the call of Wren's urgent plea to wake up. When he opened his eyes, he found her's wet and he had a headache. As he took stock, he came to another realisation he remembered. He remembered his mother. He remembered them being taken. He remembered his sister more clearly.

"Dev?" Wren prompted gently.

"What? I'm sorry. Did you say something?" He shook his head and tried to stretch out, wincing as he remembered his arm.

"I asked if you were OK. You were talking in your sleep," she told him hesitantly. He wasn't sure what he had said, but judging from her reaction, it wasn't anything good.

"I remembered," he said simply.

"You did?" she asked.

"I did, I do," he corrected, "I remember what happened, who I was."

"Is that good news?" she hedged, not entirely convinced it was.

"Yes and no. I'm glad that the mystery is solved, but I wish it hadn't happened," he explained.

"I can't say that surprises me. I watched the recording. It wasn't a comfortable watch," she confided.

"I imagine it wasn't. It wasn't exactly grand in real time either," he assured her gravely. "But it's over now."

"I hope so," Wren said in earnest.

He reached up with his good arm and tucked her hair behind her ear. She had leaned over him as he dreamt, while she'd tried to rouse him. After his fingers pushed her hair back, he reached them up further and back, curling them behind the nape of her neck, and gently tugging her down until she was close enough for him to brush his lips softly against hers in a whisper of a kiss. Pulling back as she let out a small gasp, he spoke.

"Good morning, Angel," he greeted quietly.

"Right back at you, you cheeky devil," she scolded.

"Did we hear anything about Mary's surgery?" He wondered.

"She died on the table," Wren informed him.

"I can't say I'm sorry," he admitted.

"Me neither," Wren said with sincerity, her anger obvious.

"How about everyone else? Any updates?" he asked.

"Everyone survived. Michael Ealand has vanished, though," she told him, stressing the name to imply she knew his real identity without confirming it with words.

"Yes, I'm not surprised," Dev said. He hadn't yet gotten around to thanking him.

"I'm sure he'll turn up," Wren said.

Dev laughed, "like a bad penny."

"What happens now?" Wren wondered aloud.

"We live happily ever after," Dev suggested.

"Do people get those in real life?" Wren teased, "happily ever after, I mean."

"OK, that's a fair point. Maybe we just snatch the pieces of happiness we can between the parts that go wrong," Dev shot back, giving her a playful push.

"Or maybe we should work extra hard to ensure we steal as many of them as possible," she replied, before pushing him back, careful to avoid his arm yet forcefully enough to take him by surprise. She pinned him to the hospital bed and kissed him thoroughly. His guttural groan at her action made her feel powerful. She did that to him, made him hot with want and moan her name.

"I'm not sure you kids got the hospital etiquette memo, but we don't do that here. Don't make me separate you like naughty children," the nurse chastised.

"I'm sorry," Wren mumbled, flushing pink with embarrassment.

"You should be, naughty girl," the nurse reprimanded, her eyes twinkling as she did.

The nurse checked Dev over first, then switched to check Wren's head before leaving them with a chuckle. Wren cozied up to Dev and they lay in companionable silence. Wren was happy for the first time in an extraordinarily long time.

****

Keri looked in on her brother. Phantom followed silently. They should have called him Shadow. He was annoyingly hard to shake, she thought. Seeing her brother and his white-haired beauty cuddling up, she sighed. She was happy for him. He deserved to find some peace. She couldn't say the same for herself though. She had been less than deserving thus far, selfish, and self-serving. What she deserved was penitence. Maybe she should look into that. Suddenly feeling like she didn't quite fit anywhere, she turned to go.

"Don't be a stranger, Keri," Dev said quietly, his eyes on her as she turned back with surprise. Not knowing what to say, she nodded and continued to the door. Phantom followed soundlessly. When they got outside, she whirled on him.

"Seriously, what is your deal?" she snapped. I get it we had a *"Hallmark"* moment and all of that, but that's all it was. The moment has passed. You can vanish into the night and haunt someone else, Phantom."

"I think I'll stick around a while. You seem like you're the type to attract trouble. Somebody should keep you from lighting that particular beacon," he said, deadpan.

"You're my *"Jacob Marley,"* aren't you? Should I prepare myself for three more ghosts?" she said dryly.

"Who?" Phantom asked quizzically.

"No, wait, you're Jiminy Crickett. Do you plan on being my conscience, Soulja Boy?" she taunted. "Are you going to make me a real girl?"

Phantom chuckled in surprise. Oh, she was going to be a lot of fun, he thought. His merriment only seemed to incite her anger further.

"Fine, laugh, but remember what happened to the last guy who pissed me off," she warned, threateningly.

"Give me your worst, Tinker-Hell," he cajoled in amusement.

"What did you fucking call me?" she fumed, stomping her foot indignantly.

"The likeness is uncanny," he remarked cheekily, "Now, now Tink, think happy thoughts."

"Oh, you can fuck right off, "GI Joe"," She spat in fury, storming away.

You can run, but you can't hide, Phantom thought, a devilish smile spreading into a grin, before letting her go to cool off and whistling cheerily as he headed to see Chris.

****

Raven paced back and forth, unable to make up her mind. She was outside Alec's ward and wasn't sure if she should enter it. She wasn't family. She wasn't anyone, really.

"You'll wear a hole in the floor, ItsyBit," Stephen commented, catching her off guard, "What's got you all pacey?"

"Why are you here?" she asked, trying to shift focus.

"Heading for coffee. Do you want to come? Maybe stop going back and forth, and choose a direction," he joked.

She nodded, and he turned to head to the coffee machine. Looking back at the ward one final time, she let out a groan at her stupidity and trailed along behind Stephen. It's not like she would know what to say to him even if she had gone in. He would probably have taken one look at her arrival and then been disappointed that it wasn't somebody a little more…cheerful. She had been told more than once that she was too much like hard work. Misery might like company, but unfortunately nobody wanted misery's company. Her real parents hadn't been wrong, she was nobody's first choice.

****

19th November 2014
3 months later

Keri stood alone at the graveside. Her faux family Mary and Jack were buried alongside one another. Ironic really, considering how their relationship had ended, but life's full of little ironies. As she stared at it, she wasn't entirely sure why she had come. She had plans with Dev later to see her real mother's body finally buried properly. She would be laid to rest, surrounded by Dev and his people. She wouldn't be thrown in, with no one to wish her on her way to peace. Unlike these two, she thought. Perhaps she should say a few words or something.

"Mary. Jack. How's Hell treating you?" She chuckled inappropriately, then sobered.

"I suppose this is the ending you get when you kidnap kids, steal their innocence by taking away their parents and causing unfathomable harm to others. You find yourself dying young. Youngish," she corrected and continued. "Seems like a fair exchange. I lost my childhood, enslaved to your bidding and you paid for that with your life. My cradle, your grave. May you pay dearly, for all of your sins." With that, she walked away without looking back.

****

Dev stood with his family and friends, with the exception of Gabe, who was still doing whatever he had left to do. Keri stood awkwardly beside him, not quite comfortable in the assembled crowd. She stood alone, but Dev had caught a glimpse of Phantom before he nodded and vanished from view. He didn't even want to guess at what the pair could possibly have in common. *The Phantom and the Fury sounded like a Halloween party*, he mused.

Looking to his other side, Wren winked at him encouragingly. He gave a small smile at her and studied his small company of supporters. Stephen gave him a slight nod, Raven's minuscule frame tucked under his arm protectively. Alec was watching them with an assessing gaze, before remembering himself and refocusing on his friend. Dev raised an eyebrow and smirked at him. Chris stood with his siblings, still a little subdued but towering above them. He gave Dev a chin lift. Off to the other side, his new team, Matt, Jen and Ash, stood with their heads bowed slightly in respect, The Don lifted her gaze to meet his eyes and communicated her approval.

"You okay, Dimples?" Wren whispered quietly.

"I will be," he replied simply.

He had been reinstated into his role, his suspension lifted in part due to the hard work everyone had put into clearing his name and in part due to Doctor Jean's sessions and her report clearing him for active duty. He wasn't entirely sure what had passed between his brother and the good doctor. But where they had been on good terms before, there was a decidedly frosty reception when the two crossed paths now, mostly from the Doctor's side. Stephen seemed to be put out somewhat at this development. There was a story there, that was for certain.

Returning his attention back to the grave before him, he nodded to the priest to begin. They all stood as his mother finally got the send off she deserved, each of them adding a rose to her casket as she was lowered into her grave. Keri remained stiff, not hiding the unshed tears but refusing to let them fall. Dev gave her a small hug from the side, awkwardly trying to comfort her and she relaxed her frame but still didn't relent to the emotions he knew she felt but wouldn't show.

She was a part of the proceedings, yet separate and solitary. He hoped that she found some solace before her time on this earth was over. He could never truly know what it had been like for her to grow up in the home of the two threatening figures, how it had affected her, but he hoped she could finally be free of the hold they'd had on her and find a better life for herself. Looking at Wren, he counted his blessings and wished that his sister found what he had found for himself.

Epilogue

He watched the procession from afar, and he got his first glimpse of the white-haired witch. Surveying her, he noticed she seemed different now, softer. Her tall, lithe body swayed slightly as she placed a hand on the arm of her dark-haired companion. Her long, wavy tresses hung loose down her back, framing her porcelain features, her violet eyes sparkled like amethysts as she looked up adoringly to the man beside her.

The contrast between them was both stunning and transfixing, the sight almost hypnotising to all who saw them. He studied them with both fascination and frustration. She was so close and yet so beyond his reach. As the man looked down upon her, she winked, and the rage bubbled inside of him.

No. That was not how it ended for her. She was not allowed a fairy tale ending. Her end would be met with suffering, so much suffering. By the time he finished with her, she would be a shadow of her former self. She would bend to his command. She would be the subservient subject she should have always been. She would be broken and bear his mark, cursed to smile forever through her sorrows. He would see it was so. Let the anguish begin. But before he got to that, he had a few others to take care of.

THE END

to be continued in...
Book 3 of The Haunted Past Series: Smiles of Sorrow

SMILES OF SORROW

DI Wren Jones and the MCU unit are tasked with investigating a series of savage sexual assaults that have spanned a 10 year period. With victims left brutally disfigured, including Wren's own friend, Amira. This case is no ordinary case for Wren. This is the case behind her choice to become law enforcement. However, it is far more personal than she could ever believe.

"The Smiler" is watching and waiting for his chance to capture the "white-haired witch" who casts her spell on men and brings them to ruin. He has waited a long time to show her who has the power to bring her to heel. In the meantime, he practises on his chosen prey, teaching them that their poor behaviour can and will be punished. They will be forced to smile through their sorrow, marked forever by his own brand of justice.

ABOUT THE AUTHOR

My name is Sharon Jackson, mother to a delightful daughter and related to an amazing family. I live in Milton Keynes but originate from Berkhamsted. I work as a pastry chef in a Hospice, and am an avid reader of many genres, with an insatiable thirst for knowledge. I'm also a well-travelled, adrenaline junkie that derives pleasure from finding fantastical adventures to experience; from murder mystery events, to underwater sea trekking and other eccentric yet entertaining activities. I have been reading tarot cards since the age of thirteen after being given a set that had been charmed by an Aborigine in Australia. I like curiosities, mysteries, and challenges.

Thank you for reading Snakes and Daggers and I hope you stick around for book three.

If you would like to follow me on social media then check out the links below.
Facebook
Shaz (@shaz29970) | TikTok
Sharon Jackson (@sharonjackson2439) •
Instagram photos and videos

If you appreciate the book cover and are interested in purchasing one, you can contact the artist on:
www.creativeparamita.com

Printed in Great Britain
by Amazon